# ARTIFICIAL
# FIRE

## Also by Angela Carter

*novels*

Shadow Dance
The Magic Toyshop
Several Perceptions
Heroes and Villains
The Infernal Desire Machines of Dr. Hoffman
The Passion of New Eve
Nights at the Circus

*short story collections*

The Bloody Chamber
Black Venus

*non-fiction*

The Sadeian Woman: An Exercise in Cultural History
Nothing Sacred: Selected Writings

# ARTIFICIAL FIRE

## Angela Carter

M&S

First Canadian edition

McClelland and Stewart
*The Canadian Publishers*
481 University Avenue
Toronto M5G 2E9

**CANADIAN CATALOGUING IN PUBLICATION DATA**

Carter, Angela, 1940–
   Artificial fire

Contents: Fireworks – Love.
ISBN 0-7710-1898-3

I. Title.

PR6053.A73A92 1988      823'.914      C88-093238-4

Design by T. M. Craan
Printed and bound in Canada by Friesen Printers

*Artificial Fire* contains two sections, "Fireworks" and "Love," which were published outside Canada as individual books under those titles.

   *Fireworks*:   Revised edition, 1987, by Chatto & Windus Ltd. (London).
               First edition, 1974, by Quartet Books Ltd. (U.K.).
               Published in the U.S.A. by Penguin Books, 1987.
               Copyright © Angela Carter, 1974, 1987.

               The stories were written between 1970 and 1973 and appear here in chronological order.

   *Love*:   Revised edition, 1987, by Chatto & Windus Ltd. (London).
            First edition, 1971, by Rupert Hart-Davis Ltd. (U.K.).
            Copyright © Angela Carter, 1971, 1987.

# CONTENTS

# FIREWORKS

# A SOUVENIR OF JAPAN ～

When I went outside to see if he was coming home, some children dressed ready for bed in cotton nightgowns were playing with sparklers in the vacant lot on the corner. When the sparks fell down in beards of stars, the smiling children cooed softly. Their pleasure was very pure because it was so restrained. An old woman said: "And so they pestered their father until he bought them fireworks." In this language, fireworks are called *hannabi*, which means "flower fire." All through summer, every evening, you can see all kinds of fireworks, from the humblest to the most elaborate, and once we rode the train out of Shinjuku for an hour to watch one of the public displays which are held over rivers so that the dark water multiplies the reflections.

By the time we arrived at our destination, night had already fallen. We were in the suburbs. Many families were on their way to enjoy the fireworks. Their mothers had scrubbed and dressed up the smallest children to celebrate the treat. The little girls were especially immaculate in pink and white cotton kimonos tied with fluffy sashes like swatches of candy floss. Their hair had been most beautifully brushed, arranged in sleek, twin bunches and decorated with twists of gold and silver thread. These children were all on their best behaviour because they were staying up late and held their parents' hands with a charming propriety. We followed the family parties until we came to some fields by the river and saw, high in the air, fireworks already opening out like variegated parasols. They were visible from far away and as we took the path that led through the fields towards their source they seemed to occupy more and more of the sky.

Along the path were stalls where shirtless cooks with sweatbands round their heads roasted corncobs and cuttlefish over charcoal. We bought cuttlefish on skewers and ate them as we walked along. They had been basted with soy sauce and were very good. There were also stalls selling goldfish in plastic bags and others for big balloons with rabbit ears. It was like a fairground – but such a well-ordered fair! Even the patrolling policemen carried coloured paper lanterns instead of torches. Everything was altogether quietly festive. Ice-cream sellers wandered among the crowd, ringing handbells. Their boxes of wares smoked with cold and they called out in plaintive voices, "Icy, icy, icy cream!" When young lovers dispersed discreetly down the tracks in the sedge, the shadowy, indefatigable salesmen pursued them with bells, lamps and mournful cries.

By now, a great many people were walking towards the fireworks but their steps fell so softly and they chatted in such gentle voices there was no more noise than a warm, continual, murmurous humming, the cosy sound of shared happiness, and the night filled with a muted, bourgeois yet authentic magic. Above our heads, the fireworks hung dissolving earrings on the night. Soon we lay down in a stubbled field to watch the fireworks. But, as I expected, he very quickly grew restive.

"Are you happy?" he asked. "Are you sure you're happy?" I was watching the fireworks and did not reply at first although I knew how bored he was and, if he was himself enjoying anything, it was only the idea of my pleasure – or, rather, the idea that he enjoyed my pleasure, since this would be a proof of love. I became guilty and suggested we return to the heart of the city. We fought a silent battle of self-abnegation and I won it, for I had the stronger character. Yet the last thing in the world that I wanted was to leave the scintillating river and the gentle crowd. But I knew his real desire was to return and so return we did, although I do not know if it was worth my small victory of selflessness to bear his remorse at cutting short my pleasure, even if to engineer this remorse had, at some subterranean level, been the whole object of the outing.

Nevertheless, as the slow train nosed back into the thickets of neon, his natural liveliness returned. He could not lose his old habit of walking through the streets with a sense of expectation, as if a fateful encounter might be just around the corner, for, the longer one stayed out, the longer something remarkable might happen and, even if nothing ever did, the chance of it appeased the sweet ache of his boredom for a little while. Besides, his duty by me was done. He had taken me out for the evening and now he wanted to be rid of me. Or so I saw it. The word for wife, *okusan*, means the person who occupies the inner room and rarely, if ever, comes out of it. Since I often appeared to be his wife, I was frequently subjected to this treatment, though I fought against it bitterly.

But I usually found myself waiting for him to come home knowing, with a certain resentment, that he would not; and that he would not even telephone me to tell me he would be late, either, for he was far too guilty to do so. I had nothing better to do than to watch the neighbourhood children light their sparklers and giggle; the old woman stood beside me and I knew she disapproved of me. The entire street politely disapproved of me. Perhaps they thought I was contributing to the delinquency of a juvenile for he was obviously younger than I. The old woman's back was bowed almost to a circle from carrying, when he was a baby, the father who now supervised the domestic fireworks in his evening undress of loose, white drawers, naked to the waist. Her face had the seamed reserve of the old in this country. It was a neighbourhood poignantly rich in old ladies.

At the corner shop, they put an old lady outside on an upturned beer crate each morning, to air. I think she must have been the household grandmother. She was so old she had lapsed almost entirely into a somnolent plant life. She was of neither more nor less significance to herself or to the world than the pot of morning glories which blossomed beside her and perhaps she had less significance than the flowers, which would fade before lunch was ready. They kept her very clean. They covered her pale cotton kimono with a spotless pinafore trimmed with coarse lace and she never dirtied it because she did not move. Now and then, a child came out to comb her hair. Her consciousness was quite beclouded by time and, when I passed by, her rheumy eyes settled upon me always with the same, vague, disinterested wonder, like that of an Eskimo watching a train. When she whispered, *Irrasyaimase*, the shopkeeper's word of welcome, in the ghostliest of whispers, like the rustle of a paper bag, I saw her teeth were rimmed with gold.

The children lit sparklers under a mouse-coloured sky and, due to the pollution in the atmosphere, the moon was mauve. The cicadas throbbed and shrieked in the backyards. When I think of this city, I shall always remember the cicadas who whirr relentlessly all through the summer nights, rising to a piercing crescendo in the subfuse dawn. I have heard cicadas even in the busiest streets, though they thrive best in the back alleys, where they ceaselessly emit that scarcely tolerable susurration which is like a shrill intensification of extreme heat.

A year before, on such a throbbing, voluptuous, platitudinous, subtropical night, we had been walking down one of these shady streets together, in and out of the shadows of the willow trees, looking for somewhere to make love. Morning glories climbed the lattices which screened the low, wooden houses, but the darkness hid the tender colours of these flowers, which the Japanese prize because they fade so quickly. He soon found a hotel, for the city is hospitable to lovers. We were shown into a room like a paper box. It contained nothing but a mattress spread on the floor. We lay down immediately and began to kiss one another. Then a maid soundlessly opened the sliding door and, stepping out of her slippers, crept in on stockinged feet, breathing apologies. She carried a tray which contained two cups of tea and a plate of candies. She put the tray down on the matted floor beside us and backed, bowing and apologizing, from the room whilst our uninterrupted kiss continued. He started to unfasten my shirt and then she came back again. This time, she carried an armful of towels. I was stripped stark naked when she returned for a third time to bring the receipt for his money. She was clearly a most respectable woman and, if she was embarrassed, she did not show it by a single word or gesture.

I learned his name was Taro. In a toy store, I saw one of those books for children with pictures which are cunningly made of paper cut-outs so that, when you turn the page, the picture springs up in the three stylized dimensions of a backdrop in Kabuki. It was the story of Momotaro, who was born from a peach. Before my eyes, the paper peach split open and there was the baby, where the stone should have been. He, too, had the inhuman sweetness of a child born from something other than a mother, a passive, cruel sweetness I did not immediately understand, for it was that of the repressed masochism which, in my country, is usually confined to women.

Sometimes he seemed to possess a curiously unearthly quality when he perched upon the mattress with his knees drawn up beneath his chin in the attitude of a pixy on a doorknocker. At these times, his face seemed somehow both too flat and too large for his elegant body which had such curious, androgynous grace with its svelte, elongated spine, wide shoulders and unusually well developed pectorals, almost like the breasts of a girl approaching puberty. There was a subtle lack of alignment between face and body and he seemed almost goblin, as if he might have borrowed another person's head, as Japanese goblins do, in order to perform some devious trick. These impressions of a weird visitor were fleeting yet haunting. Sometimes, it was possible for me to believe he had practised an enchantment upon me, as foxes in this country may, for, here, a fox can masquerade as human and at the best of times the high cheekbones gave to his face the aspect of a mask.

His hair was so heavy his neck drooped under its weight and was of a black so deep it turned purple in sunlight. His mouth also was purplish and his blunt, bee-stung lips those of Gauguin's Tahitians. The touch of his skin was as smooth as water as it flows through the fingers. His eyelids were retractable, like those of a cat, and sometimes disappeared completely. I should have liked to have had him embalmed and been able to keep him beside me in a glass coffin, so that I could watch him all the time and he would not have been able to get away from me.

As they say, Japan is a man's country. When I first came to Tokyo, cloth carps fluttered from poles in the gardens of the families fortunate enough to have borne boy children, for it was the time of the annual festival, Boys' Day. At least they do not disguise the situation. At least one knows where one is. Our polarity was publicly acknowledged and socially sanctioned. As an example of the use of the word *dewa*, which occasionally means, as far as I can gather, "in", I once found in a textbook a sentence which, when translated, read: "In a society where men dominate, they value women only as the object of men's passions." If the only conjunction possible to us was that of the death-defying double-somersault of love, it is, perhaps, a better thing to be valued only as an object of passion than never to be valued at all. I had never been so absolutely the mysterious other. I had become a kind of phoenix, a fabulous beast; I was an outlandish jewel. He found me, I think, inexpressibly exotic. But I often felt like a female impersonator.

In the department store there was a rack of dresses labelled: "For Young and Cute Girls Only." When I looked at them, I felt as gross as Glumdalclitch. I wore men's sandals because they were the only kind that fitted me and, even so, I had to take the largest size. My pink cheeks, blue eyes and blatant yellow hair made of me, in the visual orchestration of this city in which all heads were dark, eyes brown and skin monotone, an instrument which played upon an alien scale. In a sober harmony of subtle plucked instruments and wistful flutes, I blared. I proclaimed myself like in a perpetual fanfare. He was so delicately put together that I thought his skeleton must have the airy elegance of a bird's and I was sometimes afraid that I might smash him. He told me that when he was in bed with me, he felt like a small boat upon a wide, stormy sea.

We pitched our tent in the most unlikely surroundings. We were living in a room furnished only by passion amongst homes of the most astounding respectability. The sounds around us were the swish of brooms upon *tatami* matting and the clatter of demotic Japanese. On all the windowledges, prim flowers bloomed in pots. Every morning, the washing came out on the balconies at seven. Early one morning, I saw a man washing the leaves of his tree. Quilts and mattresses went out to air at eight. The sunlight lay thick enough on these un-paved alleys to lay the dust and somebody always seemed to be practising Chopin in one or another of the flimsy houses, so lightly glued together from plywood it seemed they were sus-tained only by willpower. Once I was at home, however, it was as if I occupied the inner room and he did not expect me to go out of it, although it was I who paid the rent.

Yet, when he was away from me, he spent much of the time savouring the most annihilating remorse. But this remorse or regret was the stuff of life to him and out he would go again the next night, or, if I had been particularly angry, he would wait until the night after that. And, even if he fully intended to come back early and had promised me he would do so, circumstances always somehow denied him and once more he would contrive to miss the last train. He and his friends spent their nights in a desultory progression from coffee shop to bar to *pachinko* parlour to coffee shop, again, with the radiant aimlessness of the pure existential hero. They were connois-seurs of boredom. They savoured the various bouquets of the subtly differentiated boredoms which rose from the long, wasted hours at the dead end of night. When it was time for the first train in the morning, he would go back to the myste-riously deserted, Piranesi perspectives of the station, discol-oured by dawn, exquisitely tortured by the notion – which probably contained within it a damped-down spark of hope – that, this time, he might have done something irreparable.

I speak as if he had no secrets from me. Well, then, you must realize that I was suffering from love and I knew him as inti-mately as I knew my own image in a mirror. In other words, I knew him only in relation to myself. Yet, on those terms, I knew him perfectly. At times, I thought I was inventing him as I went along, however, so you will have to take my word for it that we existed. But I do not want to paint our circumstantial portraits so that we both emerge with enough well-rounded, spuriously detailed actuality that you are forced to believe in us. I do not want to practise such sleight of hand. You must be content only with glimpses of our outlines, as if you had caught sight of our reflections in the looking-glass of somebody else's house as you passed by the window. His name was not Taro. I only called him Taro so that I could use the conceit of the peach boy, because it seemed appropriate.

Speaking of mirrors, the Japanese have a great respect for them and, in old-fashioned inns, one often finds them hooded with fabric covers when not in use. He said: "Mirrors make a room uncosy." I am sure there is more to it than that although they love to be cosy. One must love cosiness if one is to live so close together. But, as if in celebration of the thing they feared, they seemed to have made the entire city into a cold hall of mirrors which continually proliferated whole galleries of constantly changing appearances, all marvellous but none tangible. If they did not lock up the real looking-glasses, it would be hard to tell what was real and what was not. Even buildings one had taken for substantial had a trick of disappearing overnight. One morning, we woke to find the house next door reduced to nothing but a heap of sticks and a pile of newspapers neatly tied with string, left out for the garbage collector.

I would not say that he seemed to me to possess the same kind of insubstantiality although his departure usually seemed imminent, until I realized he was as erratic but as inevitable as the weather. If you plan to come and live in Japan, you must be sure you are stoical enough to endure the weather. No, it was not insubstantiality; it was a rhetoric valid only on its own terms. When I listened to his protestations, I was prepared to believe he believed in them, although I knew perfectly well they meant nothing. And that isn't fair. When he made them, he believed in them implicitly. Then, he was utterly consumed by conviction. But his dedication was primarily to the idea of himself in love. This idea seemed to him magnificent, even sublime. He was prepared to die for it, as one of Baudelaire's dandies might have been prepared to kill himself in order to preserve himself in the condition of a work of art, for he wanted to make this experience a masterpiece of experience which absolutely transcended the everyday. And this would annihilate the effects of the cruel drug, boredom, to which he was addicted although, perhaps, the element of boredom which is implicit in an affair so isolated from the real world was its principal appeal for him. But I had no means of knowing how far his conviction would take him. And I used to turn over in my mind from time to time the question: how far does a pretence of feeling, maintained with absolute conviction, become authentic?

This country has elevated hypocrisy to the level of the highest style. To look at a samurai, you would not know him for a murderer, or a geisha for a whore. The magnificence of such objects hardly pertains to the human. They live only in a world of icons and there they participate in rituals which transmute life itself to a series of grand gestures, as moving as they are absurd. It was as if they all thought, if we believe in something hard enough, it will come true and, lo and behold! they had done and it did. Our street was in essence a slum but, in appearance, it was a little enclave of harmonious quiet and, *mirabile dictu*, it was the appearance which was the reality, because they all behaved so well, kept everything so clean and lived with such rigorous civility. What terrible discipline it takes to live harmoniously. They had crushed all their vigour in order to live harmoniously and now they had the wistful beauty of flowers pressed dry in an enormous book.

But repression does not necessarily give birth only to severe beauties. In its programmed interstices, monstrous passions bloom. They torture trees to make them look more like the formal notion of a tree. They paint amazing pictures on their skins with awl and gouge, sponging away the blood as they go; a tattooed man is a walking masterpiece of remembered pain.

They boast the most passionate puppets in the world who mimic love suicides in a stylized fashion, for here there is no such comfortable formula as "happy ever after." And, when I remembered the finale of the puppet tragedies, how the wooden lovers cut their throats together, I felt the beginnings of unease, as if the hieratic imagery of the country might overwhelm me, for his boredom had reached such a degree that he was insulated against everything except the irritation of anguish. If he valued me as an object of passion, he had reduced the word to its root, which derives from the Latin, *patior*, I suffer. He valued me as an instrument which would cause him pain.

So we lived under a disoriented moon which was as angry a purple as if the sky had bruised its eye, and, if we made certain genuine intersections, these only took place in darkness. His contagious conviction that our love was unique and desperate infected me with an anxious sickness; soon we would learn to treat one another with the circumspect tenderness of comrades who are amputees, for we were surrounded by the most moving images of evanescence, fireworks, morning glories, the old, children. But the most moving of these images were the intangible reflections of ourselves we saw in one another's eyes, reflections of nothing but appearances, in a city dedicated to seeming, and, try as we might to possess the essence of each other's otherness, we would inevitably fail.

# THE EXECUTIONER'S BEAUTIFUL DAUGHTER

*H*ere, we are high in the uplands.

A baleful almost-music, that of the tuneless cadences of an untutored orchestra repercussing in an ecstatic agony of echoes against the sounding boards of the mountains, lured us into the village square where we discover them twanging, plucking and abusing with horsehair bows a wide variety of crude stringed instruments. Our feet crunch upon dryly whispering shifting sawdust freshly scattered over impacted surfaces of years of sawdusts clotted, here and there, with blood shed so long ago it has, with age, acquired the colour and texture of rust . . . sad, ominous stains, a threat, a menace, memorials of pain.

There is no brightness in the air. Today the sun will not irradiate the heroes of the dark spectacle to which accident and disharmony combined to invite us. Here, where the air is choked all day with diffuse moisture tremulously, endlessly on the point of becoming rain, light falls as if filtered through muslin so at all hours a crepuscular gloaming prevails; the sky looks as though it is about to weep and so, gloomily illuminated through unshed tears, the *tableau vivant* before us is suffused with the sepia tints of an old photograph and nothing within it moves. The intent immobility of the spectators, wholly absorbed as they are in the performance of their hieratic ritual, is scarcely that of living things, and this *tableau vivant* might be better termed a *nature morte* for the mirthless carnival is a celebration of a death. Their eyes, the whites of which are yellowish, are all fixed, as if attached by taut, invisible strings upon a wooden block lacquered black with the spilt dews of a millennia of victims.

And now the rustic bandsmen suspend their unmelodious music. This death must be concluded in the most dramatic silence. The wild mountain-dwellers are gathered together to watch a public execution; that is the only entertainment the country offers.

Time, suspended like the rain, begins again in silence, slowly.

A heavy stillness ordering all his movements, the executioner himself adopts beside the block an offensively heroic pose, as if to do the thing with dignity were the only motive of the doing. He brings one booted foot to rest on the grim and sacrificial altar which is, to him, the canvas on which he exercises his art and proudly in his hand he bears his instrument, his axe.

The executioner stands more than six and a half feet high and he is broad to suit; the warped stumps of villagers gaze up at him with awe and fear. He is dressed always in mourning and always wears a curious mask. This mask is made of supple, close-fitting leather dyed an absolute black and it conceals his hair and the upper part of his face entirely except for two narrow slits through which issue the twin regards of eyes as inexpressive as though they were part of the mask. This mask reveals only his blunt-lipped, dark-red mouth and the greyish flesh which surrounds it. Laid out in such an unnerving fashion, these portions of his meat in no way fulfil the expectations we derive from our common knowledge of faces. They have a quality of obscene rawness as if, in some fashion, the lower face had been flayed. He, the butcher, might be displaying himself, as if he were his own meat.

Through the years, the close-fitting substance of the mask has become so entirely assimilated to the actual structure of his face that the face itself now seems to possess a particoloured appearance, as if by nature dual; and this face no longer pertains to that which is human as if, when he first put on the mask, he blotted out his own, original face and so defaced himself for ever. Because the hood of office renders the executioner an object. He has become an object who punishes. He is an object of fear. He is the image of retribution.

Nobody remembers why the mask was first devised nor who devised it. Perhaps some tender-heart of antiquity adopted the concealing headgear in order to spare the one upon the block the sight of too human a face in the last moments of his agony; or else the origins of the article lie in a magical relation with the blackness of negation – if, that is, negation is black in colour. Yet the executioner dare not take off the mask in case, in a random looking-glass or, accidentally mirrored in a pool of standing water, he surprised his own authentic face. For then he would die of fright.

The victim kneels. He is thin, pale and graceful. He is twenty years old. The silent throng in the courtyard shudders in common anticipation; all their gnarled features twist in the same grin. No sound, almost no sound disturbs the moist air, only the ghost of a sound, a distant sobbing that might be the ululation of the wind amongst the scrubby pines. The victim kneels and lays his neck upon the block. Ponderously the executioner lifts his gleaming steel.

The axe falls. The flesh severs. The head rolls.

The cleft flesh spouts its fountains. The spectators shudder, groan and gasp. And now the string band starts to bow and saw again whilst a choir of stunted virgins, in the screeching wail that passes for singing in these regions, intones a barbaric requiem entitled: AWFUL WARNING OF THE SPECTACLE OF A DECAPITATION.

The executioner has beheaded his own son for committing the crime of incest upon the body of his sister, the executioner's beautiful daughter, on whose cheeks the only roses in these highlands grow.

Gretchen no longer sleeps soundly. After the day his decapitated head rolled in the bloody sawdust, her brother rode a bicycle interminably through her dreams even though the poor child crept out secretly, alone, to gather up the poignant, moist, bearded strawberry, his surviving relic, and take it home to bury beside her hen-coop before the dogs ate it. But no matter how hard she scrubbed her little white apron against the scouring stones in the river, she could not wash away the stains that haunted the weft and warp of the fabric like pinkish phantoms of very precious fruit. Every morning, when she goes out to collect ripe eggs for her father's breakfast, she waters with felt but ineffectual tears the disturbed earth where her brother's brains lie rotting, while the indifferent hens peck and cluck about her feet.

This country is situated at such a high altitude water never boils, no matter how deceptively it foams within the pan, so their boiled eggs are always raw. The executioner insists his breakfast omelette be prepared only from those eggs precisely on the point of blossoming into chicks and, prompt at eight, consumes with relish a yellow, feathered omelette subtly spiked with claw. Gretchen, his tender-hearted daughter, often jumps and starts to hear the thwarted cluck from a still gelid, scarcely calcified beak about to be choked with sizzling butter, but her father, whose word is law because he never doffs his leather mask, will eat no egg that does not contain within it a nascent bird. That is his taste. In this country, only the executioner may indulge his perversities.

High among the mountains, how wet and cold it is! Chill winds blow soft drifts of rain across these almost perpendicular peaks; the wolf-haunted forests of fir and pine that cloak the lower slopes are groves fit only for the satanic cavortings of a universal Sabbath and a haunting mist pervades the bleak, meagre villages rooted so far above quotidian skies a newcomer might not, at first, be able to breathe but only wheeze and choke in this thinnest of air. Newcomers, however, are less frequent apparitions than meteorites and thunderbolts; the villages breathe no welcome.

Even the walls of the rudely constructed houses exude suspicion. They are made from slabs of stone and do not have any windows to see out with. An inadequate orifice in the flat roof puffs out a few scant breaths of domestic smoke and penetration inside is effected only with the utmost difficulty through low, narrow doors, crevices in the granite, so each house presents to the eye as featureless a face as those of the Oriental demons whose anonymity was marred by no such commonplace a blemish as an eye, a nose or a mouth. Inside these ugly, unaccommodating hutches, man and domestic beast – goat, ox, pig, dog – stake equal squatting rights to the smoky and disordered hearths, although the dogs often grow rabid and rush frothing through the rutted streets like streams in spate.

The inhabitants are a thick-set, sullen brood whose chronic malevolence stems from a variety of both environmental and constitutional causes. All share a general and unprepossessing cast of countenance. Their faces have the limp, flat, boneless aspect of the Eskimo and their eyes are opaque fissures since no eyelid hoods them, only the slack skin of the Mongolian fold. Their reptilian regards possess an intensity which is in no way intimate and their smiles are so peculiarly vicious it is all for the best they smile rarely. Their teeth rot young.

The men in particular are monstrously hirsute about both head and body. Their hair, a monotonous and uniform purplish black, grizzles, in age, to the tint of defunct ashes. The womenfolk are built for durability rather than delight. Since all go always barefoot, the soles of their feet develop an intensifying consistency of horn from earliest childhood and the women, who perform all the tasks demanded by their primitive agriculture, sprout forearms the size and contour of vegetable marrows while their hands become pronouncedly scoop-shaped, until they resemble, in maturity, fat five-pronged forks.

All, without exception, are filthy and verminous. His shaggy head and rough garments are clogged with lice and quiver with fleas while his pubic areas throb and pulse with the blind convulsions of the crab. Impetigo, scabies and the itch are too prevalent among them to be remarked upon and their feet start early to decompose between the toes. They suffer from chronic afflictions of the anus due to their barbarous diet – thin porridge; sour beer; meat scarcely seared by the cool fires of the highlands; acidulated cheese of goat swallowed to the flatulent accompaniment of barley bread. Such comestibles cannot but contribute effectively to those disorders that have established the general air of malign unease which is their most immediately distinctive characteristic.

In this museum of diseases, the pastel beauty of Gretchen, the executioner's daughter, is all the more remarkable. Her flaxen plaits bob above her breasts as she goes to pluck, from their nests, the budding eggs.

Their days are shrouded troughs of glum manual toil and their nights wet, freezing, black, palpitating clefts gravid with the grossest cravings, nights dedicated solely to the imaginings of unspeakable desires tortuously conceived in mortified sensibilities habitually gnawed to suppuration by the black rats of superstition whilst the needle teeth of frost corrode their bodies.

They would, if they could, act out entire Wagnerian cycles of operatic evil and gleefully transform their villages into stages upon which the authentic monstrosities of Grand Guignol might be acted out in every unspeakable detail. No hideous parody of the delights of the flesh would be alien to them . . . *did they but know how such things were, in fact, performed.*

They have an inexhaustible capacity for sin but are inexorably baulked by ignorance. They do not know what they desire. So their lusts exist in an undefined limbo, for ever *in potentia.*

They yearn passionately after the most deplorable depravity but possess not the concrete notion of so much as a simple fetish, their tormented flesh betrayed eternally by the poverty of their imaginations and the limitations of their vocabulary, for how may one transmit such things in a language composed only of brute grunts and squawks representing, for example, the state of the family pig in labour? And, since their vices are, in the literal sense of the word, unspeakable, their secret, furious desires remain ultimately mysterious even to themselves and are contained only in the realm of pure sensation, or feeling undefined as thought or action and hence unrestrained by definition. So their desires are infinite, although, in real terms, except in the form of a prickle of perturbation, these desires could hardly be said to exist.

Their lives are dominated by a folklore as picturesque as it is murderous. Rigid, hereditary castes of wizards, warlocks, shamans and practitioners of the occult proliferate amongst these benighted mountain-dwellers and the apex of esoteric power lies, it would seem, in the person of the king himself. But this appearance is deceptive. This nominal ruler is in reality the poorest beggar in all his ragged kingdom. Heir of the barbarous, he is stripped of everything but the idea of an omnipotence which is sufficiently expressed by immobility.

All day long, ever since his accession, he hangs by the right ankle from an iron ring set in the roof of a stone hut. A stout ribbon binds him to the ceiling and he is inadequately supported in a precarious but absolute position sanctioned by ritual and memory upon his left wrist, which is strapped in a similar fashion with ribbon to an iron ring cemented into the floor. He stays as still as if he had been dipped in a petrifying well and never speaks one single word because he has forgotten how.

They all believe implicitly they are damned. A folk-tale circulates among them, as follows: that the tribe was originally banished from a happier and more prosperous region to their present dreary habitation, a place fit only for continuous self-mortification, after they rendered themselves abhorrent to their former neighbours by the wholesale and enthusiastic practice of incest, son with father, father with daughter, etc. – every baroque variation possible upon the determinate quadrille of the nuclear family. In this country, incest is a capital crime; the punishment for incest is decapitation.

Daily their minds are terrified and enlightened by the continuous performances of apocalyptic dirges for fornicating siblings and only the executioner himself, because there is nobody to cut off his head, dare, in the immutable privacy of his leathern hood, upon his blood-bespattered block make love to his beautiful daughter.

Gretchen, the only flower of the mountains, tucks up her white apron and waltzing gingham skirts so they will not crease or soil but, even in the last extremity of the act, her father does not remove his mask for who would recognize him without it? The price he pays for his position is always to be locked in the solitary confinement of his power.

He perpetrates his inalienable right in the reeking courtyard upon the block where he struck off the head of his only son. That night, Gretchen discovered a snake in her sewing machine and, though she did not know what a bicycle was, upon a bicycle her brother wheeled and circled through her troubled dreams until the cock crowed and out she went for eggs.

# THE LOVES OF
# LADY PURPLE ⟿

*I*nside the pink-striped booth of the Asiatic Professor only the marvellous existed and there was no such thing as daylight.

The puppet master is always dusted with a little darkness. In direct relation to his skill he propagates the most bewildering enigmas for, the more lifelike his marionettes, the more godlike his manipulations and the more radical the symbiosis between inarticulate doll and articulating fingers. The puppeteer speculates in a no-man's-limbo between the real and that which, although we know very well it is not, nevertheless seems to be real. He is the intermediary between us, his audience, the living, and they, the dolls, the undead, who cannot live at all and yet who mimic the living in every detail since, though they cannot speak or weep, still they project those signals of signification we instantly recognize as language.

The master of marionettes vitalizes inert stuff with the dynamics of his self. The sticks dance, make love, pretend to speak and, finally, personate death; yet, so many Lazaruses out of their graves they spring again in time for the next performance and no worms drip from their noses nor dust clogs their eyes. All complete, they once again offer their brief imitations of men and women with an exquisite precision which is all the more disturbing because we know it to be false; and so this art, if viewed theologically, may, perhaps, be blasphemous.

Although he was only a poor travelling showman, the Asiatic Professor had become a consummate virtuoso of puppetry. He transported his collapsible theatre, the cast of his

27

single drama and a variety of properties in a horse-drawn cart and, after he played his play in many beautiful cities which no longer exist, such as Shanghai, Constantinople and St. Petersburg, he and his small entourage arrived at last in a country in Middle Europe where the mountains sprout jags as sharp and unnatural as those a child outlines with his crayon, a dark, superstitious Transylvania where they wreathed suicides with garlic, pierced them through the heart with stakes and buried them at crossroads while warlocks continually practised rites of immemorial beastliness in the forests.

He had only the two assistants, a deaf boy in his teens, his nephew, to whom he taught his craft, and a foundling dumb girl no more than seven or eight they had picked up on their travels. When the Professor spoke, nobody could understand him for he knew only his native tongue, which was an incomprehensible rattle of staccato k's and t's, so he did not speak at all in the ordinary course of things and, if they had taken separate paths to silence, all, in the end, signed a perfect pact with it. But, when the Professor and his nephew sat in the sun outside their booth in the mornings before performances, they held interminable dialogues in sign language punctuated by soft, wordless grunts and whistles so that the choreographed quiet of their discourse was like the mating dance of tropic birds. And this means of communication, so delicately distanced from humanity, was peculiarly apt for the Professor, who had rather the air of a visitant from another world where the mode of being was conducted in nuances rather than affirmatives. This was due partly to his extreme age, for he was very old although he carried his years lightly even if, these days, in this climate, he always felt a little chilly and so wrapped himself always in a moulting, woollen shawl; yet, more so, it was caused by his benign indifference to everything except the simulacra of the living he himself created.

Besides, however far the entourage travelled, not one of its members had ever comprehended to any degree the foreign. They were all natives of the fairground and, after all, all fairs are the same. Perhaps every single fair is no more than a dissociated fragment of one single, great, original fair which was inexplicably scattered long ago in a diaspora of the amazing. Whatever its location, a fair maintains its invariable, self-consistent atmosphere. Hieratic as knights in chess, the painted horses on the roundabouts describe perpetual circles as immutable as those of the planets and as immune to the drab world of here and now whose inmates come to gape at such extraordinariness, such freedom from actuality. The huckster's raucous invitations are made in a language beyond language, or, perhaps, in that ur-language of grunt and bark which lies behind all language. Everywhere, the same old women hawk glutinous candies which seem devised only to make flies drunk on sugar and, though the outward form of such excessive sweets may vary from place to place, their nature, never. A universal cast of two-headed dogs, dwarfs, alligator men, bearded ladies and giants in leopard-skin loin cloths reveal their singularities in the sideshows and, wherever they come from, they share the sullen glamour of deformity, an internationality which acknowledges no geographic boundaries. Here, the grotesque is the order of the day.

The Asiatic Professor picked up the crumbs that fell from this heaping table yet never seemed in the least at home there for his affinities did not lie with its harsh sounds and primary colouring although it was the only home he knew. He had the wistful charm of a Japanese flower which only blossoms when dropped in water for he, too, revealed his passions through a medium other than himself and this was his heroine, the puppet, Lady Purple.

She was the Queen of Night. There were glass rubies in her head for eyes and her ferocious teeth, carved out of mother o'pearl, were always on show for she had a permanent smile. Her face was as white as chalk because it was covered with the skin of supplest white leather which also clothed her torso, jointed limbs and complication of extremities. Her beautiful hands seemed more like weapons because her nails were so long, five inches of pointed tin enamelled scarlet, and she wore a wig of black hair arranged in a chignon more heavily elaborate than any human neck could have endured. This monumental *chevelure* was stuck through with many brilliant pins tipped with pieces of broken mirror so that, every time she moved, she cast a multitude of scintillating reflections which danced about the theatre like mice of light. Her clothes were all of deep, dark, slumbrous colours – profound pinks, crimson and the vibrating purple with which she was synonymous, a purple the colour of blood in a love suicide.

She must have been the masterpiece of a long-dead, anonymous artisan and yet she was nothing but a curious structure until the Professor touched her strings, for it was he who filled her with necromantic vigour. He transmitted to her an abundance of the life he himself seemed to possess so tenuously and, when she moved, she did not seem so much a cunningly simulated woman as a monstrous goddess, at once preposterous and magnificent, who transcended the notion she was dependent on his hands and appeared wholly real and yet entirely other. Her actions were not so much an imitation as a distillation and intensification of those of a born woman and so she could become the quintessence of eroticism, for no woman born would have dared to be so blatantly seductive.

The Professor allowed no one else to touch her. He himself looked after her costumes and jewellery. When the show was over, he placed his marionette in a specially constructed box and carried her back to the lodging house where he and his children shared a room, for she was too precious to be left in the flimsy theatre and, besides, he could not sleep unless she lay beside him.

The catchpenny title of the vehicle for this remarkable actress was: *The Notorious Amours of Lady Purple, the Shameless Oriental Venus*. Everything in the play was entirely exotic. The incantatory ritual of the drama instantly annihilated the rational and imposed upon the audience a magic alternative in which nothing was in the least familiar. The series of tableaux which illustrated her story were in themselves so filled with meaning that when the Professor chanted her narrative in his impenetrable native tongue, the compulsive strangeness of the spectacle was enhanced rather than diminished. As he crouched above the stage directing his heroine's movements, he recited a verbal recitative in a voice which clanged, rasped and swooped up and down in a weird duet with the stringed instrument from which the dumb girl struck peculiar intervals. But it was impossible to mistake him when the Professor spoke in the character of Lady Purple herself for then his voice modulated to a thick, lascivious murmur like fur soaked in honey which sent unwilling shudders of pleasure down the spines of the watchers. In the iconography of the melodrama, Lady Purple stood for passion and all her movements were calculations in an angular geometry of sexuality.

The Professor somehow always contrived to have a few handbills printed off in the language of the country where they played. These always gave the title of his play and then they used to read as follows:

*Come and see all that remains of Lady Purple, the famous prostitute and wonder of the East!*

A unique sensation. See how the unappeasable appetites of Lady Purple turned her at last into the very puppet you see before you, pulled only by the strings of *lust*. Come and see the very doll, the only surviving relic of the shameless Oriental Venus herself.

The bewildering entertainment possessed almost a religious intensity for, since there can be no spontaneity in a puppet drama, it always tends towards the rapt intensity of ritual, and, at its conclusion, as the audience stumbled from the darkened booth, it had almost suspended disbelief and was more than half convinced, as the Professor assured them so eloquently, that the bizarre figure who had dominated the stage was indeed the petrification of a universal whore and had once been a woman in whom too much life had negated life itself, whose kisses had withered like acids and whose embrace blasted like lightning. But the Professor and his assistants immediately dismantled the scenery and put away the dolls who were, after all, only mundane wood and, next day, the play was played again.

This is the story of Lady Purple as performed by the Professor's puppets to the delirious *obbligato* of the dumb girl's samisen and the audible click of the limbs of the actors.

### THE NOTORIOUS AMOURS OF
### LADY PURPLE
### THE SHAMELESS ORIENTAL
### VENUS

When she was only a few days old, her mother wrapped her in a tattered blanket and abandoned her on the doorstep of a prosperous merchant and his barren wife. These respectable bourgeois were to become the siren's first dupes. They lavished upon her all the attentions which love and money could devise and yet they reared a flower which, although perfumed, was carnivorous. At the age of twelve, she seduced her foster father. Utterly besotted with her, he trusted to her the key of the safe where he kept all his money and she immediately robbed it of every farthing.

Packing his treasure in a laundry basket together with the clothes and jewellery he had already given her, she then stabbed her first lover and his wife, her foster mother, in their bellies with a knife used in the kitchen to slice fish. Then she set fire to their house to cover the traces of her guilt. She annihilated her own childhood in the blaze that destroyed her first home and, springing like a corrupt phoenix from the pyre of her crime, she rose again in the pleasure quarters, where she at once hired herself out to the madame of the most imposing brothel.

In the pleasure quarters, life passed entirely in artificial day for the bustling noon of those crowded alleys came at the time of drowsing midnight for those who lived outside that inverted, sinister, abominable world which functioned only to gratify the whims of the senses. Every rococo desire the mind of man might, in its perverse ingenuity, devise found ample gratification here, amongst the halls of mirrors, the flagellation parlours, the cabarets of nature-defying copulations and the ambiguous soirées held by men-women and female men. Flesh was the speciality of every house and it came piping hot, served up with all the garnishes imaginable. The Professor's puppets dryly and perfunctorily performed these tactical manoeuvres like toy soldiers in a mock battle of carnality.

Along the streets, the women for sale, the mannequins of desire, were displayed in wicker cages so that potential customers could saunter past inspecting them at leisure. These exalted prostitutes sat motionless as idols. Upon their real features had been painted symbolic abstractions of the various aspects of allure and the fantastic elaboration of their dress hinted it covered a different kind of skin. The cork heels of their shoes were so high they could not walk but only totter and the sashes round their waists were of brocade so stiff the movements of the arms were cramped and scant so they presented attitudes of physical unease which, though powerfully moving, derived partly, at least, from the deaf assistant's lack of manual dexterity, for his apprenticeship had not as yet reached even the journeyman stage. Therefore the gestures of these *hetaerae* were as stylized as if they had been clockwork. Yet, however fortuitously, all worked out so well it seemed each one was as absolutely circumscribed as a figure in rhetoric, reduced by the rigorous discipline of her vocation to the nameless essence of the idea of woman, a metaphysical abstraction of the female which could, on payment of a specific fee, be instantly translated into an oblivion either sweet or terrible, depending on the nature of her talents.

Lady Purple's talents verged on the unspeakable. Booted, in leather, she became a mistress of the whip before her fifteenth birthday. Subsequently, she graduated in the mysteries of the torture chamber, where she thoroughly researched all manner of ingenious mechanical devices. She utilized a baroque apparatus of funnel, humiliation, syringe, thumbscrew, contempt and spiritual anguish; to her lovers, such severe usage was both bread and wine and a kiss from her cruel mouth was the sacrament of suffering.

Soon she became successful enough to be able to maintain her own establishment. When she was at the height of her fame, her slightest fancy might cost a young man his patrimony and, as soon as she squeezed him dry of fortune, hope and dreams, for she was quite remorseless, she abandoned him; or else she might, perhaps, lock him up in her closet and force him to watch her while she took for nothing to her usually incredibly expensive bed a beggar encountered by chance on the street. She was no malleable, since frigid, substance upon which desires might be executed; she was not a true prostitute for she was the object on which men prostituted themselves. She, the sole perpetrator of desire, proliferated malign fantasies all around her and used her lovers as the canvas on which she executed boudoir masterpieces of destruction. Skins melted in the electricity she generated.

Soon, either to be rid of them or, simply, for pleasure, she took to murdering her lovers. From the leg of a politician she poisoned she cut out the thighbone and took it to a craftsman who made it into a flute for her. She persuaded succeeding lovers to play tunes for her on this instrument and, with the supplest and most serpentine grace, she danced for them to its unearthly music. At this point, the dumb girl put down her samisen and took up a bamboo pipe from which issued weird cadences and, though it was by no means the climax of the play, this dance was the apex of the Professor's performance for, as she stamped, wheeled and turned to the sound of her malign chamber music, Lady Purple became entirely the image of irresistible evil.

She visited men like a plague, both bane and terrible enlightenment, and she was as contagious as the plague. The final condition of all her lovers was this: they went clothed in rags held together with the discharge of their sores, and their eyes held an awful vacancy, as if their minds had been blown out like candles. A parade of ghastly spectres, they trundled across the stage, their passage implemented by medieval horrors for, here, an arm left its socket and whisked up out of sight into the flies and, there, a nose hung in the air after a gaunt shape that went tottering noseless forward.

So foreclosed Lady Purple's pyrotechnical career, which ended as if it had been indeed a firework display, in ashes, desolation and silence. She became more ghastly than those she had infected. Circe at last became a swine herself and, seared to the bone by her own flame, walked the pavements like a desiccated shadow. Disaster obliterated her. Cast out with stones and oaths by those who had once adulated her, she was reduced to scavenging on the seashore, where she plucked hair from the heads of the drowned to sell to wigmakers who catered to the needs of more fortunate since less diabolic courtesans.

Now her finery, her paste jewels and her enormous superimposition of black hair hung up in the green room and she wore a drab rag of coarse hemp for the final scene of her desperate decline, when, outrageous nymphomaniac, she practised extraordinary necrophilies on the bloated corpses the sea tossed contemptuously at her feet for her dry rapacity had become entirely mechanical and still she repeated her former actions though she herself was utterly other. She abrogated her humanity. She be-

came nothing but wood and hair. She became a marionette herself, herself her own replica, the dead yet moving
image of the shameless Oriental Venus.

The Professor was at last beginning to feel the effects of age
and travel. Sometimes he complained in noisy silence to his
nephew of pains, aches, stiffening muscles, tautening sinews,
and shortness of breath. He began to limp a little and left to
the boy all the rough work of mantling and dismantling. Yet
the balletic mime of Lady Purple grew all the more remarkable
with the passage of the years, as though his energy, channelled
for so long into a single purpose, refined itself more and more
in time and was finally reduced to a single, purified, concentrated essence which was transmitted entirely to the doll; and
the Professor's mind attained a condition not unlike that of the
swordsman trained in Zen, whose sword is his soul, so that
neither sword nor swordsman has meaning without the presence of the other. Such swordsmen, armed, move towards their
victims like automata, in a state of perfect emptiness, no
longer aware of any distinction between self or weapon. Master and marionette had arrived at this condition.

Age could not touch Lady Purple for, since she had never
aspired to mortality, she effortlessly transcended it and,
though a man who was less aware of the expertise it needed to
make her so much as raise her left hand might, now and then,
have grieved to see how she defied ageing, the Professor had no
fancies of that kind. Her miraculous inhumanity rendered
their friendship entirely free from the anthropomorphic, even
on the night of the Feast of All Hallows when, the mountain-
dwellers murmured, the dead held masked balls in the grave-
yards while the devil played the fiddle for them.

The rough audience received their copeck's worth of sensation and filed out into a fairground which still roared like a
playful tiger with life. The foundling girl put away her samisen

and swept out the booth while the nephew set the stage afresh for next day's matinée. Then the Professor noticed Lady Purple had ripped a seam in the drab shroud she wore in the final act. Chattering to himself with displeasure, he undressed her as she swung idly, this way and that way, from her anchored strings and then he sat down on a wooden property stool on the stage and plied his needle like a good housewife. The task was more difficult than it seemed at first for the fabric was also torn and required an embroidery of darning so he told his assistants to go home together to the lodging house and let him finish his task alone.

A small oil-lamp hanging from a nail at the side of the stage cast an insufficient but tranquil light. The white puppet glimmered fitfully through the mists which crept into the theatre from the night outside through all the chinks and gaps in the tarpaulin and now began to fold their chiffon drapes around her as if to decorously conceal her or else to render her more translucently enticing. The mist softened her painted smile a little and her head dangled to one side. In the last act, she wore a loose, black wig, the locks of which hung down as far as her softly upholstered flanks, and the ends of her hair flickered with her random movements, creating upon the white blackboard of her back one of those fluctuating optical effects which make us question the veracity of our vision. As he often did when he was alone with her, the Professor chatted to her in his native language, rattling away an intimacy of nothings, of the weather, of his rheumatism, of the unpalatability and expense of the region's coarse, black bread, while the small winds took her as their partner in a scarcely perceptible *valse triste* and the mist grew minute by minute thicker, more pallid and more viscous.

The old man finished his mending. He rose and, with a click or two of his old bones, he went to put the forlorn garment neatly on its green-room hanger beside the glowing, winy purple gown splashed with rosy peonies, sashed with carmine, that she wore for her appalling dance. He was about to lay her, naked, in her coffin-shaped case and carry her back to their

chilly bedroom when he paused. He was seized with the childish desire to see her again in all her finery once more that
night. He took her dress off its hanger and carried it to where
she drifted, at nobody's volition but that of the wind. As he put
her clothes on her, he murmured to her as if she were a little
girl for the vulnerable flaccidity of her arms and legs made a
six-foot baby of her.

"There, there, my pretty; this arm here, that's right! Oops a
daisy, easy does it . . ."

Then he tenderly took off her penitential wig and clucked
his tongue to see how defencelessly bald she was beneath it.
His arms cracked under the weight of her immense chignon
and he had to stretch up on tiptoe to set it in place because,
since she was as large as life, she was rather taller than he. But
then the ritual of apparelling was over and she was complete
again.

Now she was dressed and decorated, it seemed her dry wood
had all at once put out an entire springtime of blossoms for the
old man alone to enjoy. She could have acted as the model for
the most beautiful of women, the image of that woman whom
only a man's memory and imagination can devise, for the lamp-
light fell too mildly to sustain her air of arrogance and so
gently it made her long nails look as harmless as ten fallen
petals. The Professor had a curious habit; he always used to
kiss his doll good night.

A child kisses its toy before she pretends it sleeps although,
even though she is only a child, she knows its eyes are not
constructed to close so it will always be a sleeping beauty no
kiss will waken. One in the grip of savage loneliness might
kiss the face he sees before him in the mirror for want of any
other face to kiss. These are kisses of the same kind; they are
the most poignant of caresses, for they are too humble and too
despairing to wish or seek for any response.

Yet, in spite of the Professor's sad humility, his chapped and
withered mouth opened on hot, wet, palpitating flesh.

The sleeping wood had wakened. Her pearl teeth crashed
against his with the sound of cymbals and her warm, fragrant

breath blew around him like an Italian gale. Across her suddenly moving face flashed a whole kaleidoscope of expression, as though she were running instantaneously through the entire repertory of human feeling, practising, in an endless moment of time, all the scales of emotion as if they were music. Crushing vines, her arms, curled about the Professor's delicate apparatus of bone and skin with the insistent pressure of an actuality by far more authentically living than that of his own, time-desiccated flesh. Her kiss emanated from the dark country where desire is objectified and lives. She gained entry into the world by a mysterious loophole in its metaphysics and, during her kiss, she sucked his breath from his lungs so that her own bosom heaved with it.

So, unaided, she began her next performance with an apparent improvisation which was, in reality, only a variation upon a theme. She sank her teeth into his throat and drained him. He did not have the time to make a sound. When he was empty, he slipped straight out of her embrace down to her feet with a dry rustle, as of a cast armful of dead leaves, and there he sprawled on the floorboards, as empty, useless and bereft of meaning as his own tumbled shawl.

She tugged impatiently at the strings which moored her and out they came in bunches from her head, her arms and her legs. She stripped them off her fingertips and stretched out her long, white hands, flexing and unflexing them again and again. For the first time for years, or, perhaps, for ever, she closed her blood-stained teeth thankfully, for her cheeks still ached from the smile her maker had carved into the stuff of her former face. She stamped her elegant feet to make the new blood flow more freely there.

Unfurling and unravelling itself, her hair leaped out of its confinements of combs, cords and lacquer to root itself back into her scalp like cut grass bounding out of the stack and back again into the ground. First, she shivered with pleasure to feel the cold, for she realized she was experiencing a physical sensation; then either she remembered or else she believed she remembered that the sensation of cold was not a pleasurable one so she knelt and, drawing off the old man's shawl, wrapped it carefully about herself. Her every motion was instinct with a wonderful, reptilian liquidity. The mist outside now seemed to rush like a tide into the booth and broke against her in white breakers so that she looked like a baroque figurehead, lone survivor of a shipwreck, thrown up on a shore by the tide.

But whether she was renewed or newly born, returning to life or becoming alive, awakening from a dream or coalescing into the form of a fantasy generated in her wooden skull by the mere repetition so many times of the same invariable actions, the brain beneath the reviving hair contained only the scantiest notion of the possibilities now open to it. All that had seeped into the wood was the notion that she might perform the forms of life not so much by the skill of another as by her own desire that she did so, and she did not possess enough equipment to comprehend the complex circularity of the logic which inspired her for she had only been a marionette. But, even if she could not perceive it, she could not escape the tautological paradox in which she was trapped; had the marionette all the time parodied the living or was she, now living, to parody her own performance as a marionette? Although she was now manifestly a woman, young and beautiful, the leprous whiteness of her face gave her the appearance of a corpse animated solely by demonic will.

Deliberately, she knocked the lamp down from its hook on the wall. A puddle of oil spread at once on the boards of the stage. A little flame leaped across the fuel and immediately began to eat the curtains. She went down the aisle between the benches to the little ticket booth. Already, the stage was an inferno and the corpse of the Professor tossed this way and that on an uneasy bed of fire. But she did not look behind her after she slipped out into the fairground although soon the theatre was burning like a paper lantern ignited by its own candle.

Now it was so late that the sideshows, gingerbread stalls and liquor booths were locked and shuttered and only the moon, half obscured by drifting cloud, gave out a meagre, dirty light, which sullied and deformed the flimsy pasteboard façades, so the place, deserted, with curds of vomit, the refuse of revelry, underfoot, looked utterly desolate.

She walked rapidly past the silent roundabouts, accompanied only by the fluctuating mists, towards the town, making her way like a homing pigeon, out of logical necessity, to the single brothel it contained.

# THE SMILE OF WINTER ~

$B$ecause there are no seagulls here, the only sound is the resonance of the sea. This coastal region is quite flat, so that an excess of sky bears down with an intolerable weight, pressing the essence out of everything beneath it for it imposes such a burden on us that we have all been forced inward on ourselves in an introspective sombreness intensified by the perpetual abrasive clamour of the sea. When the sun goes down, it is very cold and then I easily start crying because the winter moon pierces my heart. The winter moon is surrounded by an extraordinary darkness, the logical antithesis of the supernal clarity of the day; in this darkness, the dogs in every household howl together at the sight of a star, as if the stars were unnatural things. But, from morning until evening, a hallucinatory light floods the shore and a cool, glittering sun transfigures everything so brilliantly that the beach looks like a desert and the ocean like a mirage.

But the beach is never deserted. Far from it. At times, there is even a silent crowd of people – women who come in groups to turn the fish they have laid out to dry on bamboo racks; Sunday trippers; solitary anglers, even. Sometimes trucks drive up and down the beach to and fro from the next headland and after school is over children come to improvise games of baseball with sticks and a dead crab delivered to them by the tide. The children wear peaked, yellow caps; their heads are perfectly round. Their faces are perfectly bland, the colour as well as the shape of brown eggs. They giggle when they see me because I am white and pink while they themselves are such a serviceable, unanimous beige. Besides all these visitors, the motorcyclists who come at night have left deep grooves behind them in the sand as if to say: "I have been here."

When the shadows of the evening lie so thickly on the beach it looks as though nobody has dusted it for years, the motorcyclists come out. That is their favourite time. They have marked out a course among the dunes with red wooden pegs and ride round it at amazing speeds. They come when they please. Sometimes they come in the early morning but, most often, by owl-light. They announce their presence with a fanfare of opened throttles. They grow their hair long and it flies out behind them like black flags, motorcyclists as beautiful as the outriders of death in the film *Orphée*. I wish they were not so beautiful; if they were not so beautiful and so inaccessible to me, then I should feel less lonely, although, after all, I came here in order to be lonely.

The beach is full of the garbage of the ocean. The waves leave torn, translucent furls of polythene wrapping too tough for even this sea's iron stomach; chipped jugs that once held rice wine; single sea-boots freighted with sand; broken beer bottles and, once, a brown dog stiff and dead washed up as far as the pine trees which, subtly warped by the weather, squat on their hunkers at the end of my garden, where the dry soil transforms itself to sand.

Already the pines are budding this year's cones. Each blunt, shaggy bough is tipped with a small, lightly furred growth just like the prick of a little puppy while the dry, brown cones of last year still cling to the rough stems though now these are so insecure a touch will bring them bounding down. But, all in all, the pines have a certain intransigence. They dig their roots into dry soil full of seashells and strain backwards in the wind that blows directly from Alaska. They are absolutely exposed to the weather and yet as indifferent as the weather. The indifference of this Decembral littoral suits my forlorn mood for I am a sad woman by nature, no doubt about that; how unhappy I should be in a happy world! This country has the most rigorous romanticism in the world and they think a woman who

lives by herself should accentuate her melancholy with surroundings of sentimental dilapidation. I have read about all
the abandoned lovers in their old books eating their hearts out
like Mariana in so many moated granges; their gardens are
overgrown with goosegrass and mugwort, their mud walls are
falling to pieces and their carp pools scaled over with water-
lily pads. Everything combines with the forlorn mood of the
châtelaine to procure a moving image of poignant desolation.
In this country you do not need to think, but only to look, and
soon you think you understand everything.

The old houses in the village are each one dedicated to
seclusion and court an individual sequestered sadness behind
the weather-stained, unpainted wooden shutters they usually
keep closed. It is a gloomy, aridly aesthetic architecture based
on the principle of perpetual regression. The houses are heavily shingled and the roofs are the shapes and colours of waves
frozen on a grey day. In the mornings, they dismantle the outer
screens to let fresh air blow through and, as you walk past, you
can see that all the inner walls are also sliding screens, though
this time of stiff paper, and you can glimpse endlessly receding
perspectives of interiors in brownish tones, as if everything
had been heavily varnished some time ago; and, though these
perspectives can be altered at will, the fresh rooms they make
when they shift the screens about always look exactly the
same as the old rooms. And all the matted interiors are the
same, anyway.

Through the gaping palings of certain fences, I sometimes
see a garden so harmoniously in tune with the time of year it
looks forsaken. But sometimes all these fragile habitations of
unpainted wood; and the still lives, or *natures mortes*, of rust-
ing water pumps and withered chrysanthemums in backyards;
and the discarded fishing boats pulled up on the sand and left
to rot away – sometimes the whole village looks forsaken. This
is, after all, the season of abandonment, of the suspension of
vitality, a long cessation of vigour in which we must cultivate
our stoicism. Everything has put on the desolate smile of winter. Outside my shabby front door, I have a canal, like Mariana

in a moated grange; beyond the skulking pines at the back, there is only the ocean. The winter moon pierces my heart. I weep.

But when I went out on the beach this morning with the skin on my face starched with dried tears so I could feel my cheeks crackle in the wind, I found the sea had washed me up a nice present – two pieces of driftwood. One was a forked chunk like a pair of wooden trousers and the other was a larger, greyish, frayed root the shape of the paw of a ragged lion. I collect driftwood and set it up among the pine trees in picturesque attitudes on the edge of the beach and then I strike a picturesque attitude myself beside them as I watch the constantly agitated waves, for here we all strike picturesque attitudes and that is why we are so beautiful. Sometimes I imagine that one night the riders will stop at the end of my garden and I will hear the heels of their boots crunch on the friable carpet of last year's shed cones and then there will be a hesitant rattle of knuckles on the seaward-facing door and they will wait in ceremonious silence until I come, for their bodies are only images.

My pockets always contain a rasping sediment of sand because I fill them with shells when I go onto the beach. The vast majority of these shells are round, sculptural forms the colour of a brown egg, with warm, creamy insides. They have a classical simplicity. The scarcely perceptible indentations of their surfaces flow together to produce a texture as subtly matt as that of a petal which is as satisfying to touch as Japanese skin. But there are also pure white shells heavily ridged on the outside but within of a marmoreal smoothness and these come in hinged pairs.

There is still a third kind of shell, though I find these less often. They are curlicued, shaped like turbans and dappled with pink, of a substance so thin the ocean easily grinds away the outer husk to lay bare their spiralline cores. They are often decorated with baroque, infinitesimal swags of calcified parasites. They are the smallest of all the shells but by far the most intricate. When I picked up one of those shells, I found it contained the bright pink, dried, detached limb of a tiny sea creature like a dehydrated memory. Sometimes a litter of dropped fish lies among the shells. Each fish reflects the sky with the absolute purity of a Taoist mirror.

The fish have fallen off the racks on which they have been put out to dry. These bamboo racks spread with fish stand on trestles all along the beach as if a feast was laid for the entire prefecture but nobody had come to eat it. Close to the village, there are whole paddocks filled with bamboo racks. In one of these paddocks, a tethered goat crops grass. The fish are as shiny as fish of tin and the size of my little finger. Once dried, they are packed in plastic bags and sold to flavour soup.

The women lay them out. They come every day to turn them and, when the fish are ready, they pile up the racks and carry them to the packing sheds. There are great numbers of these raucously silent, and well-muscled, intimidating women.

The cruel wind burns port-wine whorls on their dour, inexpressive faces. All wear dark or drab-coloured trousers pinched in at the ankle and either short rubber boots or split-toed socks on their feet. A layer of sweaters and a loose, padded cotton jacket gives them a squat, top-heavy look, as if they would not fall over, only rock malevolently to and fro if you pushed them. Over their jackets, they wear short, immaculate aprons trimmed with coarse lace and they tie white baboushkas round their heads or sometimes wind a kind of wimple over the ears and round the throat. They are truculent and aggressive. They stare at me with open curiosity tinged with hostility. When they laugh, they display treasuries of gold teeth and their hands are as hard as those of eighteenth-century prize-fighters, who also used to pickle their fists in brine. They make me feel that either I or they are deficient in femininity and I suppose it must be I since most of them hump about an organic lump of baby on their backs, inside their coats. It seems that only women people the village because most of the men are out on the sea. Early in the morning, I go out to watch the winking and blinking of the fishing boats on the water, which, just before dawn, has turned a deep violet.

The moist and misty mornings after a storm obscure the horizon for then the ocean has turned into the sky and the wind and waves have realigned the contours of the dunes. The wet sand is as dark and more yieldingly solid than fudge and walking across a panful is a promenade in the Kingdom of Sweets. The waves leave behind them glinting striations of salt and forcibly mould the foreshore into the curvilinear abstractions of cliffs, bays, inlets, curvilinear tumuli like the sculpture of Arp. But the storms themselves are a raucous music and turn my house into an Aeolian xylophone. All night long, the wind bangs and rattles away at every wooden surface; the house is a sounding box and even on the quietest nights the paper windows let through the wind that rattles softly in the pines.

Sometimes the lights of the midnight riders scrawl brilliant hieroglyphs across the panes, especially on moonless nights, when I am alone in a landscape of extraordinary darkness, and I am a little frightened when I see their headlamps and hear their rasping engines for then they seem the spawn of the negated light and to have driven straight out of the sea, which is just as mysterious as the night, even, and also its perfect image, for the sea is an inversion of the known and occupies half, or more, of the world, just as night does; whilst different peoples also live in the countries of the night.

They all wear leather jackets bristling with buckles, and high-heeled boots. They cannot buy such gaudy apparel in the village because the village shops only sell useful things such as paraffin, quilts and things to eat. And all the colours in the village are subfusc and equivocal, those of wood tinted bleakly by the weather and of lifeless wintry vegetation. When I sometimes see an orange tree hung with gold balls like a magic trick, it does nothing but stress by contrast the prevailing static sobriety of everything, which combines to smile in chorus the desolate smile of winter. On rainy nights when there is a winter moon bright enough to pierce the heart, I often wake to find my face still wet with tears so that I know I have been crying.

When the sun is low in the west, the beams become individually visible and fall with a peculiar, lateral intensity across the beach, flushing out long shadows from the grains of sand and these beams seem to penetrate to the very hearts of the incoming waves which look, then, as if they were lit from within. Before they topple forward, they bulge outward in the swollen shapes and artfully flawed incandescence of Art Nouveau glass, as if the translucent bodies of the images they contain within them were trying to erupt, for the bodies of the creatures of the sea are images, I am convinced of that. At this time of day, the sea turns amazing colours – the brilliant, chemical green of the sea in nineteenth-century tinted postcards; or a blue far too cerulean for early evening; or sometimes it shines with such metallic brilliance I can hardly bear to look at it. Smiling my habitual winter smile, I stand at the end of my garden attended by a pack of green bears while I watch the constantly agitated white lace cuffs on the colourful sleeves of the Pacific.

Different peoples inhabit the countries of the ocean and some of their emanations undulate past me when I walk along the beach to the village on one of those rare, bleak, sullen days, spectral wraiths of sand blowing to various inscrutable meeting places on blind currents of the Alaskan wind. They twine around my ankles in serpentine caresses and they have eyes of sand but some of the other creatures have eyes of solid water and when the women move among trays of fish I think they, too, are sea creatures, spiny, ocean-bottom-growing flora and if a tidal wave consumed the village – as it could do tomorrow, for there are no hills or sea walls to protect us – there, under the surface, life would go on just as before, the sea goat still nibbling, the shops still doing a roaring trade in octopus and pickled turnip greens, the women going about their silent business because everything is as silent as if it were under the water, anyway, and the very air is as heavy as water and warps the light so that one sees as if one's eyes were made of water.

Do not think I do not realize what I am doing. I am making a composition using the following elements: the winter beach;

the winter moon; the ocean; the women; the pine trees; the riders; the driftwood; the shells; the shapes of darkness and the shapes of water; and the refuse. These are all inimical to my loneliness because of their indifference to it. Out of these pieces of inimical indifference, I intend to represent the desolate smile of winter which, as you must have gathered, is the smile I wear.

# PENETRATING TO THE HEART OF THE FOREST  ⁓

$T$he whole region was like an abandoned flower bowl, filled to overflowing with green, living things; and, protected on all sides by the ferocious barricades of the mountains, those lovely reaches of forest lay so far inland the inhabitants believed the name, Ocean, that of a man in another country, and would have taken an oar, had they ever seen one, to be a winnowing fan. They built neither roads nor towns; in every respect like Candide, especially that of past ill-fortune, all they did now was to cultivate their gardens.

They were the descendants of slaves who, many years before, ran away from plantations in distant plains, in pain and hardship crossed the arid neck of the continent, and endured an infinity of desert and tundra, before they clambered the rugged foothills to scale at last the heights themselves and so arrive in a region that offered them in plentiful fulfilment all their dreams of a promised land. Now, the groves that skirted those forests of pine in the central valley formed for them all of the world they wished to know and nothing in their self-contained quietude concerned them but the satisfaction of simple pleasures. Not a single exploring spirit had ever been curious enough to search to its source the great river that watered their plots, or to penetrate to the heart of the forest itself. They had grown far too contented in their lost fastness to care for anything but the joys of idleness.

They had brought with them as a relic of their former life only the French their former owners had branded on their tongues, though certain residual, birdlike flutings of forgotten

African dialects put unexpected cadences in their speech and, with the years, they had fashioned an arboreal argot of their own to which a French grammar would have proved a very fallible guide. And they had also packed up in their ragged bandanas a little, dark, voodoo folklore. But such blood-stained ghosts could not survive in sunshine and fresh air and emigrated from the villages in a body, to live only the ambiguous life of horned rumours in the woods, becoming at last no more than shapes with indefinable outlines who lurked, perhaps, in the green deeps, until, at last, one of the shadows modulated imperceptibly into the actual shape of a tree.

Almost as if to justify to themselves their lack of a desire to explore, they finally seeded by word of mouth a mythic and malign tree within the forest, a tree the image of the Upas Tree of Java whose very shadow was murderous, a tree that exuded a virulent sweat of poison from its moist bark and whose fruits could have nourished with death an entire tribe. And the presence of this tree categorically forbade exploration – even though all knew, in their hearts, that such a tree did not exist. But, even so, they guessed it was safest to be a stay-at-home.

Since the woodlanders could not live without music, they made fiddles and guitars for themselves with great skill and ingenuity. They loved to eat well so they stirred themselves enough to plant vegetables, tend goats and chickens and blend these elements together in a rustic but voluptuous cookery. They dried, candied and preserved in honey some of the wonderful fruits they grew and exchanged this produce with the occasional traveller who came over the single, hazardous mountain pass, carrying bales of cotton fabrics and bundles of ribbons. With these, the women made long skirts and blouses for themselves and trousers for their menfolk, so all were dressed in red and yellow flowered cloth, purple and green checkered cloth, or cloth striped like a rainbow, and they plaited themselves hats from straw. They needed nothing more than a few flowers before they felt their graceful toilets were complete and a profusion of flowers grew all around them, so many flowers that the straw-thatched villages looked like inhabited gardens, for the soil was of amazing richness and the flora proliferated in such luxuriance that when Dubois, the botanist, came over the pass on his donkey, he looked down on that paradisial landscape and exclaimed: "Dear God! It is as if Adam had opened Eden to the public!"

Dubois was seeking a destination whose whereabouts he did not know, though he was quite sure it existed. He had visited most of the out-of-the-way parts of the world to peer through the thick lenses of his round spectacles at every kind of plant. He gave his name to an orchid in Dahomey, to a lily in Indo-China and to a dark-eyed Portuguese girl in a Brazilian town of such awesome respectability that even its taxis wore antimacassars. But, because he loved the frail wife whose grave eyes already warned him she would live briefly, he rooted there, a plant himself in alien soil, and, out of gratitude, she gave him two children at one birth before she died.

He found his only consolation in a return to the flowering wilderness he had deserted for her sake. He was approaching middle age, a raw-boned, bespectacled man who habitually stooped out of a bashful awareness of his immense height, hirsute and gentle as a herbivorous lion. The vicissitudes of a life in which his reticence had cheated him of the fruits of his scholarship, together with the forlorn conclusion of his marriage, had left him with a yearning for solitude and a desire to rear his children in a place where ambition, self-seeking and guile were strangers, so that they would grow up with the strength and innocence of young trees.

But such a place was hard to find.

His wanderings took him to regions ever more remote from civilization but he was never seized with a conviction of home-coming until that morning, as the sun irradiated the mists and his donkey picked its way down a rough path so overgrown with dew-drenched grass and mosses it had become no more than the subtlest intimation of a direction.

It took him circuitously down to a village sunk in a thicket of honeysuckle that filled with languorous sweetness the rarefied air of the uplands. On the dawning light hung, trembling, the notes of a pastoral aubade somebody was picking out on a guitar. As Dubois passed the house, a plump, dark-skinned woman with a crimson handkerchief round her head threw open a pair of shutters and leaned out to pick a spray of morning glory. As she tucked it behind her ear, she saw the stranger and smiled like another sunrise, greeting him with a few melodious phrases of his native language she had some-how mixed with burned cream and sunshine. She offered him a little breakfast which she was certain he must need since he had travelled so far and, while she spoke, the yellow-painted door burst open and a chattering tide of children swept out to surround the donkey, turning up to Dubois faces like sun-flowers.

Six weeks after his arrival among the Creoles, Dubois left again for the house of his parents-in-law. There, he packed his library, notebooks and records of researches; his most precious collections of specimens and his equipment; as much clothing as he felt would last him the rest of his life, and a crate con-taining objects of sentimental value. This case and his chil-dren were the only concessions he made to the past. And, once he had installed all those things safely in a wooden farmhouse the villagers had interrupted their inactivity long enough to make ready for him, he closed the doors of his heart to every-thing but the margins of the forest, which were to him a re-markable book it would take all the years that remained to him to learn to read.

The birds and beasts showed no fear of him. Painted magpies perched reflectively on his shoulders as he pored over the drawings he made among the trees, while fox cubs rolled in play around his feet and even learned to nose in his capacious pockets for cookies. As his children grew older, he seemed to them more an emanation of their surroundings than an actual father, and from him they unknowingly imbibed a certain ra-diant inhumanity which sprang from a benign indifference towards by far the greater part of mankind – towards all those who were not beautiful, gentle and, by nature, kind.

"Here, we have all become *homo silvester*, men of the

woods," he would say. "And that is by far superior to the preco-
cious and destructive species, *homo sapiens* – knowing man.
Knowing man, indeed; what more than nature does man need
to know?"

Other carefree children were their playfellows and their toys
were birds, butterflies and flowers. Their father spared them
enough of his time to teach them to read, to write and to draw.
Then he gave them the run of his library and left them alone,
to grow as they pleased. So they thrived on a diet of simple
food, warm weather, perpetual holidays and haphazard learning. They were fearless since there was nothing to be afraid of
and they always spoke the truth because there was no need to
lie. No hand or voice was ever raised in anger against them and
so they did not know what anger was; when they came across
the word in books, they thought it must mean the mild fretful-
ness they felt when it rained two days together, which did not
happen often. They quite forgot the dull town where they had
been born. The green world took them for its own and they
were fitting children of their foster mother, for they were
strong, lithe and supple, browned by the sun to the very colour
of the villagers whose liquid *patois* they spoke. They resembled one another so closely each could have used the other
as a mirror and almost seemed to be different aspects of the
same person for all their gestures, turns of phrase and manner
of speech were exactly similar. Had they known how, they
would have been proud, because their intimacy was so perfect
it could have bred that sense of loneliness which is the source
of pride and, as they read more and more of their father's
books, their companionship deepened since they had nobody
but one another with whom to discuss the discoveries they
made in common. From morning to evening, they were never
apart, and at night they slept together in a plain, narrow bed on
a floor of beaten earth while the window held the friendly
nightlight of a soft, southern moon above them in a narrow
frame. But often they slept under the moon itself, for they
came and went as they pleased and spent most of their time

out of doors, exploring the forests until they had gone further and seen more than ever their father had.

At last, these explorations took them into the untrodden, virginal reaches of the deep interior. Here, they walked hand in hand beneath the vaulted architraves of pines in a hushed interior like that of a sentient cathedral. The topmost branches twined so thickly that only a subdued viridian dazzle of light could filter through and the children felt against their ears a palpable fur of intense silence. Those who felt less kinship with the place might have been uneasy, as if abandoned among serene, voiceless, giant forms that cared nothing for man. But, if the children sometimes lost their way, they never lost themselves for they took the sun by day and the stars by the otherwise trackless night for their compass and could discern clues in the labyrinth that those who trusted the forest less would not have recognized, for they knew the forest too well to know of any harm it might do them.

Long ago, in their room at home, they began work on a map of the forest. This was by no means the map an authentic cartographer would have made. They marked hills with webs of feathers of the birds they found there, clearings with an integument of pressed flowers and especially magnificent trees with delicate, brightly coloured drawings on whose watercolour boughs they stuck garlands of real leaves so that the map became a tapestry made out of the substance of the forest itself. At first, in the centre of the map, they put their own thatched cottage and Madeline drew in the garden the shaggy figure of their father, whose leonine mane was as white, now, as the puff ball of a dandelion, bending with a green watering can over his pots of plants, tranquil, beloved and oblivious. But as they grew older, they grew discontented with their work for they found out their home did not lie at the heart of the forest but only somewhere in its green suburbs. They were seized with the desire to pierce more and yet more deeply into the unfrequented places and now their expeditions lasted for a week or longer. Though he was always glad to see them return, their father had often forgotten they had been away. At last, nothing but the discovery of the central node of the unvisited valley, the navel of the forest, would satisfy them. It grew to be almost an obsession with them. They spoke of the adventure only to one another and did not share it with the other companions who, as they grew older, grew less and less necessary to their absolute intimacy, since, lately, for reasons beyond their comprehension, this intimacy had been subtly invaded by tensions which exacerbated their nerves yet exerted on them both an intoxicating glamour.

Besides, when they spoke of the heart of the forest to their other friends, a veil of darkness came over the woodlanders' eyes and, half-laughing, half-whispering, they would hint at the wicked tree that grew there as though, even if they did not believe in it, it was a metaphor for something unfamiliar they preferred to ignore, as one might say: "Let sleeping dogs lie. Aren't we happy as we are?" When they saw this laughing apathy, this incuriosity blended with a tinge of fear, Emile and Madeline could not help but feel a faint contempt, for their world, though beautiful, seemed to them, in a sense, incomplete – as though it lacked the knowledge of some mystery they might find, might they not? in the forest, on their own.

In their father's books they found references to the Antiar or Antshar of the Indo-Malay archipelago, the Antiaris Toxicaria whose milky juice contains a most potent poison, like the quintessence of belladonna. But their reason told them that not even the most intrepid migratory bird could have brought the sticky seeds on its feet to cast them down here in these land-locked valleys far from Java. They did not believe the wicked tree could exist in this hemisphere; and yet they were curious. But they were not afraid.

One August morning, when both were thirteen years old, they put bread and cheese in their knapsacks and started out on a journey so early the homesteads were sleeping and even the morning glories were still in bud. The settlements were just as their father had seen them first, prelapsarian villages where any Fall was inconceivable; his children, bred in those quiet places, saw them with eyes pure of nostalgia for lost innocence and thought of them only with that faint, warm claustrophobia which the word, "home," signifies. At noon, they ate lunch with a family whose cottage lay at the edges of the uninhabited places and when they bade their hosts good-bye, they knew, with a certain anticipatory relish, they would not see anyone else but one another for a long time.

At first, they followed the wide river which led them direct-ly into the ramparts of the great pines and, though days and nights soon merged together in a sonorous quiet where trees grew so close together that birds had no room to sing or fly, they kept a careful tally of the passing time for they knew that, five days away from home, along the leisurely course of the water, the pines thinned out.

The bramble-covered river banks, studded, at this season, with flat, pink discs of blossom, grew so narrow that the water tumbled fast enough to ring out various carillons while grey squirrels swung from branch to low branch of trees which, released from the strait confines of the forest, now grew in shapes of a feminine slightness and grace. Rabbits twitched moist, velvet noses and laid their ears along their backs but did not run away when they saw the barefoot children go by and Emile pointed out to Madeline how a wise toad, squatting meditatively among the kingcups, must have a jewel in his head because bright beams darted out through his eyes, as though a cold fire burned inside his head. They had read of this phenomenon in old books but never seen it before.

They had never seen anything in this place before. It was so beautiful they were a little awe-struck.

Then Madeline stretched out her hand to pick a water lily unbudding on the surface of the river but she jumped back with a cry and gazed down at her finger with a mixture of pain, affront and astonishment. Her bright blood dripped down on to the grass.

"Emile!" she said. "It bit me!"

They had never encountered the slightest hostility in the forest before. Their eyes met in wonder and surmise while the birds chanted recitatives to the accompaniment of the river.

"This is a strange place," said Emile hesitantly. "Perhaps we should not pick any flowers in this part of the forest. Perhaps we have found some kind of carnivorous water lily."

He washed the tiny wound, bound it with his handkerchief and kissed her cheek, to comfort her, but she would not be comforted and irritably flung a pebble in the direction of the flower. When the pebble struck the lily, it unfurled its close circle of petals with an audible snap and, bewildered, they glimpsed inside them a set of white, perfect fangs. Then the waxen petals closed swiftly over the teeth again, concealing them entirely, and the water lily again looked perfectly white and innocent.

"See! It *is* a carnivorous water lily!" said Emile. "Father *will* be excited when we tell him."

But Madeline, her eyes still fixed on the predator as if it fascinated her, slowly shook her head. She had grown very serious.

"No," she said. "We must not talk of the things we find in the heart of the forest. They are all secrets. If they were not secrets, we would have heard of them before."

Her words fell with a strange weight, as heavy as her own gravity, as if she might have received some mysterious communication from the perfidious mouth that wounded her. At once, listening to her, Emile thought of the legendary tree; and then he realized that, for the first time in his life, he did not understand her, for, of course, they had heard of the tree. Looking at her in a new puzzlement, he sensed the ultimate difference of a femininity he had never before known any need or desire to acknowledge and this difference might give her the key to some order of knowledge to which he might not yet aspire, himself, for all at once she seemed far older than he. She raised her eyes and fixed on him a long, solemn regard which chained him in a conspiracy of secrecy, so that, henceforth, they would share only with one another the treacherous marvels round them. At last, he nodded.

"Very well, then," he said. "We won't tell father."

Though they knew he never listened when they spoke to him, never before had they consciously concealed anything from him.

Night was approaching. They walked a little further, until they found pillows of moss laid ready for their heads beneath the branches of a flowering tree. They drank clear water, ate the last of the food they had brought with them and then slept in one another's arms as if they were the perfect children of the place, although they slept less peacefully than usual for both were visited by unaccustomed nightmares of knives and snakes and suppurating roses. But though each stirred and murmured, the dreams were so strangely inconsequential, nothing but fleeting sequences of detached, malign images, that the children forgot them as they slept and woke only with an irritable residue of nightmare, the dregs of unremembered dreaming, knowing only they had slept badly.

In the morning, they stripped and bathed in the river. Emile saw that time was subtly altering the contours of both their bodies and he found he could no longer ignore his sister's nakedness, as he had done since babyhood, while, from the way she suddenly averted her own eyes after, in her usual playful fashion, she splashed him with water, she, too, experienced the same extraordinary confusion. So they fell silent and hastily dressed themselves. And yet the confusion was pleasurable and made their blood sting. He examined her finger and found the marks of the lily's teeth were gone; the wound had healed over completely. Yet he still shuddered with an unfamiliar thrill of dread when he remembered the fanged flower.

"We have no food left," he said. "We should turn back at noon."

"Oh, no!" said Madeline with a mysterious purposefulness that might have been rooted, had he known it, only in a newborn wish to make him do as she wanted, against his own wishes. "No! I'm sure we shall find something to eat. After all, this is the season for wild strawberries."

He, too, knew the lore of the forest. At no time of the year could they not find food – berries, roots, salads, mushrooms, and so on. So he saw she knew he had only used a pale excuse to cover his increasing agitation at finding himself alone with her so far from home. And now he had used up his excuse, there was nothing for it but to go on. She walked with a certain irresolute triumph, as though she were aware she had won an initial victory which, though insignificant in itself, might herald more major battles in the future, although they did not even know the formula for a quarrel, yet.

And already this new awareness of one another's shapes and outlines had made them less twinned, less indistinguishable from one another. So they fell once more to their erudite botanizing, in order to pretend that all was as it had always been, before the forest showed its teeth; and now the meandering path of the river led them into such magical places that they found more than enough to talk about for, by the time the shadows vanished at noon, they had come into a landscape that seemed to have undergone an alchemical change, a vegetable transmutation, for it contained nothing that was not marvellous.

Ferns uncurled as they watched, revealing fronded fringes containing innumerable, tiny, shining eyes glittering like brilliants where the ranks of seeds should have been. A vine was covered with slumbrous, purple flowers that, as they passed, sang out in a rich contralto with all the voluptuous wildness of flamenco – and then fell silent. There were trees that bore, instead of foliage, brown, speckled plumage of birds. And when they had grown very hungry, they found a better food than even Madeline had guessed they might, for they came to a clump of low trees with trunks scaled like trout, growing at the water's edge. These trees put out shell-shaped fruit and, when they broke these open and ate them, they tasted oysters. After they consumed their fishy luncheon, they walked on a little and discovered a tree knobbed with white, red-tipped whorls that looked so much like breasts they put their mouths to the nipples and sucked a sweet, refreshing milk.

"See?" said Madeline, and this time her triumph was unconcealed. "I told you we should find something to nourish us!"

When the shadows of the evening fell like a thick dust of powdered gold on the enchanted forest and they were beginning to feel weary, they came to a small valley which contained a pool that seemed to have no outlet or inlet and so must be fed by an invisible spring. The valley was filled with the most delightful, citronesque fragrance as sharply refreshing as a celestial eau-de-cologne and they saw the source of the perfume at once.

"Well!" exclaimed Emile. "This certainly isn't the fabled Upas Tree! It must be some kind of incense tree, such as the incense trees of Upper India where, after all, one finds a similar climate, or so I've read."

The tree was a little larger than a common apple tree but far more graceful in shape. The springing boughs hung out a festival of brilliant streamers, long, aromatic sprays of green, star-like flowers tipped with the red anthers of the stamens, cascading over clusters of leaves so deep a green and of such a glossy texture the dusk turned to discs of black glass those that the sunset did not turn to fire. These leaves hid secret bunches of fruit, mysterious spheres of visible gold streaked with green, as if all the unripe suns in the world were sleeping on the tree until a multiple, universal dawning should wake them all in splendour. As they stood hand in hand gazing at the beautiful tree, a small wind parted the leaves so they would see the fruit more clearly and, in the rind, set squarely in the middle of each faintly flushed cheek, was a curious formation – a round set of serrated indentations exactly resembling the marks of a bite made by the teeth of a hungry man. As if the sight stimulated her own appetite, Madeline laughed and said: "Goodness, Emile, the forest has even given us dessert!"

She sprang towards the exquisite, odoriferous tree which, at that moment, suffused in a failing yet hallucinatory light the tone and intensity of liquefied amber, seemed to her brother a perfect equivalent of his sister's amazing beauty, a beauty he had never seen before that filled him, now, with ecstasy. The dark pool reflected her darkly, like an antique mirror. She raised her hand to part the leaves in search of a ripe fruit but the greenish skin seemed to warm and glow under her fingers so the first one she touched came as easily off the stem as if it had been brought to perfection by her touch. It seemed to be some kind of apple or pear. It was so juicy the juice ran down her chin and she extended a long, crimson, newly sensual tongue to lick her lips, laughing.

"It tastes so good!" she said. "Here! Eat!"

She came back to him, splashing through the margins of the pool, holding the fruit out towards him on her palm. She was like a beautiful statue which has just come to life. Her enormous eyes were lit like nocturnal flowers that had been waiting only for this especial night to open and, in their vertiginous depths, reveal to her brother in inexpressible entirety the hitherto unguessed at, unknowable, inexpressible vistas of love.

He took the apple; ate; and, after that, they kissed.

# FLESH AND THE MIRROR ～

*I*t was midnight – I chose my times and set my scenes with the precision of the born artiste. Hadn't I gone eight thousand miles to find a climate with enough anguish and hysteria in it to satisfy me? I had arrived back in Yokohama that evening from a visit to England and nobody met me, although I expected him. So I took the train to Tokyo, half an hour's journey. First, I was angry; but the poignancy of my own situation overcame me and then I was sad. To return to the one you love and find him absent! My heart used to lump like Pavlov's dogs at the prospect of such a treat; I positively salivated at the suggestion of unpleasure, I was sure that *that* was real life. I'm told I always look lonely when I'm alone; that is because, when I was an intolerable adolescent, I learned to sit with my coat-collar turned up in a lonely way, so that people would talk to me. And I can't drop the habit even now, though, now, it's only a habit, and, I realize, a predatory habit.

It was midnight and I was crying bitterly as I walked under the artificial cherry blossom with which they decorate the lamp standards from April to September. They do that so the pleasure quarters will have the look of a continuous carnival, no matter what ripples of agitation disturb the never-ceasing, endlessly circulating, quiet, gentle, melancholy crowds who throng the wet web of alleys under a false ceiling of umbrellas. All looked as desolate as Mardi Gras. I was searching among a multitude of unknown faces for the face of the one I loved while the warm, thick, heavy rain of summer greased the dark surfaces of the streets until, after a while, they began to gleam like sleek fur of seals just risen from the bottom of the sea.

The crowds lapped round me like waves full of eyes until I felt that I was walking through an ocean whose speechless and gesticulating inhabitants, like those with whom medieval philosophers peopled the countries of the deep, were methodical inversions or mirror images of the dwellers on dry land. And I moved through these expressionist perspectives in my black dress as though I was the creator of all and of myself, too, in a black dress, in love, crying, walking through the city in the third person singular, my own heroine, as though the world stretched out from my eye like spokes from a sensitized hub that galvanized all to life when I looked at it.

I think I know, now, what I was trying to do. I was trying to subdue the city by turning it into a projection of my own growing pains. What solipsistic arrogance! The city, the largest city in the world, the city designed to suit not one of my European expectations, this city presents the foreigner with a mode of life that seems to him to have the enigmatic transparency, the indecipherable clarity, of dream. And it is a dream he could, himself, never have dreamed. The stranger, the foreigner, thinks he is in control; but he has been precipitated into somebody else's dream.

You never know what will happen in Tokyo. Anything can happen.

I had been attracted to the city first because I suspected it contained enormous histrionic resources. I was always rummaging in the dressing-up box of the heart for suitable appearances to adopt in the city. That was the way I maintained my defences for, at that time, I always used to suffer a great deal if I let myself get too close to reality since the definitive world of the everyday with its hard edges and harsh light did not have enough resonance to echo the demands I made upon experience. It was as if I never experienced experience *as* experience. Living never lived up to the expectations I had of it – the Bovary syndrome. I was always imagining other things that could have been happening, instead, and so I always felt cheated, always dissatisfied.

Always dissatisfied, even if, like a perfect heroine, I wandered, weeping, on a forlorn quest for a lost lover through the aromatic labyrinth of alleys. And wasn't I in Asia? Asia! But, even though I lived there, it always seemed far away from me. It was as if there were glass between me and the world. But I could see myself perfectly well on the other side of the glass. There I was, walking up and down, eating meals, having conversations, in love, indifferent, and so on. But all the time I was pulling the strings of my own puppet; it was this puppet who was moving about on the other side of the glass. And I eyed the most marvellous adventures with the bored eye of the agent with the cigar watching another audition. I tapped out the ash and asked of events: "What else can you do?"

So I attempted to rebuild the city according to the blueprint in my imagination as a backdrop to the plays in my puppet theatre, but it sternly refused to be so rebuilt; I was only imagining it had been so rebuilt. On the night I came back to it, however hard I looked for the one I loved, she could not find him anywhere and the city delivered her into the hands of a perfect stranger who fell into step beside her and asked why she was crying. She went with him to an unambiguous hotel with mirror on the ceiling and lascivious black lace draped round a palpably illicit bed. His eyes were shaped like sequins. All night long, a thin, pale, sickle moon with a single star pendant at its nether tip floated upon the rain that pitter-pattered against the windows and there was a clockwork whirring of cicadas. From time to time, the windbell dangling from the eaves let out an exquisitely mournful tinkle.

None of the lyrical eroticism of this sweet, sad, moon night of summer rain had been within my expectations; I had half expected he would strangle me. My sensibility wilted under the burden of response. My sensibility foundered under the assault on my senses.

My imagination had been pre-empted.

The room was a box of oiled paper full of the echoes of the rain. After the light was out, as we lay together, I could still see the single shape of our embrace in the mirror above me, a marvellously unexpected conjunction cast at random by the enigmatic kaleidoscope of the city. Our pelts were stippled with the fretted shadows of the lace curtains as if our skins were a mysterious uniform provided by the management in order to render all those who made love in that hotel anonymous. The mirror annihilated time, place and person; at the consecration of this house, the mirror had been dedicated to the reflection of chance embraces. Therefore it treated flesh in an exemplary fashion, with charity and indifference.

The mirror distilled the essence of all the encounters of strangers whose perceptions of one another existed only in the medium of the chance embrace, the accidental. During the durationless time we spent making love, we were not ourselves, whoever that might have been, but in some sense the ghosts of ourselves. But the selves we were not, the selves of our own habitual perceptions of ourselves, had a far more insubstantial substance than the reflections we were. The magic mirror presented me with a hitherto unconsidered notion of myself as I. Without any intention of mine, I had been defined by the action reflected in the mirror. I beset me. I was the subject of the sentence written on the mirror. I was not watching it. There was nothing whatsoever beyond the surface of the glass. Nothing kept me from the fact, the act; I had been precipitated into knowledge of the real conditions of living.

Mirrors are ambiguous things. The bureaucracy of the mirror issues me with a passport to the world; it shows me my appearance. But what use is a passport to an armchair traveller? Women and mirrors are in complicity with one another to evade the action I/she performs that she/I cannot watch, the action with which I break out of the mirror, with which I assume my appearance. But *this* mirror refused to conspire with me; it was like the first mirror I'd ever seen. It reflected the embrace beneath it without the least guile. All it showed was inevitable. But I myself could never have dreamed it.

I saw the flesh and the mirror but I could not come to terms with the sight. My immediate response to it was, to feel I'd acted out of character. The fancy-dress disguise I'd put on to suit the city had betrayed me to a room and a bed and a modification of myself that had no business at all in my life, not in the life I had watched myself performing.

Therefore I evaded the mirror. I scrambled out of its arms and sat on the edge of the bed and lit a fresh cigarette from the butt of the old one. The rain beat down. My demonstration of perturbation was perfect in every detail, just like the movies. I applauded it. I was gratified the mirror had not seduced me into behaving in a way I would have felt inappropriate – that is, shrugging and sleeping, as though my infidelity was not of the least importance. I now shook with the disturbing presentiment that he with his sequin eyes who'd been kind to me was an ironic substitute for the other one, the one I loved, as if the arbitrary carnival of the streets had gratuitously offered me this young man to find out if I *could* act out of character and then projected out intersection upon the mirror, as an objective lesson in the nature of things.

Therefore I dressed rapidly and ran away as soon as it was light outside, that mysterious, colourless light of dawn when the hooded crows flap out of the temple groves to perch on the telegraph poles, cawing a baleful dawn chorus to the echoing boulevards empty, now, of all the pleasure-seekers. The rain had stopped. It was an overcast morning so hot that I broke out into a sweat at the slightest movement. The bewildering electrographics of the city at night were all switched off. All the perspectives were pale, gritty grey, the air was full of dust. I never knew such a banal morning.

The morning before the night before, the morning before this oppressive morning, I woke up in the cabin of a boat. All the previous day, as we rounded the coast in bright weather, I dreamed of the reunion before me, a lovers' meeting refreshed by the three months I'd been gone, returning home due to a death in the family. I will come back as soon as I can – I'll write. Will you meet me at the pier? Of course, of course he will. But he was not at the pier; where was he?

So I went at once to the city and began my desolate tour of the pleasure quarters, looking for him in all the bars he used.

He was nowhere to be found. I did not know his address, of course; he moved from rented room to rented room with the agility of the feckless and we had corresponded through accommodation addresses, coffee shops, poste restante, etc. Besides, there had been a displacement of mail reminiscent of the excesses of the nineteenth-century novel, such as it is difficult to believe and could only have been caused by a desperate emotional necessary to cause as much confusion as possible. Both of us prided ourselves on our passionate sensibilities, of course. That was *one* thing we had in common! So, although I thought I was the most romantic spectacle imaginable as I wandered weeping down the alleys, I was in reality at risk – I had fallen through one of the holes life leaves in it; these peculiar holes are the entrances to the counters at which you pay the price of the way you live.

Random chance operates in relation to these existential lacunae; one tumbles down them when, for the time being, due to hunger, despair, sleeplessness, hallucination or those accidental-on-purpose misreadings of train timetables and airline schedules that produce margins of empty time, one is lost. One is at the mercy of events. That is why I like to be a foreigner; I only travel for the insecurity. But I did not know that, then.

I found my self-imposed fate, my beloved, quite early that morning but we quarrelled immediately. We quarrelled the day away assiduously and, when I tried to pull the strings of my self and so take control of the situation, I was astonished to find the situation I wanted was disaster, shipwreck. I saw his face as though it were in ruins, although it was the sight in the world I knew best and, the first time I saw it, had not seemed to me a face I did not know. It had seemed, in some way, to correspond to my idea of my own face. It had seemed a face long known and well remembered, a face that had always been imminent in my consciousness as an idea that now found its first visual expression.

So I suppose I do not know how he really looked and, in fact, I suppose I shall never know, now, for he was plainly an object created in the mode of fantasy. His image was already present somewhere in my head and I was seeking to discover it in actuality, looking at every face I met in case it was the right face – that is, the face which corresponded to my notion of the unseen face of the one I should love, a face created parthenogenetically by the rage to love which consumed me. So his self, and, by his self, I mean the thing he was to himself, was quite unknown to me. I created him solely in relation to myself, like a work of romantic art, an object corresponding to the ghost inside me. When I'd first loved him, I wanted to take him apart, as a child dismembers a clockwork toy, to comprehend the inscrutable mechanics of its interior. I wanted to see him far more naked than he was with his clothes off. It was easy enough to strip him bare and then I picked up my scalpel and set to work. But, since I was so absolutely in charge of the dissection, I only discovered what I was able to recognize already, from past experience, inside him. If ever I found anything new to me, I steadfastly ignored it. I was so absorbed in this work it never occurred to me to wonder if it hurt him.

In order to create the loved object in this way and to issue it with its certificate of authentication, as beloved, I had also to labour at the idea of myself in love. I watched myself closely for all the signs and, precisely upon cue, here they were! Longing, desire, self-abnegation, etc. I was racked by all the symptoms. Even so, in spite of this fugue of feeling, I had felt nothing but pleasure when the young man who picked me up inserted his sex inside me in the blue-movie bedroom. I only grew guilty later, when I realized I had not felt in the least guilty at the time. And was I in character when I felt guilty or in character when I did not? I was perplexed. I no longer understood the logic of my own performance. My script had been scrambled behind my back. The cameraman was drunk. The director had a *crise de nerfs* and been taken away to a sanatorium. And my co-star had picked himself up off the operating table and painfully cobbled himself together again according to his own design! All this had taken place while I was looking at the mirror.

Imagine my affront.

We quarrelled until night fell and, still quarrelling, found our way to another hotel but this hotel, and this night, was in every respect a parody of the previous night. (That's more like it! Squalor and humiliation! Ah!) Here, there were no lace drapes nor windbells nor moonlight nor any moist whisper of lugubriously seductive rain; this place was bleak, mean and cheerless and the sheets on the mattress they threw down on the floor for us were blotched with dirt although, at first, we did not notice that because it was necessary to pretend the urgent passion we always used to feel in one another's presence even if we felt it no longer, as if to act out the feeling with sufficient intensity would re-create it by sleight of hand, although our skins (which knew us better than we knew ourselves) told us the period of reciprocation was over. It was a mean room and the windows overlooked a parking lot with a freeway beyond it, so that the paper walls shuddered with the reverberations of the infernal clamour of the traffic. There was a sluggish electric fan with dead flies caught in the spokes and a single strip of neon overhead lit us and everything up with a scarcely tolerable, quite remorseless light. A slatternly woman in a filthy apron brought us glasses of thin, cold, brown tea made from barley and then she shut the door on us. I would not let him kiss me between the thighs because I was afraid he would taste the traces of last night's adventure, a little touch of paranoia in *that* delusion.

I don't know how much guilt had to do with the choice of this décor. But I felt it was perfectly appropriate.

The air was thicker than tea that's stewed on the hob all day and cockroaches were running over the ceiling, I remember. I cried all the first part of the night, I cried until I was exhausted but he turned on his side and slept – he saw through that ruse, though I did not since I did not know that I was lying. But I could not sleep because of the rattling of the walls and the noise of traffic. We had turned off the glaring lamp; when I saw a shaft of light fall across his face, I thought: "Surely it's too early for the dawn." But it was another person silently sliding open the unlocked door; in this disreputable hotel, anything can happen. I screamed and the intruder vanished. Wakened by a scream, my lover thought I'd gone mad and instantly trapped me in a stranglehold, in case I murdered him.

We were both old enough to have known better, too.

When I turned on the lamp to see what time it was, I noticed, to my surprise, that his features were blurring, like the underwriting on a palimpsest. It wasn't long before we parted. Only a few days. You can't keep *that* pace up for long.

Then the city vanished; it ceased, almost immediately, to be a magic and appalling place. I woke up one morning and found it had become home. Though I still turn up my coat collar in a lonely way and am always looking at myself in mirrors, they're only habits and give no clue at all to my character, whatever that is.

The most difficult performance in the world is acting naturally, isn't it? Everything else is artful.

# MASTER ~~~

*A*fter he discovered that his vocation was to kill animals, the pursuit of it took him far away from temperate weather until, in time, the insatiable suns of Africa eroded the pupils of his eyes, bleached his hair and tanned his skin until he no longer looked the thing he had been but its systematic negative; he became the white hunter, victim of an exile which is the imitation of death, a willed bereavement. He would emit a ravished gasp when he saw the final spasm of his prey. He did not kill for money but for love.

He had first exercised a propensity for savagery in the acrid lavatories of a minor English public school where he used to press the heads of the new boys into the ceramic bowl and then pull the flush upon them to drown their gurgling protests. After puberty, he turned his indefinable but exacerbated rage upon the pale, flinching bodies of young women whose flesh he lacerated with teeth, fingernails and sometimes his leather belt in the beds of cheap hotels near London's great rail termini (King's Cross, Victoria, Euston . . . ). But these pastel-coloured excesses, all the cool, rainy country of his birth could offer him, never satisfied him; his ferocity would attain the colouring of the fauves only when he took it to the torrid zones and there refined it until it could be distinguished from that of the beasts he slaughtered only by the element of self-consciousness it retained, for, if little of him now pertained to the human, the eyes of his self still watched him so that he was able to applaud his own depredations.

Although he decimated herds of giraffe and gazelle as they grazed in the savannahs until they learned to snuff their annihilation upon the wind as he approached, and dispatched heraldically plated hippopotami as they lolled up to their armpits in ooze, his rifle's particular argument lay with the silken indifference of the great cats, and, finally, he developed a speciality in the extermination of the printed beasts, leopards and lynxes, who carry ideograms of death in the clotted language pressed in brown ink upon their pelts by the fingertips of mute gods who do not acknowledge any divinity in humanity.

When he had sufficiently ravaged the cats of Africa, a country older by far than we are yet to whose innocence he had always felt superior, he decided to explore the nether regions of the New World, intending to kill the painted beast, the jaguar, and so arrived in the middle of a metaphor for desolation, the place where time runs back on itself, the moist, abandoned cleft of the world whose fructifying river is herself a savage woman, the Amazon. A green, irrevocable silence closed upon him in that serene kingdom of giant vegetables. Dismayed, he clung to the bottle as if it were a teat.

He travelled by jeep through an invariable terrain of architectonic vegetation where no wind lifted the fronds of palms as ponderous as if they had been sculpted out of viridian gravity at the beginning of time and then abandoned, whose trunks were so heavy they did not seem to rise into the air but, instead, drew the oppressive sky down upon the forest like a coverlid of burnished metal. These tree trunks bore an outcrop of plants, orchids, poisonous, iridescent blossoms and creepers the thickness of an arm with flowering mouths that stuck out viscous tongues to trap the flies that nourished them. Bright birds of unknown shapes infrequently darted past him and sometimes monkeys, chattering like the third form, leaped from branch to branch that did not move beneath them. But no motion nor sound did more than ripple the surface of the profound, inhuman introspection of the place so that, here, to kill became the only means that remained to him to confirm he himself was still alive, for he was not prone to introspection and had never found any consolation in nature. Slaughter was his only proclivity and his unique skill.

He came upon the Indians who lived among the lugubrious trees. They represented such a diversity of ethnic types they were like a living museum of man organized on a principle of regression for, the further inland he went, the more primitive they became, as if to demonstrate that evolution could be inverted. Some of the brown men had no other habitation than the sky and, like the flowers, ate insects; they would paint their bodies with the juice of leaves and berries and ornament their heads with diadems of feathers or the claws of eagles. Placid and decorative, the men and women would come softly twittering round his jeep, a mild curiosity illuminating the inward-turning, amber suns of their eyes, and he did not recognize that they were men although they distilled demented alcohol in stills of their own devising and he drank it, in order to people the inside of his head with familiar frenzy among so much that was strange.

His half-breed guide would often take one of the brown girls who guilelessly offered him her bare, pointed breasts and her veiled, limpid smile and, then and there, infect her with the clap to which he was a chronic martyr in the bushes at the rim of the clearing. Afterwards, licking his chops with remembered appetite, he would say to the hunter: "Brown meat, brown meat." In drunkenness one night, troubled by the prickings of a carnality that often visited him at the end of his day's work, the hunter bartered, for the spare tyre of his jeep, a pubescent girl as virgin as the forest that had borne her.

She wore a vestigial slip of red cotton twisted between her thighs and her long, sinuous back was upholstered in cut velvet, for it was whorled and ridged with the tribal markings incised on her when her menses began – raised designs like the contour map of an unknown place. The women of her tribe dipped their hairs in liquid mud and then wound their locks into long curls around sticks and let them dry in the sun until each one possessed a hairdo of rigid ringlets the consistency of

baked, unglazed pottery, so she looked as if her head was surrounded by one of those spiked haloes allotted to famous
sinners in Sunday-school picture books. Her eyes held the gentleness and the despair of those about to be dispossessed; she
had the immovable smile of a cat, which is forced by physiol-
ogy to smile whether it wants to or not.

The beliefs of her tribe had taught her to regard herself as a
sentient abstraction, an intermediary between the ghosts and
the fauna, so she looked at her purchaser's fever-shaking,
skeletal person with scarcely curiosity, for he was to her no
more yet no less surprising than any other gaunt manifestation of the forest. If she did not perceive him as a man, either,
that was because her cosmogony admitted no essential difference between herself and the beasts and the spirits, it was so
sophisticated. Her tribe never killed; they only ate roots. He
taught her to eat the meat he roasted over his camp fire and,
first, she did not like it much but dutifully consumed it as
though he were ordering her to partake of a sacrament for,
when she saw how casually he killed the jaguar, she soon
realized he was death itself. Then she began to look at him
with wonder for she recognized immediately how death had
glorified itself to become the principle of his life. But when he
looked at her, he saw only a piece of curious flesh he had not
paid much for.

He thrust his virility into her surprise and, once her wound
had healed, used her to share his sleeping bag and carry his
pelts. He told her her name would be Friday, which was the
day he bought her; he taught her to say "master" and then let
her know that was to be his name. Her eyelids fluttered for,
though she could move her lips and tongue and so reproduce
the sounds he made, she did not understand them. And, daily,
he slaughtered the jaguar. He sent away the guide for, now he
had bought the girl, he did not need him; so the ambiguous
couple went on together, while the girl's father made sandals
from the rubber tyre to shoe his family's feet and they walked
a little way into the twentieth century in them, but not far.

Among her tribe circulated the following picturesque folk-tale. The jaguar invited the anteater to a juggling contest in which they would use their eyes to play with, so they drew their eyes out of the sockets. When they had finished, the anteater threw his eyes up into the air and back they fell – plop! in place in his head; but when the jaguar imitated him, his eyes caught in the topmost branches of a tree and he could not reach them. So he became blind. Then the anteater asked the macaw to make new eyes out of water for the jaguar and, with these eyes, the jaguar found that it could see in the dark. So all turned out well for the jaguar; and she, too, the girl who did not know her own name, could see in the dark. As they moved always more deeply into the forest, away from the little settlements, nightly he extorted his pleasure from her flesh and she would gaze over her shoulder at shapes of phantoms in the thickly susurrating undergrowth, phantoms – it seemed to her – of beasts he had slaughtered that day, for she had been born into the clan of the jaguar and, when his leather belt cut her shoulder, the magic water of which her eyes were made would piteously leak.

He could not reconcile himself to the rain forest, which oppressed and devastated him. He began to shake with malaria. He killed continually, stripped the pelts and left the corpses behind him for the vultures and the flies.

Then they came to a place where there were no more roads.

His heart leaped with ecstatic fear and longing when he saw how nothing but beasts inhabited the interior. He wanted to destroy them all, so that he would feel less lonely, and, in order to penetrate this absence with his annihilating presence, he left the jeep behind at a forgotten township where a green track ended and an ancient whisky priest sat all day in the ruins of a forsaken church brewing fire-water from wild bananas and keening the stations of the cross. Master loaded his brown mistress with his guns and the sleeping bag and the gourds filled with liquid fever. They left a wake of corpses behind them for the plants and the vultures to eat.

At night, after she lit the fire, he would first abuse her with the butt of his rifle about the shoulders and, after that, with his sex; then drink from a gourd and sleep. When she had wiped the tears from her face with the back of her hand, she was herself again, and, after they had been together a few weeks, she seized the opportunity of solitude to examine his guns, the instruments of his passion, and, perhaps, learn a little of Master's magic.

She squinted her eye to peer down the long barrel; she caressed the metal trigger, and, pointing the barrel carefully away from her as she had seen Master do, she softly squeezed it in imitation of his gestures to see if she, too, could provoke the same shattering exhalation. But, to her disappointment, she provoked nothing. She clicked her tongue against her teeth in irritation. Exploring further, however, she discovered the secret of the safety catch.

Ghosts came out of the jungle and sat at her feet, cocking their heads on one side to watch her. She greeted them with a friendly wave of her hand. The fire began to fail but she could see clearly through the sights of the rifle since her eyes were made of water and, raising it to her shoulder as she had seen Master do, she took aim at the disc of moon stuck to the sky beyond the ceiling of boughs above her, for she wanted to shoot the moon down since it was a bird in her scheme of things and, since he had taught her to eat meat, now she thought she must be death's apprentice.

He woke from sleep in a paroxysm of fear and saw her, dimly illuminated by the dying fire, naked but for the rag that covered her sex, with the rifle in her hand; it seemed to him her clay-covered head was about to turn into a nest of birds of prey. She laughed delightedly at the corpse of the sleeping bird her bullet had knocked down from the tree and the moonlight glimmered on her curiously pointed teeth. She believed the bird she shot down had been the moon and now, in the night sky, she saw only the ghost of the moon. Though they were lost, hopelessly lost, in the trackless forest, she knew quite well where she was; she was always at home in the ghost town.

Next day, he oversaw the beginnings of her career as a markswoman and watched her tumble down from the boughs of the forest representatives of all the furred and feathered beings it contained. She always gave the same delighted laugh to see them fall for she had never thought it would be so easy to populate her fireside with fresh ghosts. But she could not bring herself to kill the jaguar, since the jaguar was the emblem of her clan; with forceful gestures of her head and hands, she refused. But, after she learned to shoot, soon she became a better hunter than he although there was no method to her killing and they went banging away together indiscriminately through the dim, green undergrowth.

The descent of the banana spirit in the gourd marked the passage of time and they left a gross trail of carnage behind them. The spectacle of her massacres moved him and he mounted her in a frenzy, forcing apart her genital lips so roughly the crimson skin on the inside bruised and festered while the bites on her throat and shoulders oozed diseased pearls of pus that brought the blowflies buzzing about her in a cloud. Her screams were a universal language; even the monkeys understood she suffered when Master took his pleasure, yet he did not. As she grew more like him, so she began to resent him.

While he slept, she flexed her fingers in the darkness that concealed nothing from her and, without surprise, she discovered her fingernails were growing long, curved, hard and sharp. Now she could tear his back when he inflicted himself upon her and leave red runnels in his skin; yelping with delight, he only used her the more severely and, twisting her head with its pottery appendages this way and that in pained perplexity, she gouged the empty air with her claws.

They came to a spring of water and she plunged into it in order to wash herself but she sprang out again immediately because the touch of water aroused such an unpleasant sensation on her pelt. When she impatiently tossed her head to shake away the waterdrops, her clay ringlets melted altogether and trickled down her shoulders. She could no longer tolerate cooked meat but must tear it raw between her fingers off the bone before Master saw. She could no longer twist her scarlet tongue around the two syllables of his name, "mas-tuh"; when she tried to speak, only a diffuse and rumbling purr shivered the muscles of her throat and she dug neat holes in the earth to bury her excrement, she had become so fastidious since she grew whiskers.

Madness and fever consumed him. When he killed the jaguar, he abandoned them in the forest with the stippled pelts still on them. To possess the clawed she was in itself a kind of slaughter, and, tracking behind her, his eyes dazed with strangeness and liquor, he would watch the way the intermittent dentellation of the sun through the leaves mottled the ridged tribal markings down her back until it seemed the blotched areas of pigmentation were subtly mimicking the beasts who mimicked the patterns of the sun through the leaves and, if she had not walked upright on two legs, he would have shot her. As it was, he thrust her down into the undergrowth, amongst the orchids, and drove his other weapon into her soft, moist hole whilst he tore her throat with his teeth and she wept, until, one day, she found she was not able to cry any more.

The day the liquor ended, he was alone with fever. He reeled, screaming and shaking, in the clearing where she had abandoned his sleeping bag; she crouched among the lianas and crooned in a voice like soft thunder. Though it was daylight, the ghosts of innumerable jaguar crowded round to see what she would do. Their invisible nostrils twitched with the prescience of blood. The shoulder to which she raised the rifle now had the texture of plush.

His prey had shot the hunter, but now she could no longer hold the gun. Her brown and amber dappled sides rippled like water as she trotted across the clearing to worry the clothing of the corpse with her teeth. But soon she grew bored and bounded away.

Then only the flies crawling on his body were alive and he was far from home.

# REFLECTIONS ⟶

*I* was walking in a wood one late spring day of skimming cloud and shower-tarnished sunshine, the sky a lucid if intermittent blue – cool, bright, tremulous weather. A coloratura blackbird perched on a bough curded with greenish may-blossom let fall a flawed chain of audible pearl; I was alone in the spring-enchanted wood. I slashed the taller grasses with my stick and now and then surprised some woodland creature, rat or rabbit, that fled away from me through long grass where little daisies and spindly branches of buttercups were secreted among gleaming stems still moist at the roots from last night's rain that had washed and refreshed the entire wood, had dowered it with the poignant transparency, the unique, inconsolable quality of rainy countries, as if all was glimpsed through tears.

The crisp air was perfumed with wet grass and fresh earth. The year was swinging on the numinous hinges of the solstice but I was ingenuous and sensed no imminence in the magic silence of the rustling wood.

Then I heard a young girl singing. Her voice performed a trajectory of sound far more ornate than that of the blackbird, who ceased at once to sing when he heard it for he could not compete with the richly crimson sinuosity of a voice that pierced the senses of the listener like an arrow in a dream. She sang; and her words thrilled through me, for they seemed filled with a meaning that had no relation to meaning as I understood it.

"Under the leaves," she sang, "and the leaves of life –" Then, in mid-flight, the song ceased and left me dazzled. My attention abstracted from my surroundings, all at once my foot turned on an object hidden in the grass and I tumbled to the ground. Though I fell on the soft, wet grass, I was shaken and winded. I forgot that luring music. Cursing my obstacle, I searched among the pale, earth-stained rootlets to find it and my fingers closed on, of all things, a shell. A shell so far from the sea! When I tried to grasp it in order to pick it up and examine it the better, I found the act unexpectedly difficult and my determination to lift it quickened although, at the same time, I felt a shiver of fear for it was so very, very heavy and its contours so chill that a shock like cold electricity darted up my arm from the shell, into my heart. I was seized with the most intense disquiet; I was mystified by the shell.

I thought it must be a shell from a tropic ocean, since it was far larger and more elaborately whorled than the shells I'd found on the shores of the Atlantic. There was some indefinable strangeness in its shape I could not immediately define. It glimmered through the grass like a cone of trapped moonlight although it was so very cold and so heavy it seemed to me it might contain all the distilled heaviness of gravity itself within it. I grew very much afraid of the shell; I think I sobbed. Yet I was so determined to wrench it from the ground that I clenched my muscles and gritted my teeth and tugged and heaved. Up it came, at last, and I rolled over backwards when it freed itself. But now I held the prize in my hands, and I was, for the moment, satisfied.

When I looked at the shell more closely, I saw the nature of the teasing difference that had struck me when I first set eyes on it. The whorls of the shell went the wrong way. The spirals were reversed. It looked like the mirror image of a shell, and so it should not have been able to exist outside a mirror; in this world, it could not exist outside a mirror. But, all the same, I held it.

The shell was the size of my cupped hands and cold and heavy as death.

In spite of its fabulous weight, I decided to carry it through the wood for I thought I would take it to the little museum in the nearby town where they would inspect it and test it and tell me what it might be and how it could have arrived where I found it. But as I staggered along with it in my arms, it exerted such a pull downwards on me that, several times, I nearly fell to my knees, as if the shell were determined to drag me, not down to the earth but into the earth itself. And then, to complete my confusion, I heard that witching voice again.

"Under the leaves – "

But, this time, when a gasp stopped the song, the voice changed at once to the imperative.

"Sic 'im!" she urged. "Sic 'im!"

Before I had a chance to do more than glance in the direction of the voice, a bullet whirred over my head and buried itself in the trunk of an elm tree, releasing from their nests in the upward branches a whirring hurricane of crows. An enormous black dog bounded towards me from the undergrowth so suddenly I saw no more than his yawning scarlet maw and lolling tongue before I went down on my face beneath him. The fright nearly bereft me of my senses. The dog slavered wetly over me and, the next thing I knew, a hand seized my shoulder and roughly turned me over.

She had called the dog away and now it sat on its haunches, panting, watching me with a quick, red eye. It was black as coal, some kind of lurcher, with balls the size of grapefruit. Both the dog and the girl glanced at me without charity. She wore blue jeans and boots, a wide, vindictively buckled leather belt and a green sweater. Her tangled brown hair hung about her shoulders in a calculated disorder that was not wild. Her dark eyebrows were perfectly straight and gave her stern face a gravity as awful as that of the shell I held in my hand. Her blue eyes, the kind the Irish say have been put in with a sooty finger, held no comfort nor concern for me for they were the eyes that justice would have if she were not blind. She carried a sporting rifle slung across her shoulder and I knew at once this rifle had fired the shot. She might have been the gamekeeper's daughter but, no, she was too proud; she was a savage and severe wood-ranger.

Why I do not know, but every impulse told me to conceal my shell and I hugged it close to me, as if my life depended on keeping it, although it was so heavy and began to throb with a wild palpitation so that it seemed the shell had disordered my own heart, or else had become my own disordered heart. But my brusque captress poked at my hands with the barrel of her rifle so roughly my bruised fingers let the shell fall. She bent forward so that her necromantic hair brushed my face and picked up the shell with amazing ease.

She examined it for a moment and then, without a word or sign to me, tossed it to her lurcher, who seized it in his mouth ready to carry it for her. The dog began to wag his tail. The rhythmic swishing of his tail upon the grass was now the only sound in the clearing. Even the trees had ceased to murmur, as though a holy terror hushed them.

She gestured me to my feet and, when I was upright, she thrust the mouth of the gun in the small of my back and marched me through the wood at gunpoint, striding along behind me while the dog padded beside her with the shell in his mouth. All this took place in unadulterated silence, but for the raucous panting of the dog. The cabbage white butterflies flickered upon the still air as if nothing whatsoever were out of the ordinary, while delicious-looking apricot and violet coloured clouds continued to chase one another across the sun according to the indifferent logic of the upper heavens, for the clouds were moved by a fierce wind that blew so high above the wood everything around me was as tranquil as water trapped in a lock, and mocked the inward perturbation that shook me.

Soon we reached an overgrown path that took us to a gate set in a garden wall where there was an old-fashioned bell-pull and, dangling above it, a bell stained with moss and rust. The girl with the rifle rang this bell before she opened the gate as if to warn whoever was at home that visitors were arriving. The

gate led into a graceful and dilapidated walled garden full of
the herbaceous splendours of early summer, hollyhocks, wall-
flowers, roses. There was a mossed sundial and a little stone
statue of a nude youth stretching his arms up out of a cuirass
of ivy. But, though the bees hummed among the flower bells,
the grass was as long as it had been in the wood and just as full
of buttercups and daisies. Dandelions expired in airy seed
heads in the flowerbeds; ragged robin and ground elder con-
spired to oust the perennials from the borders and a bright
sadness of neglect touched everything as though with dust,
just as it did the ancient brick house, almost covered with
creepers, that slept within the garden, an ancient, tumbledown
place with a look of oracular blindness in windows that were
stopped up with vines and flowers. The roof was lichened
quite over, so that it seemed upholstered in sleek, green fur.
Yet there was no peace in the dishevelled loveliness of the
place; the very plants that grew there seemed tensed in a
curious expectancy, as though the garden were a waiting room.
There was a short, crumbling flight of steps that led to a
weathered front door, ajar like the door of a witch's house.

Before the door, I involuntarily halted; a dreadful vertigo
seized me, as if I stood on the edge of an abyss. My heart had
been thumping far too hard and far too fast since I had picked
up the shell and now it seemed about to burst from too much
strain. Faintness and terror of death swept over me; but the girl
prodded me cruelly in the buttocks with her rifle so I was
forcibly marched into a country-house hall with dark stained
floorboards, a Persian carpet and a Jacobean oak chest with an
antique bowl on it, all complete yet all as if untouched for
years, for decades. A maze of dust danced in the beam of sunshine that disturbed the choked indoors air when we broke
into it. Every corner was softened by cobwebs while the indus-
trious spiders had wound filaments of geometric lace this way
and that between the crumbling furniture. A sweet, rank smell
of damp and decay filled the house; it was cold, inside, and
dark. The door swung to behind us but did not close and we

went up a staircase of worm-eaten oak, I first, she after and then the dog, whose claws clattered on the bare wood.

At first I thought the spiders had cast their nets on both sides of the stair but then I saw the workmanship that wound down the inner side of the staircase was not that of the spiders for, though it was the same colour, this web had a determinate pattern that resembled nothing so much as open-work knitting, the kind of featherlike, floating stuff from which they make courtesans' bedjackets. This knitting was part of an interminable muffler that, as I watched it, crept, with vegetable slowness, little by little downstairs towards the hall. Yard upon yard of the muffler was coiled up in airy folds on the landing and there I could hear the clack, clack, clack of a pair of knitting needles ticking away monotonously near at hand. The muffler came out of a door that, like the front door, stood a little open; it edged through the gap like a tenuous serpent.

My captress motioned me aside with the muzzle of her rifle and knocked firmly on the door.

Inside the room, someone coughed dryly, then invited us: "Come in."

It was a soft, rustling, unemphatic, almost uninflected, faded, faintly perfumed voice, like very old lace handkerchiefs put away long ago in a drawer with potpourri and forgotten.

My captress thrust me through the door before her; when I was close to her, my nostrils quivered at the vicious odour of her skin. It was a large room, part drawing room, part bedroom, for the being who lived in it was crippled. She, he, it – whoever, whatever my host or hostess may have been – lay in an old-fashioned wicker Bath chair beside a cracked marble fireplace bossed with swags and cupids. Her white hands finished in fingers indecently long, white and translucent as candles on a cathedral altar; those tapering fingers were the source of the bewildering muffler, for they held two bone needles and never ceased to move.

The volatile stitchery they produced occupied all the carpetless area of the floor and, in places, was piled up as high as

the crippled knees of its maker. There were yards and yards of
it in the room, perhaps even miles and miles of it, and I
stepped through and across it very carefully, nudging it out of
the way with my toes, to arrive where the girl directed me
with her gun, in the position of a suppliant before the Bath
chair. The crippled being who lay in it had the most regal cast
of chin and mouth imaginable and the proud, sad air of the
king of a rainy country. One of her profiles was that of a
beautiful woman, the other that of a beautiful man. It is a
defect in our language there is no term of reference for these
indeterminate and undefinable beings; but, although she acknowledged no gender, I will call her "she" because she had put
on a female garment, a loose negligee of spider-coloured lace,
unless she, like the spiders, spun and wove her own thread and
so had become clothed, for her shadowy hair was also the
colour of the stuff she knitted and so evanescent in texture it
seemed to move of its own accord on the air around her. Her
eyelids and the cavernous sockets of her eyes were thickly
stuck with silver sequins that glittered in the strange, sub-
aqueous, drowned, drowning light that suffused the room, a
light filtered through windows caked with grime and half covered by creeper, clairvoyant light reflected, with an enhanced
strangeness, by the immense mirror in a chipped gilt frame
hanging on the wall opposite the fireplace; it seemed the mirror, like the moon, was itself endowed with the light it gave
back to us.

With a touching fidelity, the mirror duplicated the room
and all it contained, the fireplace, the walls covered with a
stained white paper stippled with fronds of greenery, every
piece of neglected ormolu furniture. How pleased I was to see
my experiences had not changed me! though my old tweed suit
was stained with grass, my stick gone – left behind where I had
dropped it in the wood. And so much dirt on my face. But I
looked as if I were reflected in a forest pool rather than by
silvered glass for the surface of the mirror looked like the
surface of motionless water, or of mercury, as though it were a
solid mass of liquid kept in place by some inversion of gravity

that reminded me of the ghastly weight of the shell that now dropped at the androgyne's feet from the dog's mouth. She never stopped knitting for one moment as she nudged it with a beautiful toe painted with a rime of silver; woe gave her a purely female face.

"Only one little stitch! And I only dropped one little stitch!" she mourned. And she bowed her head over her work in an ecstasy of regret.

"At least it wasn't out long," said the girl. Her voice had a clanging resonance; mercy was a minor key that would never modify its martial music. "*He* found it!"

She gestured towards me with her gun. The androgyne directed upon me a pair of vague, too large, stagnant eyes that did not shine.

"Do you know where this shell comes from?" she asked me with a grave courtesy.

I shook my head.

"It comes from the Sea of Fertility. Do you know where *that* is?"

"On the surface of the moon," I answered. My voice sounded coarse and rough to me.

"Ah," she said, "the moon, the source of polarized light. Yes and no to your reply. It is an equivalence. The sea of fertility is a reversed system, since everything there is as dead as this shell."

"He found it in the wood," said the girl.

"Put it back where it belongs, Anna," said the androgyne, who possessed a frail yet absolute air of authority. "Before any harm is done."

The girl bent and picked up the shell. She scrutinized the mirror and took aim at some spot within it that seemed to her a logical target for the shell. I saw her raise her arm to throw the shell into the mirror and I saw her mirrored arm raise the shell to throw it outside the mirror. Then she threw the duplicated shell. There was no sound in the room but the click of the knitting needles when she threw the shell into the mirror while her reflection threw the shell out of the mirror. The shell, when it met its own reflection, disappeared immediately.

The androgyne sighed with satisfaction.

"The name of my niece is Anna," she said to me, "because she can go both ways. As, indeed, I can myself, though I am not a simple palindrome."

She gave me an enigmatic smile and moved her shoulders so that the lace negligee she wore fell back from her soft, pale breasts that were, each one, tipped by nipples of deep, dark pink, with the whorled crenellations of raspberries, and then she shifted her loins a little to display, savage and barbaric in their rude, red-purple repose, the phallic insignia of maleness.

"She can," said Anna, "go both ways, although she cannot move at all. So her power is an exact equivalent of her impotence, since both are absolute."

But her aunt looked down at her soft weapon and said gently: "Not, my darling, *absolutely* absolute. Potency, impotence in *potentia*, hence relative. Only the intermediary, since indeterminate."

With that, she caressed her naked breasts with a stunted gesture of her forearms; she could not move her arms freely because she did not stop knitting. They looked at one another and laughed. Their laughter drove icicles of fear into my brain and I did not know which way to turn.

"You see, we must do away with you," said the androgyne. "You know too much."

Panic broke over me like a wave. I plunged across the room towards the door, careless of Anna's gun in my attempted flight. But my feet were snared by the knitting and once again I plunged downwards but this time my fall half stunned me. I lay dazed while their renewed laughter darted cruelly about the room.

"Oh," said Anna, "but we shan't kill you. We shall send you through the mirror. We shall send you where the shell went, since that is where you belong, now."

"But the shell vanished," I said.

"No," replied the androgyne. "It did not vanish in reality.

That shell had no business in this world. I dropped a stitch, this morning; only one little stitch . . . and that confounded shell slipped through the hole the dropped stitch made, because those shells are all so very, very heavy, you see. When it met its reflection, it returned to its proper place. It cannot come back, now; and neither will you, after we have sent you through the mirror."

Her voice was so very gentle, yet she offered me a perpetual estrangement. I let out a cry. Anna turned to her aunt and placed her hand on her genitalia, so that the cock sprang up. It was of redoubtable size.

"Oh, auntie, don't scare him!" she said.

Then they tittered, the weird harpies, so that I was quite beside myself with fear and bewilderment.

"It is a system of equivalences," said the androgyne. "She carries the gun, you see; and I, too."

She displayed her towering erection with the air of a demonstrator in a laboratory.

"In my intermediary and cohesive logic, the equivalences reside beyond symbolism. The gun and the phallus are similar in their connection with life – that is, one gives it; and the other takes it away, so that both, in essence, are similar in that the negation freshly states the affirmed proposition."

I was more bewildered than ever.

"But do all the men in the mirror world have guns between their thighs?"

Anna exclaimed with irritation at my simplicity.

"That's no more likely than that I could impregnate you with this – " she said, pointing her gun at me, "here or in any other world."

"Embrace yourself in the mirror," said the androgyne, knitting, knitting, knitting away. "You must go, now. Now!"

Anna maintained her menace; there was nothing for it but to do as they bid. I went to the mirror and examined myself in its depths. A faint ripple ran over its surface; but when I touched it with my fingers, the surface was just as smooth and hard as it should have been. I saw that my reflection was cut off at the thighs by the gilt frame and Anna said: "Climb on a stool! Who'd want you truncated, here or there?"

She grinned in an appalling fashion and slipped back the safety catch on her rifle. So I pulled a little, cane-seated, gilt-backed chair to the mirror and clambered up. I gazed at myself in the mirror; there I was, complete from head to toe, and there they were, behind me, the androgyne weaving her ethereal coils and the armed young girl, who, now that she could kill me with one little flick of her finger, looked as beautiful as a Roman soldier plundering a North African city, with her unkind eyes and her perfume of murder.

"Kiss yourself," commanded the androgyne in a swooning voice. "Kiss yourself in the mirror, the symbolic matrix of this and that, hither and thither, outside and inside."

Then I saw, even if I could no longer be astonished, that though she knitted in both the room and the mirror, there was, within the room, no ball of wool at all; her yarn emanated from inside the mirror and the ball of wool existed only in the medium of reflection. But I did not have time to wonder at this marvel for the rank stench of Anna's excitement filled the room and her hand trembled. Out of rage and desperation, I advanced my own lips to meet the familiar yet unknown lips that advanced towards mine in the silent world of the glass.

I thought these lips would be cold and lifeless; that I would touch them but they could not touch me. Yet, when the twinned lips met, they cleaved, for these mirrored lips of mine were warm and throbbed. This mouth was wet and contained a tongue, and teeth. It was too much for me. The profound sensuality of this unexpected caress crisped the roots of my sex and my eyes involuntarily closed whilst my arms clasped my own tweed shoulders. The pleasure of the embrace was intense; I swooned beneath it.

When my eyes opened, I had become my own reflection. I had passed through the mirror and now I stood on a little, cane-seated, gilt-backed chair with my mouth pressed to an impervious surface of glass I had misted with my own breath and moistened with my own saliva.

Anna cried: "Hurrah!" She dropped her rifle and clapped her hands while her aunt, continuing, all the time, to knit, gave me a peculiarly sultry smile.

"So," she said. "Welcome. This room is the half-way house between here and there, between this and that, because, you understand, I am so ambiguous. Stay in the field of force of the mirror for a while, until you are used to everything."

The first thing that struck me was, the light was black. My eyes took a little time to grow accustomed to this absolute darkness for, though the delicate apparatus of cornea and aqueous humour and crystalline lens and vitreous body and optic nerve and retina had all been reversed when I gave birth to my mirror self through the mediation of the looking-glass, yet my sensibility remained as it had been. So at first, through the glass, I saw darkly and all was confusion but for their faces, which were irradiated by familiarity. But, when the inside of my head could process the information my topsy-turvy senses retrieved for me, then my other or anti-eyes apprehended a world of phosphorescent colour etched as with needles of variegated fire on a dimensionless opacity. The world was the same; yet absolutely altered. How can I describe it . . . almost as if this room was the colour negative of the other room. Unless – for how could I ever be certain which was the primary world and which the secondary – the other room, the other house, the other wood that I saw, transposed yet still peeping through the window in the other mirror – all that had been the colour negative of the room in which I now stood, where the exhalations of my breath were the same as the inhalations of my mirror anti-twin who turned away from me as I turned away from him, into the distorted, or else really real, world of the mirror room, which, since it existed in this mirror in this room beyond the mirror, reflected all of this room's ambiguities and was no longer the room I had left. That endless muffler or web wound round the room, still, but now it wound round contrariwise and Anna's aunt was knitting from left to right, instead of from right to left, with hands that, I realized, had they wished, could have pulled a right-hand glove over the left hand and vice versa, since she was truly ambidexterous.

But when I looked at Anna, I saw she was exactly the same as she had been on the other side of the mirror and knew her face for one of those rare faces that possess an absolute symmetry, each feature the exact equivalent of the other, so one of her profiles could serve as the template for both. Her skull was like a proposition in geometry. Irreducible as stone, finite as a syllogism, she was always indistinguishable from herself whichever way she went.

But the imperturbably knitting androgyne had turned its face contrariwise. One half of its face was always masculine and the other, no matter what, was feminine; yet these had been changed about, so that all the balances of the planes of the face and the lines of the brow were the opposite of what they had been before, although one half of the face was still feminine and the other masculine. Nevertheless, the quality of the difference made it seem that this altered yet similar face was the combination of the reflection of the female side of the face and the masculine side of the face that *did not appear* in the face I had seen beyond the mirror; the effect was as of the reflection of a reflection, like an example of perpetual regression, the perfect, self-sufficient nirvana of the hermaphrodite. She was Tiresias, capable of prophetic projection, whichever side of the mirror she chose to offer herself to my sight upon; and she went on knitting and knitting and knitting, with an infernal suburban complacency.

When I turned from the mirror, Anna was holding out her right or left hand towards me but, although I felt sure I was walking towards her and lifted up my legs and set them down again with the utmost determination, Anna receded further and further away from me. Niece and aunt emitted a titter and I guessed that, in order to come to Anna, I must go away from her. Therefore I stepped sturdily backwards and, in less than a second, her hard, thin, sunburned hand grasped mine.

The touch of her hand filled me with a wild loneliness.

With her other hand, she opened the door. I was terribly afraid of that door, for the room that contained the mirror was all that I knew, and therefore my only safety, in this unknown world that Anna, who now smiled inscrutably at me, negotiated as skilfully as if she herself, the solstice in person, went on curious hinges between this place and that place unlike her aunt, who, since she was crippled, could not move unless her condition of permanent stasis meant she was moving too fast for me to see, with a speed the inertia of the eye registered as immobility.

But, when the door creaked open on everyday, iron hinges that had never been oiled in this world or any other world, I saw only the staircase up which Anna had led me, down which she would now lead me, and the muffler that still curled down to the hall. The air was dank, just as it had been. Only, all the alignments of the stairwell had been subtly altered and the light was composed of a reversed spectrum.

The webs of the spiders presented structures of white fire so minutely altered from those I had passed on my way upstairs that only memory made me apprehend how their geometrical engineering had all been executed backwards. So we passed under the spectral arch they had prepared for us and out into the open air that did not refresh my bewildered brain, for it was as solid as water, dense and compact, of an impermeable substance that transmitted neither sound nor odour. To move through this liquid silence demanded the utmost exertion of physical energy and intellectual concentration, for gravity, beyond the mirror, was not a property of the ground but of the atmosphere. Then Anna, who understood the physical laws of this world, exerted a negative pressure upon me by some willed absence of impulse and to my amazement I now moved as if propelled sharply from behind along the path to the gate, past flowers that distilled inexpressible colours from the black sky above us, colours whose names only exist in an inverted language you could never understand if I were to speak it. But the colours were virtually independent of the forms of the about spread umbrellas of petals as thin yet as hard as the shoulder blade of a rabbit, for the flesh of the flowers was calcified and lifeless; no plant was sentient in this coral garden. All had suffered a dead sea-change.

And the black sky possessed no dimension of distance, nor gave none; it did not arch above us but looked as if it were pasted behind the flat outlines of the half-ruinous house that now lay behind us, a shipwreck bearing a marvellous freight, the female man or virile woman clicking away at her needles in a visible silence. A visible silence, yes; for the dense fluidity of the atmosphere did not transmit sound to me as sound, but, instead, as irregular kinetic abstractions etched upon its interior, so that, once in the new wood, a sinister, mineral, realm of undiminishable darkness, to listen to the blackbird was to watch a moving point inside a block of deliquescent glass. I saw these sounds because my eyes took in a different light than the light that shone on my breast when my heart beat on the other side of it, although the wood through whose now lateral gravity Anna negotiated me was the same wood in which I had been walking when I first heard her sing. And I cannot tell you, since there is no language in this world to do so, how strange the antithetical wood and sweet June day were, for both had become the systematic negation of its others.

Anna, in some reversed fashion, must still have been menacing me with her gun, since it was her impulse that moved me; on we went, just as we had come – but Anna, now, went before me, with the muzzle of her gun pressed in the belly of nothingness, and the dog, her familiar, this time in the van. And this dog was white as snow and its balls were gone; on this side of the mirror, all dogs were bitches and vice versa.

I saw wild garlic and ground elder and the buttercups and daisies in the fossilized undergrowth now rendered in vivacious yet unnamable colours, as immobile arabesques without depth. But the sweetness of the wild roses rang in my ears like a peal of windbells for the vibrations of the perfumes echoed on my eardrums like the pulse of my own blood since, though they had become a kind of sound, they could not carry in the same way that sound did. I could not, for the life of me, make up my mind which world was which for I understood this world was coexistent in time and space with the other wood – was, as it were, the polarization of that other wood, although it was in no way similar to the reflection the other wood, or this wood, might have made in a mirror.

The more my eyes grew accustomed to the dark, the less in common did the petrified flora seem to have with anything I knew. I perceived all had been starkly invaded with, yes, shells, enormous shells, giant and uninhabited shells, so we might have been walking in the ruins of a marine city; the cool, pale colouring of those huge shells now glowed with a ghostly otherness and they were piled and heaped upon one another to parody the landscape of the woodland, unless the trees parodied them; all were whorled the wrong way round, all had that deathly weight, the supernatural resonance of the shell which seduced me and Anna told me in a soundless language I understood immediately that the transfigured wood, fertile now, only of metamorphoses, was – for how could it be anything else – the Sea of Fertility. The odour of her violence deafened me.

Then, once again, she began to sing; I saw the mute, dark, fire burning like Valhalla in *Götterdämmerung*. She sang a funeral pyre, the swan's song, death itself, and, with a brusque motion of her gun, she forced me forward on my knees while the dog stood over me as she tore open my clothes. The serenade smouldered all around us and I was so much at the mercy of the weight of the air, which pressed down on me like a coffin lid, and of the viscosity of the atmosphere, that I could do nothing to defend myself, even if I had known how, and soon she had me, poor, forked thing, stretched out upon a bank of shells with my trousers round my knees. She smiled but I could not tell what the smile meant; on this side of the mirror, a smile was no clue whatsoever to intention or to feeling and I did not think she meant to do me a good deed as she un-buckled her uncouth leather belt and stepped out of her jeans.

Parting the air with the knives of her arms, she precipitated herself upon me like a quoit on a peg. I screamed; the notes of my scream rose up on the air like ping-pong balls on a jet of water at a funfair. She raped me; perhaps her gun, in this system, gave her the power to do so.

I shouted and swore but the shell grotto in which she rav-ished me did not reverberate and I only emitted gobs of light. Her rape, her violation of me, caused me atrocious physical and mental pain. My being leaked away from me under the visitation of her aggressive flesh. My self grew less in agony under the piston thrust of her slender loins, as if she were a hammer and were forging me into some other substance than flesh and spirit. I knew the dreadful pleasure of abandonment; she had lit my funeral pyre and now would kill me. I felt such outrage I beat in the air behind my head with my helpless fists as she pumped away indefatigably at my sex, and to my sur-prise, I saw her face cloud and bruises appear on it, although my hands were nowhere near her. She was a brave girl; she only fucked the harder, for she was intransigent and now resembled the Seljuk Turks sacking Constantinople. I knew there was no hope for me if I did not act immediately.

Her gun lay propped against the shells beside us. I reached the other way and seized it. I shot at the black sky while she straddled me. The bullet pierced a neat, round, empty hole in the flat vault of the heavens but no light, no sound, leaked through; I had made a hole without quality but Anna let out a ripping shriek that sent a jagged scar across the surface of the wood. She tumbled backwards and twitched a little. The dog growled at me, a terrible sight, and leaped at my throat but I quickly shot her, also, in this negative way and, now free, there remained only the problem of the return to the mirror, the return to the right-hand side of the world. But I kept tight hold of the gun, by grasping it loosely, because of the guardian of the mirror.

To return to the house, I struck out from the shell grotto

where Anna lay, in the opposite direction from the one we had come from. I must have fallen into a mirror elision of reflected time, or else I stumbled upon a physical law I could not have guessed at, for the wood dissolved, as if the blood that leaked from Anna's wound was a solvent for its petrified substance, and now I found myself back at the crumbling gate before her juices were dry on my cock. I paused to do up my fly before I made my way to the door; I used my arms like scissors to snip through the thickness of the atmosphere, for it grew, moment by moment, less liquid and more impalpable. I did not ring the bell, so great was my outrage, so vivid my sense of having been the plaything of these mythic and monstrous beings.

The knitting curled down the stairs, just as I expected, and, in another moment, I saw, on a staccato stave, the sound of the needles.

She, he, it, Tiresias, though she knitted on remorselessly, was keening over a whole dropped row of stitches, trying to repair the damage as best she could. Her keening filled the room with a Walpurgisnacht of crazy shapes and, when she saw I was alone, she flung back her head and howled. In that decompression chamber between here and there, I heard a voice as clear as crystal describe a wordless song of accusation.

"Oh, my Anna, what have you done with my Anna – ?"

"I shot her," I cried. "With her own weapon."

"A rape! She's raped!" screamed the androgyne as I dragged the gilt chair to the mirror and clambered up on it. In the silvered depths before me, I saw the new face of a murderer I had put on behind the mirror.

The androgyne, still knitting, kicked with her bare heels upon the floor to drive her Bath chair over the wreathing muffler towards me, in order to attack me. The Bath chair cannoned into the chair on which I stood and she rose up in it as far as she could and began to beat me with her tender fists. But, because she did not stop knitting, she offered no resistance when I brought my ham-hand crashing down on her working face. I broke her nose; bright blood sprang out. I turned to the mirror as she screamed and dropped her knitting.

She dropped her knitting as I crashed through the glass
    through the glass, glass splintered round me driving
unmercifully into my face
      through the glass, glass splintered
        through the glass –
          half through.

Then the glass gathered itself together like a skilful whore
and expelled me. The glass rejected me; it sealed itself again
into nothing but mysterious, reflective opacity. It became a
mirror and it was impregnable.

Balked, I stumbled back. In Tiresias' bed-sitting room, there
was the most profound silence, and nothing moved; the flow of
time might have stopped. Tiresias held her empty hands to her
face that was now irretrievably changed; each one snapped
clean in two, her knitting needles lay on the floor. Then she
sobbed and flung out her arms in a wild, helpless gesture.
Blood and tears splashed down on her robe, but in a baleful,
hopeless way she began to laugh, although time must have
started again and now moved with such destructive speed
that, before my eyes, that ageless being withered – a quick
frost touched her. Wrinkles sprang out on her pale forehead
while her hair fell from her head in great armfuls and her
negligee turned brown and crumbled away, to reveal all the
flesh that sagged from the bone as I watched it. She was the
ruins of time. She grasped her throat and choked. Perhaps she
was dying. The muffler was blowing away like dead leaves in a
wind that sprang up from nowhere and raced through the
room, although the windows stayed shut tight. But Tiresias
spoke to me; she spoke to me once again.

"The umbilical cord is cut," she said. "The thread is broken.
Did you not realize who I was? That I was the synthesis in
person? For I could go any way the world goes and so I was
knitting the thesis and the antithesis together, this world and
that world. Over the leaves and under the leaves. Cohesion
gone. Ah!"

Down she tumbled, the bald old crone, upon a pile of wisps
of unravelled grey wool as the ormolu furniture split apart and

the paper unfurled from the wall. But I was arrogant; I was undefeated. Had I not killed her? Proud as a man, I once again advanced to meet my image in the mirror. Full of self-confidence, I held out my hands to embrace my self, my anti-self, my self not-self, my assassin, my death, the world's death.

# ELEGY FOR A FREELANCE ➤

*I* remember you as clearly as if you'd died yesterday, though I don't remember you often – usually I'm far too
busy. But I told the commissar about you, once. I asked him if
I'd done the right thing; would he have done the same? But he
said, if I wanted absolution, that he was the last person to ask
for it, and, besides, everything is changed now, and we are not
the same.

I remember that I was living high up in an attic, in a house
in a square. Most of the windows in the other houses round the
square were boarded up and planks were nailed across the
doors but they were not uninhabited. Although all these
houses were waiting to be pulled down, they contained a handful of small, scarcely licit households whose members crept in
and out through secret entries, lived by candlelight, slept upon
the filthy mattresses the dossers who lived there before them
had used and ate stews made from vegetable picked out of the
greengrocers' garbage cans and butchers' bones begged for dogs
that did not exist.

But our landlord – it was legal to own private property, to
rent it out, in those days – refused to sell his house to the
speculators who wanted to pull the entire terrace down. He'd
spent the Blitz in his house; it was his foxhole. He pulled the
carious walls up snug around his ears and felt himself envel-
oped in a safety that, although it was fictive, he believed in
completely. He rented his rooms out at old-fashioned rents
because he did not know that times had changed; how could
he? He never left home. He was confined to a chair and almost

blind. His room was his world, his house the unknown universe he knew of but never ventured into. Everything else was
unknowable. He did not even know that the boys who lived in
the basement filled milk bottles with petrol in their back
room and made explosions.

A girl lived with them in the basement. She was fifteen. Her
face was pale, mild and plump and always seemed a little
surprised that she found herself stumbling under the weight of
a pregnancy that had stunned her. She hardly ever spoke and
moved with the heaviness of somebody moving under water.
You kept a rifle in our room and loved to sit and scan the
square and the street below us from the open window.

A young man and a girl came to do yoga in the square every
morning. They adopted the tree position. A child on the
swings swung more and more idly; he twisted round to watch
them. They always had the same audience, the children in the
playground and the apprentice sniper. They unfurled their
right legs from the hip and reefed them in at the knee in order
to place the soles of their bare right feet against the inner sides
of their upper left thighs. They joined their hands together as
if in prayer and then raised their joined hands above their
heads. In order to keep their balance, they fixed their eyes on
the worn grass in front of them with the utmost concentration.
They maintained this position for an entire minute – I
watched the hand on my watch move – and then they returned
their right feet to the ground as they lowered their hands and
arms and now raised their left legs in order to repeat the exercise. When it was over, they decorously stood on their heads.
They were rapt with devotion.

X watched them through the sights of his rifle while they
went through the entire repertory of movements. I was scared
out of my wits when he slipped back the safety catch and did
not dare say anything. I knew the couple below by sight. They
squatted in a house on the other side of the square. They were
harmless as the pigeons who lived on the roof. When they had
finished, they went away again. X replaced the safety catch
and laughed. I was very frightened of him in his feral moods

but he told me an authentic assassin ought to be as indifferent as the weather and, when he scanned the square, all he was doing was practising indifference.

I went into his world when I fell in love with him and felt only a sense of privilege in its isolation. We had purposely exiled ourselves from the course of everyday events and were proud to live in parentheses. I went out for a little air at night, sometimes, when the streets were flooded with the ghastly yellow light that bleaches the blood that runs out of road accidents so that it doesn't look real. I used to walk through the streets for miles and I would clap my hands with childlike pleasure, I would enthusiastically applaud the detonating railway stations.

It hardly seemed possible the city could survive that summer. The sky opened like the clockwork Easter eggs the Tsars gave one another. The night would part, like two halves of a dark shell, and spill explosions. Because I lived in a house full of amateur terrorists, I felt I myself lit the fuses and caused these displays of pyrotechnics. Then I would feel almost omnipotent, just as X did, when he sat with his rifle above the square at the window of my room.

I was living high up in an attic. I hung over the summer in my attic as though it were the gondola of a balloon. London lay below me with her legs wide open; she was a whore sufficiently accommodating to find room for us in her embraces, even though she cost so much to love.

She is so old she ought to be superannuated, you said, the old cow. She paints so thickly over the stratified residue of yesterday and the day before yesterday and the day before the day before's cosmetics you can hardly make out the wens and blemishes under all the layers of paint, graffiti and old posters – voluptuous, oppressive, corrupt, self-regarding London marinating in the syrup of her own decay like *baba au rhum*, while the property speculators burrow away at her guts with the vile diligence of gonococci.

A feverish, hysterical glamour played over this wasting city like summer lightning. While I watched it, the city changed shape. Towers of steel and glass thrust their way through the soft, soiled velvet rind of the rotting fruit. Nobody lived in those towers; how could anybody live there – like the architecture of the Third Reich, they looked as if they were intended to be most beautiful in ruins. Amongst this architecture of desolation, haunting the fat-infested rubble, mendicants and proselytizers rang bells and rattled tambourines as they offered to the passer-by a bewildering variety of salvations. Those in saffron robes who had shaved their heads invoked the gods of the Indian subcontinent though our neighbours told us we ought to trust in Jesus. But *our* salvation would be gelignite; the basement of the house in which I lived had become a little arsenal. Any wise child can get a hand grenade together; it was the time of the Children's Crusade.

It was a strange, suspended time. The city had never looked more beautiful but I did not know, then, that it seemed to me beautiful only because it was doomed and I was the innocent slave of bourgeois aesthetics, that always sees an elegiac charm in decay. I remember velvet nights spiked with menace and the beautiful showers of sparks when an amateur incendiarist ignited a police station. My house was always full of the shimmering sound of the trees in the square moving in the wind, so that it seemed the sea was rushing through the corridors, the rooms.

I was living on the fourth floor although I had such vertigo that the sight of any abyss, however insignificant, excited in me, almost intolerably, the desire to plunge. I was quite helpless before the attraction of gravity. I was overwhelmed. I became powerless. Therefore to live on the fourth floor meant that every day began with a small triumph of will over instinct. I wanted to jump; but I must not jump. Pallor, shallow breathing, a prickle of cold sweat – I exhibited all the symptoms of panic, as I did when I met X. *That* was like finding myself on the edge of an abyss but the vertigo that I felt then came from a sense of recognition. This abyss was that of my own emptiness; I plunged instantly, for my innocence was so perfect that I saw in this submission the height of sophistication.

It was as lovely a summer as those that precede wars. The West Indian lady who ran the neighbourhood launderette always wore a small felt hat with a veil, as if she were determined to keep up appearances even in the most extreme circumstances. She pushed the dirt around the floor with a sodden mop and, when her tasks were finished, she would sit on a chair and read her well-thumbed Bible aloud to herself in that ineffable, querulous lilt, like the voice of a reproachful bird. Sometimes she would exclaim over the things she found in the book; when I looked over her shoulder, once, while she was crying: HOSANNA! I saw she was reading the Apocalypse.

The squatters consecrated the house next door. All night long, while we fixed up our explosive devices in the basement, they chanted: BABY JESUS, BABY JESUS, BABY JESUS.

I would not have believed Lenin was right when he said there was no place for orgy in the revolution, even if I had read Lenin. What we were about in bed seemed to be activity that could in itself overturn the world. X's lycanthropic eyes glowed in the dark like fuses. I found most pleasure of all in the delicious dread that seized me when he clung too close. I wanted to be the Madonna of the Barricades; I would have shot anybody you told me to but only if they did not get hurt. I felt I needed to understand nothing beyond my own sensations. I felt, as primitives do, that ceremonials such as the ones we made could revivify dead earth. Your kisses along my arms were like tracer bullets. I am lost. I flow. Your flesh defines me. I become your creation. I am your fleshly reflection.

("Libido and false consciousness characterized sexual relations during the last crisis of Capital," says the commissar.)

A man constructs his own fate out of his sense of the world. You engaged in conspiracies because you believed the humblest objects were engaged in a conspiracy against you. Your conviction was contagious; it impressed me. "Even the strawberries smell of blood, this summer," you remarked with anticipatory relish. I found you more and more often at the window, practising indifference.

You described the state of permanent revolution to me. It

sounded like a series of beautiful explosions. Volcano after
volcano would erupt under their own internal stresses in an
endless reduplication of ecstasy. When the bed creaked beneath us, it sounded like the *Liebestod* from *Tristan and Isolde*
performed with vehemence by a military band. The grand design of glorious convulsions you depicted was so beautiful I
wept; but we would begin, you said, in small ways, we would
begin with a single shooting. You made assassination sound as
enticing as pornography. A, B and C were suspicious of me
since you abandoned the basement for my bed. Now we were
all gripped in the same obsession, they treated me more politely. *Folie à deux, à trois, à quatre.* We were living on the crater
of a volcano and felt the earth move beneath us. What stirring
times! What seismographic times!

("The bourgeoisie turned politics into an aspect of romanticism," says the commissar. "If it was only an art form, how
could it threaten them?")

The city unravelled like knitting as the transport workers'
strikes imposed vast distances between its various sections
but we never went beyond walking distance of our house so
the strikes did not affect us.

Our house was tall and narrow. Worn steps led down to the
area. Our landlord lived in the front room on the ground floor.
He crouched in front of his television set making what sense
he could out of the random flickering that was all his eyes
registered, poor old thing, with his stick and his cats. He had a
sink and a gas ring and a little cupboard where he kept his
cats' fish. He boiled up their dinners twice a week and stored
their food in a plastic washing-up bowl when it was cooked.
The house stank of stale fish; we had to burn incense all the
time to cancel out the smell. He spread his table with clean
newspapers and set out the fish for his cats in separate saucers.
They all jumped up to eat. There was a soup plate full of water
which, although it was refreshed each day, always managed to
drown a fly or two by lunchtime, and a saucer of milk that had
turned into junket by the six o'clock news. His three-legged
chairs were balanced on piles of old newspapers and uphol-

stered with cast-off garments. Cats of all colours sat upon the sideboard amongst the empty brown ale bottles, the open cans of condensed milk, the stopped clock, the yellowing circulars, the football coupons, the curded milk bottles, the plaster Alsatian dog with one ear chipped. There he sat, a king in his kingdom, thumping upon the floor when the conspirators in the basement went *bang!* by accident.

Once a week, in turn, we visited him to pay our rents for we were determined to be scrupulous and, if you must have a landlord at all, it's best if he's purblind. It was like paying tribute to a holy statue. Age had drawn his yellow, freckled skin so tight across his skull his head shone like polished bone and his eyes had faded to the innocent blue of baby ribbon – wandering, rheumy eyes, gummed at the corners. His bony fingers clutched the handle of his stick with a certain balked ferocity.

He was afraid of us, I suppose, and so he pretended to be fierce. In the pub, they said he kept roll upon roll of banknotes stored in Old Holborn tins tucked away here and there amongst the clutter. He ingested his rents like a sponge but he suspected nothing although the cats did and threshed their tails when we went into his room. Sometimes they spat. The ginger one once scratched you.

A middle-aged transvestite lived on the first floor but he was too immersed in his aberration to pay us much attention. He ventured out for little walks around the square in the dusk that tenderly veiled his eccentricity, tottering on his five-inch heels, spiking the ground before him in the manner of a climber with the point of his long, furled umbrella. He wore a black gaberdine two-piece with a pencil skirt for these expeditions and slung a fox-fur round his neck. The mask hung over his left shoulder and kept a good lookout behind with its little, beady eyes. Above him, a slack-witted unmarried mother pigged it with her brood. She did the old man's shopping for him, when she remembered, but he only wanted the fish, twice a week, a can or two of beans and the occasional bottle of brown ale.

A perpetual twilight dominated that house, with its characteristic odours of stale cooking, phantom bacon, lavatories and
the cats who pissed in the hall. The bulbs on the stairways
were always blown. It was an old, dark house; it was a cave. We
saw visions on the walls. It was a slum. It was a citadel. That
was the time of the freelance assassins; our cell was self-sufficient and took no orders nor cognizance of any other cell in
the cancerous growth of the deathwardly inclining city. You
had the plausibility of a Nechaev; to plot a murder became
your sole preoccupation.

You arbitrarily selected a member of the cabinet. We con-
sulted the I Ching, we threw the coins. The oracle seemed to
be propitious, although, as always, its tone was guarded. We
drew lots. Inexorably, the marked card found you. In the full
consciousness of a young man about to become an assassin,
you made love to me like the storming of the Bastille. But then
I found you'd somewhere encountered an obstacle to indifference for now you were crying, though, when I asked why you
were crying, you hit me.

Our neighbours were chanting so loudly they might have
been chanting in the same room and I had no curtains at the
window so the glaring, yellow light balefully illuminated your
unhappy face, but I was too much under your spell to guess
why you were crying. Hadn't everything been decided? Tomorrow we would go and murder the politician. I would ring the
doorbell and then you would fire the gun. I could not understand why you were crying, you had so successfully impressed
me with the model simplicity of the plan, so that I was sure we
were in the right. I went to sleep again, sulking because I had
been hit. The monotonous, droning chant – BABY JESUS, BABY
JESUS, BABY JESUS – lulled me to sleep.

What an awakening! – there was so much blood on your
shirt. You spilled the banknotes over me. They were in tight
little blue rolls that bounced off my body, unfurling as they
fell to the floor. Such a lot of money! I blinked in the violet
dawn, astounded at the extravagance of your hysteria. You
sobbed and babbled and hurled the furniture to the ground,

smashed cups, overturned the wastepaper basket. I made you tea and slyly stoked up the mug with sleeping pills. I choked it down you and got you into the bed I had vacated for I could never lie in the same bed with you, now. I stayed with you until I was certain you were sleeping and locked the door behind you.

A, B and C had finished the night's work and were frying eggs and bread on their gas ring. A's girl lay on the mattress under her belly which was the size and shape of a dirigible, round enough, big enough to rise up into the air and carry her away with it from this vale of tears, over the rainbow, to a happy land far, far away. I told them what you had said to me, that you killed him for practice. We had intended to be such philosophic assassins! But what were your existential credentials when you murdered the landlord? Was it the dress rehearsal for an assassination or the audition of an assassin?

The old man lay on the floor in his rank pyjamas. His debilitated, senescent tool dangled out of his yellowed fly. The cats milled about him, mewing ravenously. There was blood on their whiskers and on their inquisitive paws. X had smashed in the old man's skull and he'd tumbled off the bed in his death agony. In spite of his age and weakness, he had put up a struggle; we could see the signs of it all over the room. The bedclothes were disordered and his little night-table had been knocked over. The chamber-pot it contained had fallen out on its side, spilling its contents on the floor. Then X must have gone through every cupboard and drawer in the room to find the fabled tobacco tins of money. We looked at the evidence in silence though all the time the neighbours went on wailing very loudly. We could hear them downstairs, even here, on the ground floor. The cats pressed against us, yowling, and I thought I had better feed the cats because I did not want them to practise necrophagy upon the landlord. I opened the food cupboard and took out their fish. I spread the table and laid out their meal as if nothing had happened. They all jumped up and tucked in, purring as they swallowed their dinners.

We had not let A's girl into the room because of her condition. Now, from behind the lace curtain, we saw her, with her shawl flung carelessly round her shoulders, pursuing her burden as it stumbled away down the street. A said: "She's broken – she's gone for the police." I rushed out of the house and ran after her. I soon caught up with her; she was too fat to run fast. She wept. She said how much she always disliked X; that he had cold eyes. Then she fainted. A came and helped me carry her back to the basement. Shortly after that, she went into labour. The neighbours continued to chant: BABY JESUS, BABY JESUS, BABY JESUS. While I held A's girl's frightened, hot, sticky hand and A heated water, B and C took some rope, went to my attic and tied X up. They said he was too surprised to struggle when they woke him. He must have felt it was the revolt of the toys.

Then a police car drew up outside and we shrank into ourselves, we were so scared. Poor Susie moaned and tore at the mattress on which she lay. But the police had come for our neighbours. The transvestite had complained about the noise and we watched from the area steps as the police took an axe to the boards that were nailed over the front door and entered it. A little while later, they came out again, half leading, half carrying the dazed and shaking occupants, who were all as white as sheets, tranced, emaciated, their eyes staring as still they mumbled their orisons, too limp and listless to protest.

I sterilized my nail scissors in the gas jet and A held his wailing son in his arms after I cut the cord. But, however pleased A was to be a father, he insisted on a fair trial for X. Perhaps, even then, B and C didn't quite trust me; I'd been a rich girl. But X confessed everything to us all quite freely.

We tried him in the attic. We left Susie downstairs nursing her baby. We untied X's legs and let him sit down on a chair but we did not untie his arms. He confessed as follows; he seemed agonizingly torn between humiliation and self-justification.

"I wasn't sure, I wasn't sure of myself. I kept thinking, what if I blow it? If I'd blown the whole thing, hadn't been able to pull the trigger, had just stood there in the doorway staring vacantly at him. What if I can't kill when I want to kill and am in the right to kill? What if I were paralysed? What if I'd spent so long looking at people through the sights of a rifle and holding back from shooting that I could never shoot? Fear I'd be weak shook me.

"What good did the landlord do to anyone? Sitting in his room, sucking in his rents. Nobody loves him. He's significant to nobody. He's hardly alive at all, he can't talk, hardly, he's almost blind, squatting like a toad on all that money.

"I was in a frenzy, I prayed. Yes, I did. The fear I'd fail threw me into a frenzy. I prayed and the answer came. I left her sleeping and took the gun and went to his room. He didn't wake up when I went in but the cats all woke and stretched themselves and jumped off the chairs and the sideboard and the bed and came towards me, mewing; it was a tide of fur with eyes and mouths in it. He woke up when he heard the cats and began to mew, too. "Who's there, pussies, what's the matter, pussies?" I had nothing against him when I went into the room – nothing. It was only an exercise in self-control.

"But I began to hate him when I saw how helpless he was. When I saw how easy it would be to kill him, nothing to it, than I began to hate him. I raised the rifle and looked at him through the sights. The sights changed the way I saw him. Through the sights of the rifle, now I saw he was not human, not even an old wreck of humanity. He was only an object to be extinguished. He asked some menacing person he could not see if that person had come for his money. When I realized that person was I, I thought that I might just as well take his money, while I was here, since he offered it to me. But I said nothing and my hands were shaking. He told me not to kill him. That was how he reminded me I *could* kill him, if I wanted to. Up till then, I had not wanted to but when he called me his murderer, I became so. He sealed his own fate. It was his own fault, what happened.

"Next door they were chanting away like mad things. He rolled about on his filthy bed clutching his head with his hands as if his hands would protect it. His pyjamas burst open and the old flesh spilled on the sheets. I felt nauseated to see his old flesh. My fingers tightened on the trigger. The cats screamed and pressed against my legs. The ginger one scratched me. They reared up on their hind legs and snarled, I could have sworn they were attacking me. How disgusting the old bedbug was, now he was at my mercy! But just as I was about to shoot, I thought: what a noise the gun will make. It will be much louder than the chanting, even. The noise will wake Sister Boy. Sister Boy will wake and throw his negligee round his shoulders and come and see what is the matter. The woman upstairs will wake, or her kids will wake. They'll all come down, even the four-year-old, wiping the sleep out of its eyes. I thought of a holocaust – mow them all down. But I was too self-restrained.

"I lowered the gun. He was fumbling in his little night-table, where he keeps his pisspot. The night-table rocked, he was fumbling so. Out jumped the pisspot and crashed on the ground. All the cats puffed out their fur, stuck up their backs and hissed and shrank away from me, because the crash of the pisspot startled them, but he was rummaging for his savings in the night-table and found one little tin. He shook the bank-notes all over the floor, they were rolled up in the tin like curling papers, they fell in the spilled piss and the cats pounced on them and began to pat them this way and that way with their paws. He scooped up some banknotes in his fists and shoved them towards me. He said: "Take it, it's all I've got." But I knew he had lots of other old tobacco tins full of money, doesn't everybody say so? When he tried to buy me off so cheaply, I lost all mercy and bludgeoned him about the head with the butt of the rifle until he stopped moving."

He looked at us as though he was certain we understood everything perfectly. I closed my eyes; I had the sensation of falling. Yet, when I opened my eyes, the abyss remained; I stood only upon its brink. Now my eyes were open, perception, lucidity became my new profession. At the conclusion of his story, X began to cry like a child, as though he were to be pitied, and then I felt most afraid of him, in case I began to pity him. While we watched him snivelling, we grew older. He cried like a baby and we became his parents. We must decide what would be best for him. Now I was his mother, they his father and we saw our common responsibility as his cause in the random nature of his effect.

"It must be worst for you," A said to me, because I'd been the lover of this person; but the same terror gripped us all, for our complicity with him was over once he had acted only for himself and by himself and now we could stand apart from him and, in judging him, judge ourselves.

I will try and describe you better. I am glad you died before the barricades went up. We served our time and took our punishment upon them but I would not have liked to have you beside me with a machine-gun because you were your own hero, always your own hero, and would not have taken orders easily. But you might have made an exceptional Kamikaze pilot, had you not been so scared of dying. You made us believe you were our leader; so, while you were ordering us about, how could we become a confederacy? We were in the deepest complicity with you; we admired your paranoia. While we admired it, we believed it formed an explanation of events in itself. But I was always a little afraid of you because you clung to me far too tightly and made me come with the barbarous dexterity of a huntsman eviscerating a stag.

After we heard X's confession, we gave him some water to drink and tied up his arms again before we gagged him, in case he tried to cry to Sister Boy or the unmarried mother below for help. Then we went down to the basement to discuss what we should do with him. A's girl was suckling her baby. She seemed obscurely but entirely content with her own miracle. She was angry we had locked her into the basement and said she would never leave A because he was the father of her child but I thought she said that due to the emotion generated in the generation of the baby and we should still be wary of her. A cooked her some brown rice and vegetables and added a couple of eggs, because she needed nourishment. After a great deal of discussion, B took some food to X also, but X dashed the dish to the floor. He was petulant, now, B told us; he thought we were behaving irrationally.

He had quite recovered his old self-confidence, it seemed, but we no longer retained confidence in him. We reached our decision in unison, although C – what memories of old movies! – at first wanted to lock X alone in my attic with a revolver and let him take his own way out. But our consensus convinced C that X would not have done so, had we given him the chance.

B took a coil of stout rope from the cupboard under the sink. We waited until dark; we listened desultorily to the radio and heard the army had been called in to break the car-workers' strike but we were all stricken with such dreadful gravity at the unexpected turn of events in our cell that the news did not move us. Our private situation seemed to us far more significant.

X was in a foul state since we had not untied him all day so now he rolled in his own excrement and stank. He was in a filthy temper and cursed us but, when he saw the rope, first he laughed to try to bluff his way out of the noose; and then he blubbered – there is no other word for his collapse in tears and pleadings. He seemed astonished we were capable of acting without him. A held the revolver. It wasn't far to Hampstead Heath.

We forced X along with his arms bound and the muzzle of the revolver in his back. We did not meet many others on the streets; those whom we did pass by edged away from us, they must have thought we were all drunk, and the Heath itself was empty apart from a distant bonfire that marked, probably, the camp of some homeless family. By now the moon was up; we soon found a suitable tree.

When X realized there was no hope for him, he relapsed into silence but, when I slipped the noose round his neck, he asked me if I loved him. I was surprised at that – it seemed to me so far from the point; but I replied, yes, I *had* loved him and I tested the running knot. B and C pulled the rope. Up, he went, like a flag. There was a russet-coloured moon of ominous size too low above the whispering bushes; he danced exuberantly for five minutes beneath it after the click when his neck broke. His bowels opened. What a mess!

When it hung limp, we cut his body down and threw it in the undergrowth. A vomited and B wept a little, but C and I covered it with leaves, like the robins in *Babes in the Wood*. I retained such a ferocious calm that C said to me, you are turning into a tiger lady when I always thought you were such a pussycat. I think that justice had been done, although we ourselves had been the perpetrators of both crime and punishment and we did not dig a hole to bury X because we wanted to leave a loophole in which the everyday circumstances of justice might catch up with us. We were beginning to behave with a certain dignity. Our illogic began to approach a kind of harsh virtue, although we looked at one another with veiled, estranged eyes; who were we, what were we becoming?

Was it possible we could have done what we had done; how could it have been possible we had planned what we had intended?

A's girl and the child slept quite peacefully in the basement where we made ourselves tea that did not taste any different from the tea we had drunk before we hanged him.

Now B revealed an intransigent morality. He wanted us to go to the police, make a clean breast of all and take our punishment, since we had done nothing of which we ourselves were ashamed. But A had his baby son to think of and wanted to take Susie and his child to a Welsh mountain where he had friends on a commune, there to recuperate from these excesses in the clean air. Apropos of nothing, he declared he'd never be able to look at meat again and would walk on the other side of the road when he passed a butcher's shop. He sat on the mattress by the sleeping girl and looked, every moment, more and more like an ordinary husband and father. But C and I did not know what to do, now, nor what to think. We felt nothing but a lapse of feeling, a dulled heaviness, a despair.

The pure, cool light of early September touched the contents of the room with fastidious fingers; we looked at the day with mild surprise, that it should be as bright as any other day, brighter, in fact, than most. Then I felt a drop like a heavy raindrop fall on the back of my hand but it was not a raindrop, for the sun was shining, nor a drip from a leaking cistern, because the landlord's room was directly over our heads. This was a red drop. Horror! It was blood; and, looking up, I saw the stain on the ceiling where the old man's blood was leaking through. Soon he would begin to smell.

We began to argue. Should we dig a hole in the backyard and bury the old man in it, pack our few things and leave the house under false names for secret destinations, as A wanted to do; or should we throw ourselves upon the law, as B thought was right? Instinct and will, again; I was poised on the window ledge of a fourth floor of a building I had never suspected existed and I did not know which was will and which was instinct that told me to jump, to run. While we were discussing these things, we heard a low rumble in the distance. We thought it was thunder but, when A turned on the radio to find out what time it was, only martial music was playing and the newsflash informed us the coup had taken place; the army was in power, as if this was not home but a banana republic. They were encountering some resistance in the north but were rapidly crushing it. All the time we had been plotting, the generals had been plotting and we had known nothing. Nothing!

The thunder grew louder; it was gun and mortar fire. The sky soon filled with helicopters. The Civil War began. History began.

# LOVE

One day, Annabel saw the sun and moon in the sky at the same time. The sight filled her with a terror which entirely consumed her and did not leave her until the night closed in catastrophe for she had no instinct for self-preservation if she was confronted by ambiguities.

It had happened as she walked home through the park. In the system of correspondences by which she interpreted the world around her, this park had a special significance and she walked along its overgrown paths with nervous pleasure, especially in certain yellow, tarnished lights of winter when the trees were bare and the sun, as it set, rimmed the branches with cold fire. An eighteenth-century landscape gardener planned the park to surround a mansion which had been pulled down long ago and now the once harmonious artificial wilderness, randomly dishevelled by time, spread its green tangles across the high shoulder of a hill only a stone's throw from a busy road that ran through the city dockland. All that remained of the former mansion were a few architectural accessories now the property of the city museum. There was a stable built on the lines of a miniature Parthenon, housing for Houyhnhnms rather than natural horses; the pillared portico, especially effective under the light of a full moon, never to be entered again by any horse, functioned only as a pure piece of design, a focal point in the green composition on the south side of the hill where Annabel rarely ventured for serenity bored her and the Mediterranean aspect of this part of the park held no excitements for her. She preferred the Gothic north,

where an ivy-covered tower with leaded ogive windows
skulked among the trees. Both these pretty whimsies were
kept securely locked for fear of the despoliation of vandals but
their presence still performed its original role, transforming
the park into a premeditated theatre where the romantic imagination could act out any performance it chose amongst set-
tings of classic harmony or crabbed quaintness. And the magic
strangeness of the park was enhanced by its curious silence.
Footfalls fell softly on the long grass and few birds sang there,
but the presence all around of the sprawling, turbulent city,
however muffled its noises, lent such haunted, breathless
quiet an unnatural quality.

The park maintained only a single, still impressive entrance, a massive pair of wrought-iron gates decorated with
cherubs, masks of beasts, stylized reptiles and spearheads from
which the gilding flaked, but these gates were never either
open or closed. They hung always a little ajar and drooped
from their hinges with age; they served a function no longer
for all the railings round the park were gone long ago and
access everywhere was free and easy. The park was on such
high ground it seemed to hang in the air above a vast, misty
model of a city and those who walked through it always felt
excessively exposed to the weather. At times, all seemed nothing but a playground for the winds and, at others, an immense
drain for all the rain the heavens could pour forth.

Annabel went through the park in a season of high winds
and lurid weather, early one winter's evening, and happened to
look up at the sky.

On her right, she saw the sun shining down on the district
of terraces and crescents where she lived while, on her left,
above the spires and skyscrapers of the city itself, the rising
moon hung motionless in a rift of absolute night. Though one
was setting while the other rose, both sun and moon gave forth
an equal brilliance so the heavens contained two contrary
states at once. Annabel gazed upwards, appalled to see such a
dreadful rebellion of the familiar. There was nothing in her
mythology to help her resolve this conflict and, all at once, she

felt herself the helpless pivot of the entire universe as if sun, moon, stars and all the hosts of the sky span round upon herself, their volitionless axle.

At that, she bolted from the path through the long grass, seeking cover from the sky. Wholly at the mercy of the elements, she lurched and zig-zagged and her movements were so erratic, apparently at the whim of the roaring winds, and her colours so ill-defined, blurred by the approaching dusk, that she might herself have been no more than an emanation of the of the place or time of year.

At the crest of the hill, she flung up her hands in a furious gesture of surrender and pitched herself sideways off the path, concealing herself behind a clump of gorse where she lay moaning and breathless for a few moments. The wind tied strands of her hair to spikes of gorse and thus confirmed her intuition that she should not budge one inch until the dreadful, ambiguous hour resolved itself entirely to night. So there she stayed, a mad girl plastered in fear and trembling against a thorn bush suffering an anguish which also visited her when pressed just as close to the blond flesh of the young husband who slept beside her and did not know her dreams, although he was a beautiful boy whom anybody else would have thought well worth the effort of loving.

She suffered from nightmares too terrible to reveal to him, especially since he himself was often the principal actor in them and appeared in many hideous dream disguises. Sometimes, during the day, she stopped, startled, before some familiar object because it seemed to have just changed its form back to the one she remembered after a brief, private period impersonating something quite strange, for she had the capacity for changing the appearance of the real world which is the price paid by those who take too subjective a view of it. All she apprehended through her senses she took only as objects for interpretation in the expressionist style and she saw, in everyday things, a world of mythic, fearful shapes of whose existence she was convinced although she never spoke of it to anyone; nor had she ever suspected that everyday, sensuous human practice might shape the real world. When she did discover that such a thing was possible, it proved the beginning of the end for her for how could she possess any notion of the ordinary?

Her brother-in-law once gave her a set of pornographic photographs. She accepted the gift absently, without doing him the courtesy of investigating the complex motives behind it, and she examined the pictures one by one with a certain impersonal curiosity. A glum, painted young woman, the principal actress (torso and legs sheathed in black leather, sex exposed) eyed the camera indifferently as though it were no business of hers she was blocked at every orifice; she went about her obscene business with neither relish nor disgust, rather with the abstract precision of the geometrician so that these stark juxtapositions of genitalia, the antithesis of the erotic, were cold as Russia when nights are coldest there and possessed chiefly the power to affront. Annabel, comforted and reassured by these indifferent arrangements of bizarre intersecting lines, became convinced they told a true story. For herself, all she wanted in life was a bland, white, motionless face like that of the photographic whore so she could live a quiet life behind it, because she was so often terrified when the pictures around her began to move, as she thought, of their own accord and she could not control them.

So these photographs were cards in her private tarot pack and signified love.

As she waited for the sun to set, she had ample time to refresh and embellish her initial terror and was finally seized with the conviction that this night, of all nights, it would never disappear at all but lie stranded for ever above the horizon so she would have to stay nailed to the hillside. At these times, she thought of her husband as a place of safety although, when she was face to face with him, she could find no means of telling him her fears since his brother was her only intermediary between her private experience and the common one; and, this time, it was he who rescued her so she learned to trust him a little more.

But when she first met the boy who became her brother-in-law, he frightened her more than anything had done until that date.

Before they were married, when she was living with Lee, who was then a student, Lee came home from a lecture one February afternoon to find his brother had returned from North Africa unannounced. The newcomer sat on the floor at right angles to the wall in the recesses of a black, hooded, Tunisian cloak which concealed every part of him but for long fingers which drummed restlessly against his knee. On the other side of the room, Annabel sat in a similar position, shielding her face with her hair. An air of mutual mistrust filled the room. Lee dropped a string bag containing groceries on the floor and went to feed the dying fire.

"Hi, Alyosha," said Buzz.

Lee knelt beside him to hug and kiss him.

"I have a dose," enunciated Buzz with precision.

"You want to eat?"

Buzz padded after Lee into the adjoining kitchen and, grasping him from behind, pressed his fingertips against the base of Lee's throat until Lee went limp.

"I don't like her," said Buzz and released him.

When Lee could speak, he said: "Try that unarmed combat stuff on me again and I'll smash you against the fucking wall."

"Bad . . ." said Buzz effortfully . . . "vibes . . ."

Lee shrugged and broke eggs into a pan of hot fat.

"But I don't like her!" wailed Buzz childishly. He wound the cloak round himself to hide. "And you're knocking her off, aren't you; you're screwing her all night."

Lee menaced him briefly with the breadknife and he fell back, whimpering, for knives, his favourite weapon, impressed him horribly when they were turned against him. He crouched on the floor like a dog to eat his food in the tent of the black cape and Annabel still sat where they had left her, in the dark.

"That's my brother," said Lee pleasantly.

"What's wrong with him?"

"Gonorrhoea."

"Pardon?"

"A venereal disease," explained Lee.

"Apart from that."

"He's a freak."

She appeared to consider this gravely for a few minutes. Then she said: "Come here."

She embraced Lee with such unexpected passion he started to shiver, murmuring her name and running his hands over her body. As they toppled sideways to the floor, the lights in the room flashed on and Buzz's shadow fell over them like that of an avening angel for he spread out his arms so the folds of the cloak made wings. He attacked them both impartially and, catching Lee unprepared, soon succeeded in subduing him; when he adopted the traditional pose of the victor, his knee in Lee's belly, he snarled:

"Don't ever let me catch you at it again!"

But time passed and Buzz and Annabel became, in a sense, accomplices and then they left Lee out of their plottings for he understood neither of them, although he loved them both.

Buzz never went out without a camera; that night of January, when he found her on the hill, he took several photographs of her without her knowledge as soon as he saw her angular, familiar body stretched out against the bush in the strange light. Then he knelt beside her without speaking till there was nothing but honest moonlight before he led her home to the flat in a Victorian square, where they all three lived together. She stood in the dark porch fumbling for her latch-key with chilly fingers stiff with fright which could not find their way about the satchel which also contained her sketchbooks and a few things, a model soldier, three tubes of white gouache and a bar of chocolate, which she had stolen that day at lunchtime. Buzz dug into the bag and found her key, took the chocolate bar, kissed her cheek and ran off for he had arranged a party in the flat that night and had some preparatory business to do. He liked organizing parties for he always hoped something terrible would happen when so many people intersected upon one another. He was, as usual, in a state of suppressed nervous excitement.

In their room, Lee lay face down on the carpet in front of the fire, perhaps asleep. The walls round him were painted a very dark green and from this background emerged all the dreary paraphernalia of romanticism, landscapes of forests, jungles and ruins inhabited by gorillas, trees with breasts, winged men with pig faces and women whose heads were skulls. An enormous bedstead of dull since rarely polished brass, spread with figured Indian cotton, occupied the centre of the room which was large and high but so full of bulky furniture in dark woods (chairs, sofas, bookcases, sideboards, a round mahogany table covered with a fringed, red plush cloth, a screen covered with time-browned scraps) that one had to move around the room very carefully for fear of tripping over things. Heavy velvet curtains hung at the windows and puffed blue dust at a touch; a light powder of dust covered everything. On the mantelpiece stood the skull of a horse amongst a clutter of small objects such as clockwork toys, stones of many shapes and various bottles and jars.

All this heterogeneous collection seemed to throb with a mute, inscrutable, symbolic life; everything Annabel gathered around her evoked correspondences in her mind so all these were the palpable evidence of her own secrets and the room expressed a hermetic spiritual avarice. In her way, she was a miser. In this oppressive room, Lee was as out of place as a goatherd's son trapped in a witch's house for he always took about with him a peasant or rustic breath of open air. He lay on the carpet and traced the threadbare warp with his finger. She moved almost silently but he heard her come in and raised his head. His eyes were of the clearest, most beautiful, most intense blue though always rimmed with reddish inflammation. He put out his hand and caught hold of one of her naked feet, which were both caked with damp earth from the hillside.

"Trampling in graves again," he said for he took her otherworldliness lightly. "Oh, my duck, you'll catch your death."

The local evening newspaper drifted apart leaf from leaf in the draught caused by Annabel's entrance. Lee trapped the paper and pointed out a blurred photograph.

"Joanne. Joanne Davis. She's in my form at school. I teach her. Sweet Jesus, can you credit it?"

He was a schoolteacher for a living and worked in a comprehensive school. His pupil was a buxom blonde who wore a bikini with a sash over her bosom identifying her as the winner of a minor beauty contest. She revealed her teeth in a smile as brilliantly artificial as those of acrobats.

"She has no academic bent," said Lee. "Sixteen, she is. I'm an old man to her. I'm Mr. Collins and sometimes even 'sir'."

He was twenty-four, old enough for this to sadden him, but Annabel indifferently stirred the paper with her toes. She was so full of the terror of the park she could barely think of anything else and she rehearsed the simple sentence carefully before she asked him if supper was ready so that no tremor in her voice should betray her agitation. He nodded and abandoned the attempt to chat with her; they did not speak to one another, much. She evaded his hands and padded out into the kitchen to inspect the food he had prepared in case it contained snakes and spiders while Lee rose and found her antique lace tablecloth in the drawer of an enormous sideboard which was decorated with small, carved lions' heads with brass rings in their noses. He did not hear her return but saw her suddenly materialize in the dusty surface of the sideboard mirror, which was subtly warped, so her face looked as if it were reflected in water. All was as it should be in the kitchen and she gave him a smile of such unexpected sweetness that he turned, put his arms around her and hid his face in her hair, for he was having an affair with another woman, as was only to be expected.

"What did you do today, love?"

"I drew the model," she said indifferently.

Her apparent indifference to the world outside her own immediate perceptions had ceased to hurt Lee but never failed to bewilder him for he always tried to be as happy as he could, himself. They had lived together for three years but still, when he was with Annabel, Lee was like a lone explorer in an unknown country without a map to guide him. Genuine explorers rarely smile for what they have undergone wipes the smiles from their faces for good; Lee was not yet quite ready to join that select and aristocratic company but he was already very much changed from what he had been and his marvellous smile was a far less frequent event than in the days before he met her, for until then he had been perfectly free.

This freedom had been the result of an unusual combination of circumstances. Neither he nor his brother carried through life the name he had been born with. Lee had undergone three changes of forename, from Michael to Leon to his own choice of diminutive borrowed from some now forgotten Saturday-morning cinema Western, Lee, and he arrogantly retained the last name into adult life for he was not ashamed of his romanticism. The aunt who cared for both of the boys changed his name to Leon, for Trotsky. She was a remarkable woman, a canteen cook and shop steward who worked her fingers to the bone to support the two boys and inculcated in them a sense of pride and a certain critical severity which, in adulthood, they both expressed sufficiently in their separate ways, though neither in a way of which their aunt would have approved.

Buzz, however, had renamed himself. At four years old, he selected this mysterious monosyllable from the credits of a television cartoon film and after that he insisted it was his own name and his only name; he refused to answer to any other and so he soon acquired it permanently. He said he liked the word because it hung in the air for a long time after him but Lee guessed he liked the persistent irritation of the sound. Their aunt changed their original surname to her own by deed poll after their mother, her sister, forfeited her social personality in such a spectacular manner that she became a legend in the neighbourhood where they lived.

On Empire Day at the primary school which Lee attended

when he was a small child, there was an annual festival with a display of flags, patriotic tableaux and country dancing. This celebration reached its climax when a selection of infants filed on to the playground in their best clothes with, attached by string, a card bearing a single letter around each neck so that, assembled in a line, they spelled out in total the motto of the school, a Kantian imperative: DO RIGHT BECAUSE IT IS RIGHT. Upon a blowing day in June, in his sixth year, Lee carried the letter S when his mother, naked and painted all over with cabbalistic signs, burst into the crowded playground and fell writhing and weeping on the asphalt before him.

When Lee attained the age of reason and acquired his aunt's pride, he was glad his mother had gone mad in style. There could be no mistaking her intention nor could her behaviour be explained in any other terms than the onset of a spectacular psychosis in the grand, traditional style of the old-fashioned Bedlamite. She progressed to unreason via no neurotic back alleyway nor let any slow night of silence and darkness descend upon her; she chose the high road, operatically stripping off her clothes and screaming to the morning: "I am the whore of Babylon." His aunt took him to visit her in hospital from time to time but she was beyond recall and failed to recognize them as if they had been, at the best of times, chance and unmemorable acquaintances. So, soon after they went to live with their aunt, she saw the logic of the child when the younger brother insisted on changing his name. She changed Michael's for him as well and blotted out the family name with her own.

In the street where the brothers lived with their aunt during their childhood, it always seemed to be Sunday afternoon. It is becoming increasingly difficult to find such streets, though they used to exist in large numbers in all our great cities – those quiet terraces of artisans' dwellings where the sunlight falls on cracked paving stones and smoky brick with a peculiar sweetness and the winds seem never chill nor boisterous. In summer, they hang protectors of faded canvas over the front doors to prevent the sun from peeling off still more of paint blistered already by suns of many summers and old men sit outside in shirtsleeves on kitchen chairs, as if put out to air upon the pavement. On the low window ledges, one might find, here, a pie set out to cool or a jelly to set, there, a dreaming cat; the windows themselves are hung with half-curtains of coarse lace or display dusty, unlifelike plants in green glazed pots and plaster Alsatian dogs, though now and then one catches glimpses of those tiny, brown front rooms flickering in the light of coal fires – rooms which, in winter, seem to promise all the warmth in the world. A gentle, respectable serenity pervades these scenes of urban pastorale. In such a street, behind scalloped lace, their aunt ferociously refused to submit to cancer in the style of a revolutionary, in a room full of yellowing pamphlets. It took her a whole, stifling, oppressive summer to die but all the time she died magnificently. That autumn, Lee went away to university and Buzz left London with him. The following year, the GLC pulled their old street down so all they had left was a few memories.

The brothers lived together in the university town. Lee was like a ploughboy and Buzz like a nightbird; Lee was sentimental while Buzz was malign; Lee's sensuality was equalled only by Buzz's perversity but they stayed together because they were alone in a world with which both felt themselves subtly at variance. Both walked warily, with the marvellous, collected walk of gunfighters of the Old West, and they were quick to take offence. They had the air of visitors who do not intend to stay long. Their mother's madness, their orphaned state, their aunt's politics and their arbitrary identity formed in both a savage detachment for they found such detachment necessary to maintain their precarious autonomy. From earliest childhood, they were accustomed to fighting, though Lee was better at it.

Lee was an honest orphan; his father had been a railwayman killed in the course of duty but after her husband's death, the wife had gone on the game and Buzz was fathered by an American serviceman who left behind him nothing but a crude, silver, finger-ring decorated with a skull and crossbones. Buzz created an authentic savage from this shadow. He became convinced the man had been an American Indian and claimed as proof his own straight, coarse, sooty hair, high cheekbones and sallow complexion. Sometimes the tribe he favoured most were the Apaches but, in less aggressive moods, he thought he might be a Mohawk since he had no fear at all of heights and often walked on roofs. Lee went to a grammar school but Buzz went to a secondary modern school. There, with a passionate stubbornness that earned his brother's unwilling respect, he steadfastly refused to learn anything useful.

He worked sporadically in factories, down at the docks or else serving or washing up in cafés. At the times he was not working, he lived off his brother and sometimes stole. He was taller than Lee and dressed himself in rags. He had neither talents nor aptitudes, only a disconcertingly sharp intelligence and a merciless self-absorption. He had long, thin hands as if expressly formed for picking and stealing, and he bit his nails down to the half-moon. He lived at a conscious pitch of melodrama; once, filling out a form for some job or other he never achieved, he wrote down against the space marked: INTERESTS, the two words, sex and death.

"Don't let's exaggerate," said Lee gently.

Lee looked like Billy Budd, or a worker hero of the Soviets, or a boy in a book by Jack London. He was of medium height and sturdy build; his eyes were blue and looked like the eyes of a seafarer partly because of the persistent slight reddening of the rims due to a chronic slum-child infection he did not shake off as he grew up. His hair was the colour of hay, his complexion fresh and only the lack of a front tooth took away the suspicion he might be simple-minded for it gave his gapped but dazzling smile a certain ambiguity. Like most people who happen to be born with a degree of physical beauty, he had become self-conscious very young in life and so profoundly aware of the effect of his remarkable appearance on other people that, by the age of twenty, he gave the impression of perfect naturalness, utter spontaneity and entire warmth of heart.

"Alyosha," said Buzz with contemptuous admiration. "Bloody Alyosha."

Buzz's conversation was composed of unnerving silences interspersed with rare outbursts of intense but often disconnected speech. His huge, heavily lidded eyes (the irises large and dark, the pupils white and gleaming) were as disconcerting in his immobile face as if real eyes had moved within those faces the ancient Egyptians painted on their coffin lids. He had been grievously exposed to his mother's madness; her persistent delusion that her sallow, dark baby, child of a dark stranger, was touched with the diabolic, had warped his development to a certain extent and, besides, blighted him with a sense he might be cut out for some extraordinary fate though he had no idea what such a fate might be. But Lee bubbled with frank, engaging good humour though an air of alienation surrounded them; both appreciated they were exotics. They got on well together and it never occurred to either they might live apart.

They moved disinterestedly in the floating world centred loosely upon the art school, the university and the second-hand trade and made their impermanent homes in the sloping, terraced hillside where the Irish, the West Indians and the more adventurous of the students lived in old, decaying houses where rents were low. They were curiously self-contained so that people rarely mentioned them separately but always as the Collins brothers, like bandits. They knew of, and encouraged, this practice. But, the winter he was eighteen, Buzz disappeared precipitously to North Africa with a group of acquaintances leaving Lee to continue his studies alone in the flat they occupied at that time. They thought of this flat as another temporary place to stay awhile; in fact, they would find themselves living there for some years. It was to become their home.

This flat comprised two rooms separated by flimsy double doors and a kitchen, partitioned off by hardboard from the room at the front of the house. This front room, Lee's room, had long windows opening on to a balcony and, at that time, it was quite bare but for an alarm clock on the mantelpiece and a number of books cleverly stacked one on top of the other. He stored a mattress in a built-in cupboard, together with his clothes, and took it out at night to sleep on. It was a large room; the walls and also the floorboards were painted white. The room echoed at the slightest sound or movement and Lee took off his shoes in the house, in the Japanese manner. Besides, he walked very quietly.

At that time, his room was always extraordinarily tidy, white as a tent and just as easy to dismantle but this was not ascetic barrenness. Because of its whiteness and uninterrupted space, the room was peculiarly sensitive to the time of day, to changes in the weather and to the seasons of the year. It changed continually and without any volition on Lee's part at all. There was nothing inside it to cast shadows but the movements of Lee himself and his brother, though the branches of the trees in the square outside shivered across this radiant interior in a variety of shadow shapes and, at night, the lights of the city played mysteriously across the endless walls. When he opened the window the winds rushed through.

Furnished entirely by light and shade, the characteristics of the room were anonymity and impermanence. There were no curtains at the windows for the room was so indestructibly private there was no need to hide anything, so little did it reveal. In this way, Lee expressed a desire for freedom; in the last years of his adolescence, freedom was his grand passion and a principal condition of freedom, it seemed to him, was lack of possessions. He also remained cool and detached in his dealings with women for freedom from responsibilities was another prerequisite of this state. So his sentimentality found expression in the pursuit of a metaphysical concept of liberty. When he was thirteen and Buzz eleven, he persuaded his brother to run away with him to Cuba to fight for Castro. Buzz stole a Spanish phrase-book from W.H. Smith's and they got as far as Southampton before the police found them. Their aunt was furious but gratified. The act was principally the expression of a sentimentality so pure it became his greatest virtue, in one sense, since his sentimentality often, when he grew up, made him act against his desires.

Buzz sent Lee some hash wrapped up in a djellabah from Marrakesh, for a Christmas present, and the brothers did not see one another for six months. During this time, Lee met the woman who later became his wife; on New Year's morning, he woke up on a strange floor to find an unknown young girl in his arms. She opened her eyes and some kind of hunger, some kind of despair in her narrow face caught at Lee's very tender heart. The room was full of darkness, silence and stale air. On a sofa, a young man and a girl twined together under a Paisley shawl; he murmured in his sleep and then a mouse rattled across the floor. Lee's unexpected visitor turned her head sharply at the noise, shivered and wept. He took her home with him and gave her some breakfast. When she told him her name was Annabel he knew at once she was middle-class and, by her nervous manner, he guessed she was a virgin.

Annabel ate a little, drank her tea and covered her face with her hands so he could not watch her any more. Her movements were spiky, angular and graceful; how was he to know, since he was so young, that he would become a Spartan boy and she the fox under his jacket, eating his heart out. The Japanese peasantry had an awed respect for foxes, who, they believed, could enter a person's body either through the breast or else the space between the flesh of a finger and any one fingernail. When the fox was inside, it would harangue its host until he lost his reason but Lee felt no need to beware of her. He smiled at her, leaned across the table and drew her hands away from her face, a pale face, mostly eyes. When he found out how friendless she was, he took her to live with him.

She sat in his white, empty room all day gazing at the wall. At intervals, he fed her and caressed her. Then, one morning while he was at a lecture, she took her pastel crayons and drew a tree on the section of the wall at which she habitually stared. She drew with such conviction she must have been sketching the tree in her mind for a long time for it was a flourishing and complicated tree covered with flowers and many coloured birds. At that, Lee judged the time had come. As he guessed, she was a virgin. He fetched a towel to wipe away the blood. She asked, would it be any better when she was used to it? He replied, "Yes, love, of course, love," though the sight of her curiously pointed teeth disturbed him and when she asked in a voice of pure curiosity: "Why should you want to do this to me?" he was bereft of an answer. All at once his strong and graceful young body seemed to him a fragile and unnecessary appurtenance; her eyes reflected him in strange contours and he could not tell whether she saw him as he thought he was or not or what it was she saw in him, with her huge eyes which too much weeping seemed to have given the shape of tears laid on their sides. He realized he could supply her only with a physiological answer while she would never be satisfied with less than an existential one and he became melancholy but she was full of questions and soon drew his hand to the region of her fresh wound although it was not passion which moved her but, perhaps, curiosity. This happened on a very cold day towards the end of January, when snow was falling outside.

Two months before he met her, she tried to commit suicide by taking an overdose of sleeping tablets but the warden of the hostel where she lived found her in time. At the hospital where she was taken, she exhibited such marked stress symptoms at the suggestion she leave the art school where she was a student and return to her parents that they judged it best to leave her exclusively under the warden's kindly eye. The warden was a liberal woman in her forties who hoped nothing better for Annabel than that at last she might find someone to love her. Her room-mate at the hostel took her to a party on New Year's Eve. Annabel sat by herself in a corner and looked, first at some old magazines she found on the floor and, next, at the figures before her in the candlelight. She saw a series of interesting conjunctions of shapes and one or two disturbing faces and then she went to sleep. She woke up again because she was cold.

It was so late that all the lights were out and the candles

burned down to stubs. Most of the guests had gone though a
couple were making love on a sofa and several others were
sleeping on the floor. Annabel was so cold she arbitrarily selected one boy and went to lie down beside him to keep herself
from freezing. "Whom have we here?" he said in the morning.
Later, the warden visited him and was, of course, charmed; she
thought he was sweet-tempered and stable and happily con-
fided Annabel to his care.

He did not expect her to stay with him but she did so. Soon
she brought in a record player from her old room. As he had
suspected, she liked baroque harpsichord music best of all. He
called upon reserves of tact, gentleness and sensitivity formed
during his aunt's last illness to cope with her vagarious moods;
she was capable of every shade of melancholy from a sweet
sadness to the bleakest despair. He was used to having somebody to care for and, because his brother was away, he cared
for her. She slept beside him and occasionally, out of pure
curiosity, embraced him. Sometimes he succeeded in eliciting
a small, tremulous response from her but, more often, not,
though he often woke in the mornings to find her, awake
already, staring at him fixedly with her peculiarly luminous
eyes as if blasting him with Platonic intimations he did not
understand. Then his initial disquiet would briefly revisit him
and he suspected that her visionary eyes pierced his disarming
crust of charm to find beneath it some other person who was,
perhaps, himself.

He was attracted to her because he was unsure of his effect
upon her and became increasingly attached to her because of
her strangeness which seemed to him qualitatively different
but quantitively akin to the strangeness he himself felt, as
though both could say of the world: "We are strangers here."
Fish in the deep sea are luminous so that they can recognize
one another; might not men and women also exude some kind
of speechless luminescence to those akin to them? He felt a
sense of unspoken contact with her, like that of two people
from different countries who do not speak one another's language thrust together in a third whose language neither under-

stands. Besides, for the first month they lived together, he was sleeping with the wife of his philosophy tutor, although it took him several years to realize that a logical remedy for some of his and Annabel's discontents might be the presence of a complacent third, and a disaster to understand, still later, that it was not an entirely satisfactory solution.

This woman was perhaps five years older than Lee and he felt a certain derisive affection for her, though he continued with the affair because he was sure he was irrelevant to her and their experience appeared to cross over one another's in a perfectly abstract manner with no recognition of each other's individual natures. She was a tiny, sullen brunette, the mother of three small children. She had the gritty texture of the chronically unhappy and treated the young lover she had acquired out of spite and boredom with savage contempt, except for certain glimpses of her all-consuming discontent as she clung to him in the aftermath. "It is like screwing the woman's page of the *Guardian*," he told Buzz but he never mentioned her to anyone else out of indifference rather than discretion.

She made cool and practical arrangements. He went to see her twice a week, in the afternoons, when her children were at their play group and also on Thursday evenings, when they were in bed and her husband took an evening class on the concept of mind. They always made love in the spare room on a sheetless bed under a framed reproduction of a Picasso blue-period harlequin with a bloom of dust on the glass. During the entire course of the affair, she never solicited so much as a single piece of information from Lee concerning his family, his environment or his ambitions; she showed no curiosity of any kind about him at all. He thought this was very interesting.

Anyway, she was a great convenience for him; he took a certain pleasure in coupling with the wife of a man who taught him ethics; she left most of his evenings free; and he felt, with a puritanical sense of satisfaction inherited from his aunt, that he was learning something important about the middle class. But when he arrived one Thursday evening in early February, he found her in a filthy mood and followed her, with a more than usually wary tread, into the terra incognita of the living room.

Unknown but by no means unpredictable. On a guard before the fire, small garments steamed. He saw she had been reading *The Second Sex*, which lay face down on the floor. The walls were beige, a cerebral Mondrian print hung over the home-made hi-fi and bits of plastic toy scattered the rush matting. Lee gave himself his private grin of wry pleasure, a facial expression he preferred to conceal from the world most of the time in case it gave too much away.

The weather remained cold; he squatted down on the matting and warmed his hands at the fire. He wondered if he should buy some rush matting for Annabel lay full length on the cold, hard boards for hours on end and he often thought she looked as if she were on a slab in a morgue. He did not like to be a prey to such melodramatic imagery. His other love – that is if Annabel were to be defined as his lover – anyway the other woman – and was she the Other Woman or simply another woman? – anyway, this particular woman seated herself in an armchair and drew her legs up defensively beneath her, thus making herself impregnable. She wore jeans, a checkered shirt, her feet were bare and her long, dark hair was caught at the nape by a rubber band. She twirled her wedding ring around her finger, a sure sign of repressed annoyance, and she was mute.

Lee rocked back and forth on his heels, holding out his hands to the electric bars. Tonight, he looked like Barnaby Rudge. Mentally he wandered through his wardrobe of smiles, wondering which one to wear to suit this ambiguous occasion. At a very early age, Lee discovered the manipulative power of his various smiles and soon learned to utilize them in order to smooth his passage through life for he liked to have an easy time of it; that was what he called being happy. He selected a tentative and encouraging smile; it clicked into position so smoothly you would have sworn he wore his heart upon his face. As soon as the smile materialized, she burst into speech.

"You have shacked up with some bird, I hear," she said.

"Yeah," said Lee slowly, scenting trouble. "So what?"

She made a dismissive gesture with her hands, got up and started to prowl around the room.

"Of course, I can hardly expect you to be faithful to me."

"So that's it!" thought Lee and knew the affair was at an end. He chose his words carefully.

"I dunno. You've got every right to *expect* me to be faithful to you but whether I am or not, that's a different kettle of fish, isn't it?"

She continued to stalk around the room so stormily he became embarrassed for her as her behaviour seemed far in emotional excess of the circumstances.

"Why didn't you tell me yourself?"

"No business of yours."

"Thank you," she said ironically.

"Look," said Lee. "Something's biting you over and above me pulling a piece of stray."

"To hear you talk, who would ever believe you were an undergraduate?"

At that, Lee decided to hurt her feelings.

"Here, are you scared I'll give you crabs or something, or some vile disease?"

When she kicked him with her naked foot, he realized this analysis was correct and, as he went sprawling, he began to laugh. This made her angrier than ever.

"Couldn't you have told me about this girl yourself?"

"I haven't got a talking mouth," said Lee. He returned again to his oriental squat and turned upon her vengefully the full, disconcerting force of his dazzling smile for it had never occurred to him to tell her about Annabel since this other woman was so unimportant to him. Not that Annabel was, as yet, important to him. She lit a cigarette curtly, averting her head so as to regain her composure. It was a pleasant room, full of books and newspapers. Lee read a spine or two.

"You are quite irrelevant to me, a thing. An object. The first time I slept with you, it was an *acte gratuit*. An *acte gratuit*," she repeated with some irritation for he did not seem to understand her. "Do you know what I mean?"

Lee said nothing, out of spite.

"It was meaningless and absurd. It was a contentless act but, then, everything was contentless as if nothing cast any shadow, except my children and I couldn't communicate with them."

She fell silent. Lee glanced at her from under his lashes, half sorry for her, half extremely irritated. The silence lengthened. At last he stood up.

"Well, I'd better be getting along," he said.

"You're a rat," she said. "You rat."

Lee wanted nothing except to get out of the house as quickly as he could and would have agreed to anything she said. He nodded briskly.

"Yeah, I'm a rat," he said. "A rat of working-class origins," he amplified.

At that, she jumped up and pummelled him with her fists. He caught hold of her wrists and hit her once. She subsided immediately and touched her cheek wonderingly with her fingertips.

"She's got funny eyes," said Lee. "I quite like her, if you want to know. She doesn't say much. And she'll probably have to go when my brother comes home, anyway."

In moments of stress, his grammar-school accent collapsed completely. He was surprised to appreciate the extent of his agitation and also to hear his own words; since he never spoke anything but the truth, he must have become attached to Annabel. He was bewildered and blinked a little. Due to his chronic eye infection, his eyes watered under bright lights, weariness or strain; the lights were low but his eyes began to water. She pulled away her hands for the touch of his skin had become unbearable to her and gazed at him with wonder as she recalled his past physical tenderness. She was full of unbelieving pain to realize at last such caresses had been quite involuntary and, in a sense, nothing to do with her, no kind of tribute.

"What the fuck do you want from me, anyway?" demanded Lee with some brutality. "You want me to ask you to leave your husband and come and live with me?"

"I'd never do that," she said immediately.

"Well, then," said Lee and sighed. At this time, he did not appreciate shades of meaning. He thought a door must either be open or closed and that, in general, people meant what they said. Besides, he was poor and could not have afforded to support her and her children, even if he had wanted to. His eyes were watering so badly the dark young woman before him shimmered.

"I could make things very unpleasant for you at the university," she said.

Now it was his turn to be shocked.

"So it's true what my aunt told me about the duplicity of the bourgeoisie?"

Then the baby wailed and its mother gave a small shriek and twitched a little. Lee was filled with angry sadness.

"Ah, come off it," he said. "You had what you wanted, didn't you?"

"You have a cold heart, I must say."

"What?"

"You lay me and you don't give two straws –" Her hair was coming loose from its band and her face was flushed.

"What is it that's troubling you, honestly, I mean, troubling you so much?"

"Go away," she said. "I feel degraded."

Lee was deeply offended and demanded, shocked: "Here, how can you possibly find sex degrading?"

She stopped short, taken aback, shot him a puzzled look and then took a deep breath.

"I could have you thrown out of the university."

"Yeah, well," said Lee slowly for he was beginning to realize she was attracted to him because she thought he was a thug. "Yeah, well; then I'd come and beat you up, wouldn't I? Me and my bruvver, we'd both come."

She had seen his brother in the street.

"Dear God," she said. "I really think you would."

She might have wished, all the time, that Lee would fall in love with her to lend the whole encounter a little more significance but if this was so he did not realize it. It seemed to him she had used him as a screen on which to project her own discontents, a fair exchange. He had a simple sense of justice.

"Go away, Leon Collins," she said.

Lee realized she had learned his name by glancing through her husband's class list for nobody ever called him Leon, not even his teachers, face to face. But, then, he did not know her first name, either. Diminishing screams of the still-untended baby followed him down the stairs.

"Well," thought Lee, "you live and learn."

But he was very bewildered and extremely ill at ease. His room reverberated with harpsichord arpeggios. Annabel had let the fire die down to a few red coals so all was a glowing darkness intermittently punctuated by headlights of passing cars which flickered through the uncurtained windows to play like the aurora borealis on the body of the girl on the white floor, which was the only object to disturb the emptiness of the room but for her record player. The music ended and the needle hiccupped over vacant grooves. Lee went to switch it off and she caught his arm.

"You smell of outdoors," she said. "But you've been with some woman."

"Well, yes and no," said Lee, who always spoke the truth. "Does it hurt your feelings?"

He spoke very gently because her distress was so impassive. She shook her head wordlessly and the tears came pouring down without a sound.

"Then why are you crying?"

"I thought you wouldn't come back."

"Oh," said Lee, nonplussed. Her huge, grey eyes were fixed on his face; his own eyes began to scald again as if burned by her metaphysical fire. He thought she was making some monstrous demand on him but he could not interpret it and, trapped in this strange regard, he found he was trembling so much he had to put out his hand to support himself on the floor. He was astonished to discover he was so touched by this grief, perhaps because it seemed evidence he was important to her in some mysterious way he could not fathom. The longer he stared into her eyes, the greater grew his confusion until, at last, with both relief and fear, he saw her newly magic outlines were those of a thing that needed to be loved. He thought: "Oh, God, I should have recognized her sooner." So his stoic senti-mentality betrayed him. He kissed her hesitantly and though she did not open her mouth she placed her hands on his shoulders underneath his heavy jacket. He shrugged off his coat and spread it out to shield her from the hard floorboards. She lay back compliantly and did not take her gaze from him so he was still trembling from her scrutiny as he entered her.

But, even if they now acknowledged the state of love, their lovemaking was still permeated by unease for she understood the play of surfaces only superficially; she was like a blind man at a firework display who can only appreciate the fires in the air by interpreting their various degrees of magnificence through the relative enthusiasms of the noisy crowd. The na-ture of the dazzlement was dimly apprehended, not known.

On his return, Buzz seethed with jealous fury for a long time. In structure, the flat was an L-shaped ballroom divided by double doors which now served as a wall but this wall was very thin and Buzz, in his narrow cot, could hear each word and movement the lovers made. Every night he lay sweating at the unmistakable creakings and groans, writhing as he imag-ined their unimaginable privacy. He pressed his dark face into the pillow, cursed them bitterly and slowly became obsessed with the idea of stabbing them both as they slept together. He lovingly fingered his Moroccan knife and watched them dur-ing the day while, at night, he swore and masturbated. Lee was aware of the tensions ravaging his brother but was soon too much preoccupied with tensions of his own to pay them any attention for he could not ignore there was no magic implosion of the flesh in Annabel. He could evoke from her only those faint sighs and shudders the sensitive and perverse membrane of his brother's ear transformed to shrieks and cries. She seemed to grow more and more fascinated by the appearance of his face and body but she had no memory of skin to compare the feel of his skin with and seemed to like, best of all, the sensation of intimacy she experienced in bed with him; she had often read about such intimacy. She began a series of pictures of him. She drew her first picture the morning after their first authentic night, when certain implicit avowals had been made; in this picture, he looked like a golden lion too gentle to ever eat meat. Over the years, she drew and painted him again and again in so many different disguises that at last he had to go to another woman to find out the true likeness of his face.

When Buzz stole his first camera, the flat was given over entirely to the cult of appearances. Buzz used the camera as if to see with, as if he could not trust his own eyes and had to check his vision by means of a third lens all the time so in the end he saw everything at second hand, without depths. He developed and printed the pictures in his back room and pinned them on the walls until he was surrounded by frozen memories of the moment of sight; to have them in a condition where he could hold them in his hand gave him a sense of security. He took innumerable photographs of Lee and Annabel and obtained some relief by means of this kind of voyeurism so the atmosphere in their home grew less strained, though they often woke up in the morning to find him perched on the end of the bed, clicking away. And he padded round after them, continually catching them unawares, so they were caught in all manner of situations and often wore expressions of startled irritation in the completed photographs. Cardboard crates of prints and negatives slowly accumulated in Buzz's room.

Lee had two old photographs which were precious to him. Neither brother had anything left from their childhood besides these photographs. One showed a line of clean children carrying letters which together formed the exhortation: DO RIGHT BECAUSE IT IS RIGHT; the other was of a large, stern, middle-aged woman outstaring the camera with a brother on either side of her. She was their aunt. The brothers looked themselves already, though one was eleven and the other nine, and leaned back on their heels in characteristic, defensive/aggressive stance but the aunt stood straight enough to out-face a battalion and shame them. Annabel looked at the photograph of the aunt and then at Lee. Putting her finger to his cheek, she removed a tear but he did not want her to think he was really crying.

"That's no authentic tear, love: my eyes, they water easily."

In fact, this tear both was and was not authentic. His eye disease rendered his tears ambivalent. But, since he had the simple heart of one who boos the villain, when, as he often did, he found he was crying, he usually became sad. Whether his tears were the cause or the effect of a grief or if this grief, when it was experienced, would define itself to him as a reaction to some arbitrary stimulus such as the picture of the dead woman whom he had loved or as a reflection on common mortality – these were questions he had not yet chosen or chosen to need to ask himself. So he usually pretended he was not crying although he had the habit of crying easily.

These were his two iconic photographs, that of a child named Michael and that of a family group. Buzz gave him a picture of himself and Annabel in bed asleep and that made a third, an image of a lover. Lee and Annabel looked like Daphnis and Chloë or Paul and Virginia; Lee, tangled in her very long hair, lay in the crook of her naked shoulder for she was taller than he and they looked as beautiful and peaceful as if made in heaven for one another. Lee kept these photographs in an envelope with their three birth certificates and, later, his marriage certificate. But he could find no causal connection between his three photographed faces. The infant, the child and the adolescent or young man whose face was still so new, unused and incomplete seemed to represent three finite and disconnected states. Looking in the mirror, he saw the face of a stranger to any of them with features which had been filtered through his wife's eyes and subjected to so many modifica-

tions in the process that it was no longer his own. There
seemed no connecting logic between the various states of his
life, as if each had been attained, not by organic growth but by
a kind of convulsive leap from condition to condition. He felt
no nostalgia for the innocence he found upon his old, cast-off
faces, only a fierce indignation he should ever have been innocent enough to surrender his freedom. For now his once desert
room where he had lived as aridly alone as Crusoe on his
island with only Buzz for a sullen, undutiful Friday – now this
room was choked with things, painted out in thick, dark colours and filled with such a rich, sombre gloom one took a deep
breath before stepping over the threshold, knowing one was
about to plunge into another, heavier kind of air.

In this cavernous, mysterious room, he hugged her tightly
for he knew that duplicity thrives on physical contact. Here,
where she and her furniture were sunk together in the same
dream, she had at least a shape and an outward form; she had
the same status as a thing, as her sofa possessed, or her sideboard with the lions' heads. Here, she was an object composed
of impervious surfaces. But when she walked beside him down
the street in her randomly assembled clothes, she was quite
wispy and tenuous, like a phantom rag-picker. She was tall and
very thin. Her hands were long and the veins stuck out from
them in thick bunches like the veins on the freckled hands of
old women. Her feet, also, bulged with swollen and protuber-
ant veins. Because of her meagre build, she seemed still taller
than she was, a sparse, grotesquely elegant, attenuated girl
with a narrow face and hair so straight it fell helplessly down
around her as a mute tribute to gravity. She had prehensile
toes that could pick up a pencil and sign her name. She stole.

Lee was horrified to find she stole. She stole food from super-
markets and books from bookshops; she stole paints, ink,
brushes and small items of clothing. Her parents were wealthy
and gave her a large allowance but still she stole and Lee had
always regarded thievery as the legitimate province only of the
poor. He thought it morally proper the poor should steal as
much as they could but, since money was given one only in

order to buy things with and so keep the wheel of the economy in motion, then it was the duty of the rich (the hub of the wheel) to purchase as much as they were able. Nevertheless, she continued to steal in spite of his stern disapproval and this proclivity proved one of the many things she and her brother-in-law held in common.

They married when her parents found out she and Lee were living together. Lee had taken his final examinations, obtained a mediocre degree and registered with the university's department of education for a teacher training course. His brother greeted this action with snarling derision but Lee was forced to support his household, who were either unable or unwilling to support themselves. Annabel informed her parents of her change of address without giving them any further details and they assumed she shared a flat with another girl. She visited them occasionally and, towards the end of the summer, they happened to be passing through the city on the way to Cornwall and came ringing the door bell early one morning.

Buzz was awake and working in the dark room he had improvised from his own quarters. It was a warm day and he wore nothing but a pair of filthy white sailor trousers holed, here and there, with acid. His Apache or Mohawk hair hung past his shoulders and he reeked of incense and chemicals. He went to answer the door and found a man and a woman in casual, expensive clothes who smelled of soap and money, odours alien to him. Because of his perversity, he led them into Lee's room through his own, past walls papered with pictures of their only daughter frequently unclothed and often in the arms of a man but they managed to retain their equanimity although Buzz's room was packed full of his fetishes, which included knives, carcasses of engines salvaged from the scrapyard and all his tanks of chemicals. He had also boarded up the windows to keep the light out. If Lee's room was like a fresh sheet of paper, Buzz's was like a doodling pad but the many objects which filled it were so eclectic in nature and lay about so haphazardly where he had let them fall that it was just as

difficult to gain any hints from it towards the nature of whoever lived there.

Though Lee's room was already less pristine than it had
been. A forest of trees, flowers, birds and beasts had invaded
the walls so Lee and Annabel lay together on the narrow mattress like lovers in a jungle. She had already bought a red plush
sofa, a round table and a stuffed fox in a glass case so the
general effect, since it was that of transition between one extreme state and its polar opposite, would have been peculiarly
disturbing if Annabel's parents had not had eyes only for their
daughter and the gardener's boy, the covers pushed off them
for the heat, sleeping.

"Wake up," said Buzz. "It's her mum and dad."

Annabel shivered but stayed fast asleep. Lee, however,
prised open his seccotined eyes and gave his tribute of tears to
the glorious morning. When he saw a man in a dark suit looking down at him, he thought the worst had happened and it
was a plain-clothes man come to look for hash or appropriated
property. He rolled over and extended his wrists.

"It's a fair cop," he said.

Immediately they took Annabel away with them and the
brothers sat brooding in a room which seemed so under-fur-
nished without her they knew they both would not be at ease
in it again until her return. They felt incomplete without her
presence; without any conscious volition of her own, by a
species of osmosis, perhaps, since she was so insubstantial,
somehow she had entered the circle of their self-containment.
When her parents discovered that Lee was a graduate, in spite
of appearances, they decided he might be a rough diamond and
became a little more conciliatory but they still refused to let
him see her unless he married her which at last he agreed to
do, out of pride. Her mother wanted a white wedding and a
church.

"My aunt would turn in her grave," said Lee.

It was finally arranged the wedding should take place in the
registry office of the town in which the brothers lived. A date

was fixed and a licence obtained. Annabel remained with her parents in the Home Counties for the interim period and the brothers stayed where they were. As soon as he became aware that he was about to do something irreversible, Lee began to drink heavily for he could not have gone through with the marriage unless he passed the time before it in a state of oblivion. Annabel was quite incomprehensible to him and he already knew she was unbalanced; yet his puritanism demanded he should be publicly responsible for her. He was overcome with conflicting apprehensions.

One January morning, Annabel woke up and found it had been snowing so there was no apparent difference between the world outside and the world inside. Snow lay thickly on top of the wrought-iron curlicues of the balcony and caked the bare branches of the trees in the square; yet still the grey sky was full of soft, whirling flakes and every sound was silenced as if the snow pressed fingers in the ears. The room was full of white light reflected from outside and the only difference was that here it was not snowing for everything was as white as the extreme, unimaginable North except for the red enamel alarm clock, which now rang. Lee, still asleep, flung out one arm to depress the button; she took a technical pleasure in observing the musculature of his shoulders and the play of snowlight on the golden down which covered them for he was of a furry texture. He was colourful to look at and also reminded her of Canova's nude, heroic statue of Napoleon in Wellington House. She was grateful for his warmth. She watched the daily struggle to open his eyes and then he smiled to recognize her, hugged her, kissed her cheek and rooted about on the white floor beside him for his discarded clothes. She was especially pleased when she caught a glimpse of his leonine left profile. She found him continuously interesting to look at but it hardly occurred to her the young man was more than a collection of coloured surfaces and she had never learned to think of herself as a living actor, anyway. She did not even think of herself as a body but more as a pair of disembodied eyes – when she thought about herself at all, that is. She was eighteen, secretive and withdrawn since childhood. Her favourite painter was Max Ernst. She did not read books. Lee got her breakfast and built up a roaring fire.

It was too snowy to think of going to the art school. She lay against his very white pillow and drank her tea peacefully. She had chosen an old white flannel shirt of his to wear in bed and he thought this wilful and perverse attire was a simple, sexual defence, for which he forgave her. It was unnecessary to have forgiven her for she did not know it defended her. Though she had shared a bed with him for three weeks, she never thought of it as a place for anything but sleeping in. Therefore she did not know she had anything to protect while Lee assumed all manner of virginal hedging on her part and, unconcerned, waited for her to make up her mind. He picked up his books, put on several layers of clothing and went out into the snow for he was a conscientious student. For a while she watched the flames in the grate. Then she crept from the bed and, like Bluebeard's wife, sneaked into the forbidden territory of Buzz's room, where the air struck damp and chill.

Even before it became officially a dark room, it was very dark for the window opened on to a blank wall and, since his avocation was trading, it was also cluttered up with many odd objects as well as his ongoing fetishes. Everything was cold, miserable and arbitrary, a rummage sale presided over by many pictures of Red Indians cut out of books.

"What is your brother like?"

"An Apache, sometimes."

She wandered about picking things up and putting them down again. She examined Buzz's clothes which were kept spilling out of a tea chest, selected a ragged vest dyed purple and a pair of orange crushed-velvet trousers, took off Lee's shirt and donned these garments to find out what Buzz felt like or what it might feel like to be Buzz. But his old clothes felt like any other greasy and unwashed old clothes and she was disappointed. She already felt a vague interest in him, just as she felt more comfortable in his room than she did in Lee's, although she now returned to it for warmth. She opened his neat cupboard, took out the box of pastel crayons she kept on his shelf, knelt on the mattress and, out of boredom, began to draw the tree Lee so seriously misconstrued as, perhaps, a tree of life when it was more nearly related (for him, at least) to the Upas Tree of Java, the fabulous tree that casts a poisoned shade.

Lee came home at lunchtime, glowing with cold and his hair full of snow. Removing his shoes and socks in the kitchen, he padded silently into his room to find it strewed, still, with bedclothes and breakfast dishes and a figure, now on tiptoe, adding a gaudy parrot to the topmost branch of a colourful tree. Dark hair hung down the back of a familiar vest and for a moment he thought his brother was back unexpectedly but the draughtsmanship was infinitely superior to anything of which Buzz was capable and she turned to him, offering him an unemphatic smile.

"Well, well," said Lee.

The crumbling pastels had showered the bed with polychromatic grit and Lee was annoyed to see such a mess, though pleased she had at last been sufficiently moved to do something, whatever it was. So he thought the time was right for, at the back of his mind, he had always intended to lay her some time or other. He knelt on the mattress beside her and put his arm around her waist. She took this for only another of the small caresses he often gave her. When he buried his face in the cool flesh of her belly, she pretended to herself she was preoccupied with the position of the parrot which, she judged, should have been, perhaps, an inch or two further to the left but this pretence could not protect her for long because he kissed her breasts and the red crayon dropped from her hand.

Seized with intimations of an invasion of privacy, she looked down at his rough blond head with bewilderment for the sensation of his touch had no effect on her. The castle of herself was clearly about to be invaded and, though the idea of it surprised her, the actual indifference of her response told her she would submit indifferently and she thought: "Why not? Why not?"

She made no effort to undress herself, to see what he would do, so he took his brother's clothes off her; he had to raise her limp arms to draw off the vest and part her legs to remove the trousers. She watched him all the time without appreciating the extraordinarily erotic effect of her passivity, her silence and her enquiring eyes, comforted by memories of the nursery because he undressed her as if she were a little girl. Then he took off his own clothes. She was half perplexed and half amused at the sight of his erection but somehow affronted by his general air of insouciance for she knew this was supposed to be an event of some significance for her. He lay down beside her again and she examined his face for some indication of what he would do next. He seemed to expect some advance on her part so she tentatively put her arms around his neck, or perhaps she did this because she had read somewhere, in a magazine, perhaps, that this was what she was supposed to do. She would have liked some instructions on how to behave for it is a hard thing to make love when one has few, if any, ideas of common practice. He seemed to be experiencing some private kind of pleasure from these contacts of surface upon surface and the interaction of skin and she bemusedly resented his privacy since she felt privacy was her exclusive property and nobody else had much right to it. When he kissed her, she knew enough to open her lips and allow him to explore the interior of her mouth; at the soft pressure of his tongue on her own, she let out a muffled, involuntary moan which was, rather, a question although Lee paid it no heed and nudged open her legs with his knee. She made no movements either of complicity or denial and was surprised how mysterious his actions were when he put his hand between her legs.

Then, unexpectedly, they had a conversation. He asked when she would have her next period and she told him, in two or three days' time, and he said: that's perfectly splendid, ducks, and gave her an honest and unpremeditated smile. In the deep focus of the embrace, he was more interesting to look at than she would ever have imagined and this never previously encountered smile enchanted her so much she kissed him of her own accord. She felt rather than saw his pleasure when she did so and this bewildered her even more for she was accustomed only to seeing.

"Here," he said, "you won't get much out of it this time, probably, but I'll try not to hurt you. Anyway" (he added puritanically) "you ought to have had it by your age; whatever do they teach you at them schools." She felt it served him right when she saw he was nonplussed at so much blood.

Lee wondered if it were one of those cases, well-known in medical literature, where rupture of the hymen brought on a fatal haemorrhage? And still she could not understand the function of it, nor see how, with one thing and another, he began to be very much afraid though she soon saw she could hurt him as badly with her silences as he could ever afflict her by any other means. After the blood dried, she also learned that, if she concentrated very hard, the touch of his hand released infrequent but marvellous images inside her head. So she gazed at him with wonder, as if he might be magic, and he looked at her nervously, as if she might not be fully human.

They rolled all over the pastel crayons scattered on the sheets so her back was variegated with patches and blotches all the colours of the rainbow and Lee was also marked everywhere with brilliant dusts, both here and there also darkly spotted with blood, each a canvas involuntarily patterned by those workings of random chance so much prized by the surrealists.

She was fortunate in her first lover in so far as he was kind, gentle and experienced; she was unfortunate in that soon he began to love her and, after that, could not leave her alone. As for Annabel, she was like a child who reconstructs the world according to its whims and so she chose to populate her home with imaginary animals because she preferred them to the drab fauna of reality. She quickly interpreted him into her mythology but if, at first, he was a herbivorous lion, later he became a unicorn devouring raw meat and she never saw him the same twice, nor did these pictures have any continuity except for the constant romanticism of the imagery. She had no control over them, once they existed. And, as she drew him, so she saw him; he existed for her only intermittently.

Waking in the middle of the night, she sometimes saw white birds, perhaps albatrosses, frozen in the middle of the ceiling; if she could not make out their outlines, precisely, that made them even more terrifying and there was no comfort to be got from the man sleeping beside her for he had undoubtedly become another, some other thing. She lay immobile under the covers listening to the menacing thunder of his breathing and did not dare stretch out her hand to touch him for fear of encountering the leathern surfaces of a dragon's wing. One night Lee woke in the grip of a dream and reached out for her while she was asleep. She screamed so loudly Buzz sprang awake and darted to defend her.

"I thought you were an incubus," she said to Lee when the ensuing confusion had died down. Then they had to make tea and so on, in the false cheerfulness of five in the morning. Still, whatever he was, he grew necessary to her and she even played with the idea of bearing his children, though these children existed solely in the terms of her mythology, were purely symbolic and quite undemanding, related not to fantasies of motherhood but to certain explicit fantasies she had of totally engulfing him which she occasionally experienced with extraordinary intensity when he penetrated her, as if, drawing him through her hairy portals, he could be forever locked up inviolably inside her, reduced himself to the condition of an embryo and, by dissolving in his own sperm, become himself his own child. So, by impregnating her, he would cease to exist.

Because she gave Lee so large, if so ambiguous, a role in her mythology, she wished, gently, to reduce him to not-being.

She allowed her parents to take her away but she knew she would come back in the end. It was all the same to her whether she married Lee or not though he regarded it as a legal contract. Her parents bought her a white dress to be married in but she forgot to put it on that morning and dressed herself as usual in jeans and tee shirt, although her mother made her change her clothes and brushed out her hair for her. Annabel stood beside her parents in front of the registry office, kicking at the plaster in the wall with a bored air, wearing a thin, pretty dress of white silk she had not chosen for herself while she waited for things to continue as they had done before. It was a hot day in July and the courtyard was full of the suave perfume of lime trees. The mother wore a suit of coffee-coloured lace. Lee was twenty minutes late, blanched, shaking and still fairly drunk. The ragged brother sat cross-legged outside during the ceremony as immobile as a veritable Apache with his camera slung round his neck like a talisman.

"Oh, my darling," said Annabel's mother. "It's not what I would have wished for you."

Lee wrote his name in the register.

"What an unusual name," said the mother with a faint note of hope. "Leon."

Lee realized that if they were foreign, some of their eccentricities might be excused so he bared his teeth in a snarl and said: "I was named for Trotsky, the architect of the Revolution."

At that, he remembered his aunt and thought his heart might break as he stood in the cool, bright building for he had abandoned all the hopes with which his aunt had named him, if he had ever understood them at all. "Betrayed to the bourgeoisie!" he thought and, once outside, lurched against the wall as if to face the firing squad. The brilliant morning shot him through the eyes with darts of glass and he was crushed by the conviction that he had done something irreparable. He saw the man and the woman grimacing at his brother and his new wife, their daughter, and all transmitted signs and messages not one of which any of the others could interpret. Words flew out of their mouths like birds, up and away, and all were behaving well, even Buzz, though he looked fresh from a visit to the tomb of Edgar Allan Poe for he had found a black suit somewhere.

No wonder the daughter saw only appearances. Despite the eccentricity of his behaviour, the uncouthness of his accent and the length of his hair, the parents were so impressed at the sight of the camera they thought Buzz might be a respectable Bohemian and would, one day, grow rich for they had read how photographers were the new aristocracy. So the camera was sufficient justification for the boy's wild appearance and both cast strained glances at the drunk, sick and shattered bridegroom as if they thought their daughter had made the wrong choice, if she was going to marry into Bohemia anyway, that is, and since she was so good at art, they might as well resign themselves. After all, they had let her go to art school. But Lee looked like a seaman after a week's leave in a rough port and could be incorporated into no tender system of dreams or hopes. Annabel lifted up her hand which wore a wedding ring. The morning fell apart. Overcome with nausea, Lee ran inside the registry office. He found the lavatory and vomited for a long time.

When he crept back nervously into the sunshine, shielding his hurt eyes with his hand, he found his abrupt departure had broken the frail bond of the wedding group who now stood each one far apart from the others and looked abstractedly outwards in different directions. The white carnation in the father's buttonhole would have brought tears to Lee's eyes if his eyes had not been full of tears already.

"You're covered in white," said Buzz. "How bridal, how apt."

"There was a window."

"I suppose you tried to climb through it and run away, then."

"You bet."

Buzz laughed and brushed the whitewash off Lee's shoulder. Lee was white as the plasterwork and running with sweat but he said: "Nothing personal, love," to Annabel and she took hold of his clammy hand where her parents had insisted he, too, should wear a ring.

Soon the parents drifted wanly away and the Collinses, now legally augmented by their third, returned to their quarter, up the hill, past the university, attracting to them a procession of chance acquaintances on the way so the boisterous party which arrived at the house was more Réné Clair than Antonioni and Lee, who thought it was immoral to be unhappy, soon regained his good humour. But that night Buzz had a paranoid *crise* because he smoked too much and Lee fought with him for about an hour, to keep him still.

Annabel folded herself up in a corner in her wedding dress which was very grubby by now and covered her ears with her hands for Buzz was screaming dreadfully. The light was that of a church at Christmas for they had lit a great many candles and the flickering room smelled of melted wax. The people who came to celebrate the wedding drifted out into the night for most of them knew from experience to leave the brothers well alone when they were wrestling with demons and, at last, Lee got a handful of sleeping tablets down Buzz's throat, half led and half dragged him to the safety of his narrow cot and held him till he went to sleep.

Annabel, altogether too white and sinister in the soft light, was slowly blowing out the candles one by one. Because of the indifference natural to her, Lee thought she showed no interest in what had happened to Buzz though she might have been too frightened to want to speak of it. However, he was too embarrassed at so much hysteria to do anything but act as if nothing out of the ordinary had occurred. Besides, she would have to get used to that sort of thing, if she was to live with them for ever. They went to bed together and it was no better and no worse than any other time except that Lee found it more difficult than usual, for he remembered that a door can be only open or closed and he had made some formal promises, before witnesses, that he ought not to sleep with any other woman again until the end of his natural life which meant, perhaps another forty years. Unless Annabel died. Barricaded behind her immobility, Annabel felt nothing but forgot the wedding ceremony almost immediately. Next morning, she started to paint the walls dark green.

In the rich, dark room his touch told her he could not deceive her but she said: "If you deceive me, I'll die," and he hugged her more closely, on the brink of treacherous tears, for she did not even suspect him after they had lived together for so long. She would as soon have thought that her coronation mugs, her Staffordshire pottery figure of Prince Albert and her brass bedstead itself be unfaithful to her or her own clothes commit adultery. He occupied the most important place among these possessions she had bought at auction sales or which Buzz obtained for her; they went to the city tip together, too, and raked through ashes for objects. And they went out stealing while Lee was at work, to come home with their arms full of things, many of them useless.

Lee deluded himself that, since he was not emotionally involved with the girl, Carolyn, he was not, significantly, unfaithful to his wife. In the period of introspection which followed the inevitable catastrophe, he had ample time to ironically applaud the extent of his self-deceit but now he had neither the time nor the inclination to do so nor any intimation a catastrophe might be near for he thought that he had finally established an equilibrium and now things could go on for ever.

"Sleeping with Annabel is like reading Samuel Beckett on an empty stomach," he said to Carolyn as he walked her home through deserted streets in the small hours. Though he spoke primarily to clarify the situation to himself and so excuse it (for he felt some premonitions of guilt) it came through to her as a seduction speech; it interested her in him. When they reached her room, he blinked at the light and inspected her posters and paper flowers curiously. He had forgotten how far Annabel's gloomy interior deviated from a young girl's norm. Momentarily embarrassed, Carolyn halted with her fingers on the fastening of her fur jacket, for something in his manner suggested that though they had returned to her room with only one purpose, the act seemed too intimate to be performed by people so unfamiliar to one another.

"Do right because it is right," thought Lee but the motto was no help at all since it only implied the question of the nature of the right.

She laughed out of embarrassment and enquiry; the space between them vanished immediately. Contentless sexuality is the most puritanical of all pleasures since it is pure experience devoid of any extrasensory meaning and Lee suddenly appreciated the iron will of the wife of his tutor in ethics, who had been strong enough to evade the perils of the aftermath in which confidences may be exchanged and information gathered. Carolyn told him how she was in love with someone who was in love with some other person and, in return, he felt bound to offer her a few behavioural snapshots of Annabel, such as Annabel drawing her deceitful tree that winter morning; Annabel flipping his penis between her fingers and asking, "What is it for?" and Annabel being beaten. But he realized these were not so much pictures of actual events, even though they had all happened, but somehow the terms in which he was forced to describe them turned them into stills from expressionist films, stark, grotesque and unnatural. So he talked a little more, though, by trying to formulate and coherently relate the exact truth about certain aspects of their relationship, he inflated these details out of all proportion and, as soon as he showed her Annabel being beaten, he knew he had gone too far.

He and Annabel sometimes played chess for she liked to handle the pieces of a red and white Chinese ivory set that Buzz had somehow acquired for her; she would fall into a reverie, her eyes fixed vacantly on the board caressing the knight or castle in her hand while Lee gnawed his fingernails and waited for some startling, irrational move which would throw his mathematical attack into disarray.

"She plays chess from the passions and I play it from logic and she usually wins. Once, I took her queen and she hit me."

Though, he recalled, not sufficiently brutally to require that he tie her wrists together with his belt, force her to kneel and beat her until she toppled over sideways. She raised a strangely joyous face to him; the pallor of her skin and the almost miraculous lustre of her eyes startled and even awed him. He was breathless with weeping, a despicable object.

"That will teach you to take my queen," she said smugly. There were bruises on her shoulders and breast when she took off her sweater to go to bed. She stroked herself thoughtfully and suggested: "I should like a ring with a moonstone in it."

Her transparency astonished him but he was guilty enough to go and look for a moonstone ring the next day. But there were no moonstones to be bought in the city so he found her a print of Millais' "Ophelia" in a second-hand shop because Annabel often wore the same expression and she seemed surprised and contented enough with that, though he suspected she bore him a concealed grudge.

"What was she doing?" asked Carolyn. "Was she trying to humiliate you?"

"Maybe. It's a roundabout way of doing it, though."

Already he felt remorse that he had told this story in such a way that he himself appeared in a good light, for so he betrayed Annabel when he did not know who she thought he was when he beat her. As he returned home, the street lights were winking out and the birds singing. He often went out without Annabel and came home late for his friends bored her but this time she woke up as he slid into the bed and said: "I had a bad dream. It was morning and you weren't here and were never coming back." He closed his eyes and pressed his face into the pillow but could not forbear to take hold of her terrible, hot, sticky hand for he knew he was her only friend although she did not like him much.

"Sometimes I surprise her in front of a mirror, practising smiling," Lee told his new mistress and it was true, as far as it went, for he often found Annabel smiling to herself in the mirror and he could not think what else she might be doing if it was not practising how to smile.

"Oh, darling, she does sound a bitch," said Carolyn with false lightness; she was not an imaginative girl.

His face went as blank as if all capacity for expression had dropped straight out of it and Carolyn learned, in that moment, that a woman in love can never afford to reveal what feelings she may have towards her lover's wife. This knowledge in itself would have been worth the emotional price of the whole experience to Carolyn but, by the end of the affair, she had acquired so much miserable information about men and women she almost decided to give up relationships for good for, if she fell in love with Lee to distract herself, the cure proved worse than the disease.

She was a student of English literature and knew both brothers by sight and by word of mouth; they had an attractive reputation of danger because Buzz was a petty criminal and all kinds of rumours went around about the three-cornered household. Carolyn saw the wife once or twice in the street and dismissed her from her mind for Carolyn was far prettier than Annabel, much more passionate and three times as comprehensible. She was not at all prepared for the overwhelming jealousy she began to feel for this shadowy figure. It was as if she found herself cast willy-nilly in the role of the Other Woman and now she had to learn the entire traditional script, no matter how crippling she found it to her self-esteem. So, much later the same evening that Annabel had been terrified by the sun and moon, Carolyn arrived at Lee's flat with some of her friends because Buzz was giving a party and Carolyn could use it as an excuse to infiltrate Lee's home.

Buzz stuck candles by their own grease on to every flat surface and Lee helped him, half in hopes the house would catch fire and burn down for Buzz had told him about the scene on the hill. He had tried to talk of it to Annabel, she could not or would not answer him and now he was in a mood of savage depression. Buzz, half naked, had covered himself in stripes of red and black greasepaint. He pushed Annabel's bed into a corner, cleared away enough of their common junk to make a dancing space and opened the double doors to create a single, large, L-shaped room. By the time Carolyn and her cover arrived, the party could be heard half a block away and the hosts were lost among the guests.

Annabel sat wrapped in a flowered silk shawl making right

angles to the wall on her brass bed, still too frozen with fear to drink from the glass of red wine she held in her hand. When Lee felt her eyes upon him, he thought she was privately accusing him of hypocrisy and soon grew in the mood for violence. The brothers danced together, a put-on or come-on for which they were notorious, an exotic display. Loud music played. Carolyn detached herself from her group and edged down the room until she reached the long windows. She slipped the catch on one window and let in a breath of cold air which made the candle flames around her quiver and sent coruscating lights up and down the shining surface of her white satin dress. Lee saw her and was by now drunk enough to give her his most dazzling smile. Her principal distinguishing feature was an air of tranquil self-confidence and he thought it was both plausible and even inevitable she might light him out of Juliet's tomb into some kind of promised land.

Afterwards, the events of the night seemed, to all who participated in them, like disparate sets of images shuffled together anyhow. A draped form on a stretcher; candles blown out by a strong wind; a knife; an operating theatre; blood; and bandages. In time, the principal actors (the wife, the brothers, the mistress) assembled a coherent narrative from these images but each interpreted them differently and drew their own conclusions which were all quite dissimilar for each told himself the story as if he were the hero except for Lee who, by common choice, found himself the villain.

"You're crying," said Carolyn, touched.

He did not bother to correct her. He stood by the window and looked out across the tops of the leafless trees to the few windows still left glowing in the houses on the other side of the square.

"We all stole a car, once. Well, it wasn't so much stealing, more like taking and driving away, they told me I was too timorous for authentic stealing. I opened the glove compartment and found a leaflet that promised you a thousand destinations. Think of that."

Carolyn, mystified, could not see the point.

"What happened then?"

"We couldn't decide where to go," said Lee and laughed.

Annabel glimpsed the nacreous shimmer of Carolyn's dress intermittently through the shoulders of the dancers. The music continued to play extremely loudly. Buzz, magnificently painted, sat briefly beside her.

"All right, are you?"

She nodded. They both watched Lee's leonine left profile bent over the head of the girl in white.

"She's done up like a bride," said Annabel softly, so that nobody could hear her.

"Sure you're all right?" demanded Buzz, quivering in the expectation of disaster.

"Give me your ring."

He slipped his father's silver ring on to her thin forefinger, the only one it would fit, and she allowed him a ghostly smile.

"Now I'm invisible," she said with satisfaction. Since they often played inscrutable games together, he thought no more about it but smiled and kissed her before he went away. She drew the shawl around her shoulders and set her feet on the ground. It is hard to say if she actually thought she was invisible; at least, she felt as if she might be. She picked her way delicately towards the window, drew aside the curtain and pressed her face against the cool glass. She saw, in the most immediate, domestic terms, a recreation of the sun and moon in appalling harmony.

Carolyn had become so obsessed with Lee that she had lost all sense of discretion or any sense at all. The landlord had replaced the rusted wrought iron of the lower part of the balcony by some graceless wooden boards so they were concealed from the street but Annabel gazed through the window at them like an infatuated spectre. The spectacle was as silent as if it took place under water and the arrangement of interlocking lines was familiar enough in itself; but this girl's face was vividly contorted, not bland and impassive like that of the whore in the photograph and Lee was lost to her in a secret, ultimate privacy. She could not incorporate this manifestation of his absolute otherness anywhere into her mythology, which was an entirely egocentric universe, and she felt a grieving jealousy of the act itself, which she understood only in symbolic terms.

"If you deceive me, I'll die," repeated Annabel as if it were a logical formula. If she felt relief and even pleasure each time she herself evaded real contact with him, knowing the magic castle of herself remained unstormed, she thought perhaps he kept the key to the castle, anyway, and one day he might turn against it and rebel. But when she saw the rebellion in action, she was forced to desperate measures to disarm him for she might, possibly, perhaps, hopefully, be able by these means to turn an event that threatened to disrupt her self-centred structure into a fruitful extension of it. She let the curtain fall back into place and turned from the window. The party went on as if nothing had happened and Buzz was deep in conversation with a Black man in dark glasses so she could get no help from him. It was practical help rather than comfort she wanted. Because she went stealing with Buzz and they shared the secret of the ring, she did not regard Buzz as too much separate from herself but it was Lee she loved and Lee she now intended to wound.

She went immediately to the bathroom to kill herself in private. Fortunately it was unoccupied. After she locked the door, she remembered she should have borrowed one of Buzz's knives and stabbed herself through the heart. She was irritated to realize she would have to make do with an undignified razor blade but quickly cut open both her wrists with two clean, sweeping blows and sat down on the floor, waiting to bleed to death. She had always bled very easily. She guessed, however, it would take some time to bleed to death. Her wrists ached but she was as content as if she had won another game of chess by unorthodox means.

"They've locked us out," said Lee.

Carolyn pulled the white dress around her shoulders and laughed.

"I'm absolutely filthy," she said luxuriously. To be discovered locked out with him in a state of erotic disarray was as public an announcement of their liaison as she could wish and she thought how simple things would now become, a face-to-face confrontation between the Wife and the Other Woman, a certain victory. She wound her arms round him as he tapped at the pane until a blonde girl let them in. Carolyn was too preoccupied with the management of her satin skirts to take any notice of this amazing young woman, whose sullen face, round and white as a saucer of milk, seemed to float in an enormous cloud of peroxide hair, and Lee was too sunk in thought to recognize her until she said: "Good evening, Mr. Collins," giggled and added, "sir."

She was dressed as an incipient tart in a tight, white polo-neck sweater, stretch denim trousers and high-heeled boots; only her fat, pale, discontented lips and the startling fairness of her skin hinted at how young she was, the beauty queen of the evening paper, Lee's pupil, to whom he taught current affairs and who now discovered him in a compromising position amidst scenes of drunkenness and drugged debauch.

"Dear God, who brought you, Joanne?"

"Don't worry," she said. "I won't breathe a word."

So he was trapped into complicity with a schoolgirl. Carolyn, looking round, was disappointed to see none of her friends left in the room. Even Buzz had vanished, although the music still played. Lee became edgy and nervous.

"I'll take you home."

She found her fur wrap on Buzz's cot, beneath some offensive pictures of Lee and Annabel. They left the remains of the party and, as at their first meeting, walked through the quiet streets together as if alone in the world. Suddenly she emitted a rich, low chuckle and pressed his hand but he was by now quite sober and in a state of great agitation for he had behaved more foolishly than he would ever have believed possible.

"The last time my mother communicated to anyone, it was to say she knew she was the Whore of Babylon," he said, but he was thinking mainly about Annabel. Carolyn turned wide eyes to him; he had never mentioned his mother to her before and she thought this must be the beginning of a further stage of intimacy.

"Tell me about your mother," she said encouragingly.

"She's locked up," said Lee. "Certified."

She had not expected him to sound so cruel.

"Poor Lee," she said tentatively.

"We was better off with the aunt, wasn't we. You don't want to live with a mad woman, do you, not at the impressionable age."

A few days later, Buzz showed him the pictures he had taken on the hill. He could never have imagined such terror in her face for he had little capacity for metaphysical dread himself; otherwise, he had foreseen exactly how she would look for the woman in the playground and the girl on the hill were already superimposed on one another in his mind so that to speak of his mother was to speak of Annabel. He noticed his grammar-school accent had given way entirely so he knew he was under stress. Besides, his eyes burned.

"Your aunt . . . your aunt brought you up?"

"Yes. Both of us. She – "

He could not finish the sentence and left it hanging in the air. Carolyn grew sad and a little apprehensive to find no increase but a diminution of intimacy, for he had suddenly become unresponsive to her and she shivered, sensing, perhaps, the imminent loss of a little of her marvellous assurance. She lived in a terrace built out on a cliff over a river, a silent place.

"Are you coming in?"

He gave her a curious look of mild reproof and she felt a premonition of sorrow.

"Lee?"

She stood and beseeched him in the cold midnight in her pretty, silly clothes. But Lee knew he walked some kind of tightrope above a whirlpool, though he believed that the knowledge itself might be enough to avert a fall if he walked carefully and, even if he now intended to break with Carolyn, he was sufficiently sentimental or else, perhaps, vain enough to go upstairs with her. But her room made him vertiginous and he had to keep from the window in case he jumped out. Then he knew he could no longer live at everyday altitudes and had been deceiving himself. He succumbed to guilt immediately.

"What have I done wrong?" she asked like a miserable child, confronted with an indifference which opened with the magic speed of a Japanese water flower, and now Lee oscillated sickly between two focuses of guilt, his mistress and his wife. Yet all he had wanted from Carolyn, in the first place, had been a little, simple affection and she, from him, pleasure, although now she was in such a tranced and helpless state she thought she would be lonely without him for the rest of her life.

"I don't know you," said Lee. "I don't know you at all, do I?"

It was an excuse or an attempt at an explanation rather than a complaint but she was cut to the heart for she did not realize they had only intersected by chance upon one another and exchanged spurious, self-contradictory falsehoods as if flashing lights in one another's faces.

Lee saw the ambulance from the top of the street and broke into a run. He was in time to see them carry Annabel from the house, wrapped in a blanket, and then Buzz spat at him. Buzz was still painted like a fiend and fixed at last upon a situation which fired all his histrionic opportunism.

"I broke the door down and you was off screwing and she dying, wasn't she?"

Lee felt nothing but surprise. Perhaps one of the ambulance men held Lee off him; anyway, soon he found himself in the casualty ward of the hospital giving Annabel's name and address to a nurse. He spelled the name "Annabel" twice out loud and then found he could not stop repeating the letters unless he kept his hand in front of his mouth. Annabel was nowhere to be seen. A man whose face had been smashed by a bottle lay on a bench, swearing. A pale child inserted sixpence in a machine and withdrew a paper cup of coffee. Another nurse (though perhaps it was one of the first two or one of the onlookers or, indeed, another nurse altogether) offered Buzz a sedative. Lee continued to feel nothing but shock. Annabel on a stretcher, covered up with blankets, vanished through a pair of swing doors. Somebody was trying to inject Buzz with something. What was the child doing here; she could be no more than twelve years old, sitting on a bench, swinging her legs and giggling. Admitted to a night ward without flowers, Annabel would wake in the worst of fears and think herself still dead, if she woke at all, that is.

Once out in the hospital yard, bundled outside by who knew how many nurses, orderlies and extras, Buzz attacked his brother again but Lee broke free and ran for it. The hospital was perhaps a mile and a half away from the quarter where they lived and Lee made his way up the hill by short cuts and back alleys, glancing behind him from time to time, but he soon shook Buzz off and at last found himself in front of Carolyn's house as a church tower somewhere in the city below struck three. He rang Carolyn's bell and she opened the door. Her tawny hair hung down the back of a crimson satin kimono but the yellow light of the street lamps took all her colours away. She saw such misery in his face she grew breathless for she had lain on her narrow bed all the time since he had left her, staring into the darkness, imagining him beside her.

"I knew you'd come back," she said. "I just knew."

"Oh, my love, it's not that," he said, ashamed. "Let me in for a while, I can't go home."

"What's the matter?"

"It's very melodramatic," said Lee. "You would hardly believe it."

They went up the stairs to her room and the lights switched off automatically behind them. Once inside her door, she was startled to see him so grotesquely smeared with Buzz's greasepaint and filthy from the chase through the streets. He dropped his jacket on the floor and lay down on her bed. She did not know what to do and moved about her room uneasily; she was not dressed properly for receiving bad news. Lee found and lit a cigarette, unpleasantly aware that everything he did or said could not fail to breathe stale cliché for he had seen so many scenes of this nature in "B" feature films, it seemed, in

reality, second hand. How was he, then, to invest the horrify-
ing with dignity?

"She . . ."

"Pardon?" she said.

"She tried to end it all, love, she almost did it. My Annabel,
that is, Annabel to whom I'm married, that is."

She lay down beside him and he stroked her hair. She had no
vocabulary to deal with the event, either; besides, she had
thought of herself only as the Other Woman, never as a Femme
Fatale. "Good heavens," she thought. "I must be dangerous."

"Can I sleep here? I want to keep away from my brother, he's
in a homicidal mood."

"Yes. Of course." She found she was crying a little and
thought Lee must also be crying when it was only the scalding
of his hypocritical eyes. As soon as they were in bed together,
he did something he could never afterwards explain away or
justify to himself; he performed an act which was, in the stric-
test sense, gratuitous. Because she was female, naked and
available, he fucked her while she continued to cry, aware of
some gross impropriety but quite unable to resist it. He appeared to be behaving in a perfectly involuntary way, as if to
prove to himself he was indeed a villain untouched by any
normal human sentiments, and thus extracted from himself a
false confession to convince himself, in retrospect, he was
immoral, although, at the time, he was not thinking of anything at all. Then he fell into a profound sleep from which he
was awakened by the insistent ringing of a bell.

"It's the post, I expect," she said. "I won't be a minute."

He could scarcely tear his eyes open but he felt the inrush
of cold air into the bed when she left it and heard the rustle of
her kimono and the pad, pad, pad of her bare feet. His reactions
were extremely slow and he did not say: "Don't go, it's my
brother," until she had left the room. After a moment, he heard
her scream.

The light of early morning flooded the hallway for the front
door was wide open and Carolyn leaned against the porch
cupping her face in her hands. Blood poured through the

cracks between her fingers. Buzz, oddly shamefaced, stood on the doorstep with his hands dangling loosely by his sides, and though he carried his camera, he had not taken any pictures.

"I hit her," he said. "I think I broke her nose."

"We'll have to take her to hospital," said Lee and began to laugh.

"If you had come down first, I would have killed you." Buzz showed the knife he held in readiness. He regained a little of his eldritch composure as he did so, cloaked, dark, menacing and fully armed. All the tenants of the rooms in the house peered from their individual doorways to witness the amazing scene and Lee was suddenly exasperated.

"Ah, come off it," he said. At that, Buzz flung the knife down at his foot as in the old game of daring-with-a-knife they used to play at primary school. The knife stuck quivering in the wooden door jamb. Lee, stark naked, turned and offered to the spies on the staircase the appalling brilliance of his most artificial smile before he pulled out the knife, offered the hilt back to Buzz and shut the front door on him. Carolyn, bleeding profusely, preceded him back up the stairs.

"Please don't call the police, it's a family matter," said Lee to a woman in a dressing gown.

Carolyn jumped when he touched her but dressed herself and he went to telephone a taxi. He took her into the casualty ward and they attended to her at once. The wounded man and the child had gone but the nurses were the same as before.

"I see you left your brother behind this time," said the sister, folding her white lips sternly. She was an austere, grey woman of about fifty.

"Annabel," he said. "Please?"

"Your private morals are nothing to do with me," said the sister.

"What the fuck do you mean?" demanded Lee. "Let me see my wife, won't you?"

"She's awake," said the sister. "I must say," she added with distaste, "you do have a high casualty rate among your women-folk, don't you?"

Her slight Scots accent lent a steely precision to her speech.

"Tell me about Annabel. I'm legally married to Annabel; doesn't that give me any rights?"

"She had a little breakfast; a boiled egg, toast."

"Can I see her?"

"She refuses to see you," the sister replied with an air of grim satisfaction.

Lee sank down on the bench where the bottled man had lain.

"Point-blank?"

"She threatens worse if you persist in trying to see her."

"I see," said Lee heavily.

"We're going to move her to a very pleasant psychiatric hospital as soon as it's possible, Mr. Collins. You must realize your wife is a very disturbed girl, very sick. Your wife is a girl in need of care, of loving care . . . "

Lee knew the woman judged him and found him wanting and this seemed only fair and just. The nurse reminded him of his aunt, who would have forgiven no act which seemed to her immoral. At that, Lee was convulsed by the knowledge of sin and guilt. Nothing in his education had prepared him for such ravagement and he could guess at no absolution. Besides, his aunt would have mocked the notion for to forgive is only to obliterate and what good does that do?

A changed girl, Carolyn came out through a pair of swing doors. Her reddish brown hair was caked and spiked with dried blood and a muzzle of bandages obscured her pretty face completely. She would not look Lee in the eye and hardly spoke to him as she brusquely brushed past him towards the open air. It was now about eight o'clock on a Sunday morning. Lee had nowhere to go but back to the flat and nothing to do there but clean the bathroom of blood before the rest of the residents in the house, who all shared the bathroom, discovered it had become an abattoir overnight. His clothes were spattered with Carolyn's blood, also, and soon he saw himself as a red-handed butcher to whom both women seemed no more than curious meat. He had no equipment to deal with abnormal states of mind and his composure utterly deserted him. He entered a delirious state of wilful self-abandonment.

When Annabel found she remained alive, she did not know, at first, how to reconcile herself to it until she hit upon the device of believing herself invisible as long as she wore the skull ring, though she constantly wondered why, if this were so, so many people seemed to be able to see her. This question absorbed her completely and she did not rest in her mind until she found an answer which satisfied her.

"How do you see me?" she asked Buzz. He picked at his lower lip with his fingernail for a while and then replied: "In fits and starts."

"That's not good enough," she said ominously and relapsed into speculation.

"Mrs. Collins still refuses to see you," another sister told Lee, whose home was now unbearable for the tap dripped Annabel's tears and the very sofa seemed re-upholstered with her anguish. At last Buzz led him by the hand to an interview with Annabel's psychiatrist for by now Lee was unable to negotiate the city on his own and could not see where he was going. To compound his distress, he had been drinking heavily during the past fortnight and afterwards he could remember nothing between leaving his house and arriving as if miraculously translated into the warm interior of a cosy hospital with hardly a movement at all on his own part. Buzz abandoned his brother in a room full of faded chintz and old magazines where he waited forty minutes, staring vacantly at an empty wall; intermittently he saw the face of his mother as it had looked after she had been dipped in the petrifying well of madness. Then a nurse came and showed him up a linoleum staircase which shone as if it had been gilded and Lee felt sure it reached almost as high up to heaven as Jacob's ladder although he turned off, as instructed, at the first landing and entered the

whitest of offices. Here, he found a young woman seated behind an impressive desk. She was dressed entirely in black and
lavishly hung about with hair of metallic yellow. Her eyes
were concealed behind tinted glasses and her voice was as if
smoked also, dark-toned and husky.

"Mr. Collins?"

"Well, yes and no," replied Lee who always spoke the truth.
A look of curiosity passed across her face. She gestured him to
sit down.

"A regulation chair of tubular steel," observed Lee and slith-
ered from it to the ground. Where he lay, he saw how the walls
of the room converged upon him from all four corners and
crawled for refuge under the desk itself, where he found himself confronted by the woman's high, brown boots in such an
unnatural perspective that the feet were enormous and the
uppers soared above him like mill chimneys. The boots were
so beautifully polished they appeared irradiated from within.

"A kind of expressionist effect," he said.

"Pardon?"

"Everything is subtly out of alignment. Shadows fall awry
and light no longer issues from expected sources."

"Do you go to the cinema often?"

"Now and then. It stops us all from having to talk to one
another though she never follows the story, she only looks at
the pictures."

Since she wore no stockings, the grain of skin appeared to
simulate the leather; he stroked her knee and, meeting with no
response either in the negative or the affirmative, he explored
the outer thigh and then the inner thigh until at last his
fingers sank into the hot, wet, hairy cleft itself. At the moment
of intimate contact, he experienced a sudden, violent explo-
sion inside his head and instantly re-lived the night of the
catastrophe in its entirety.

When the debris cleared, he found himself sprawling on the
floor at the other side of the room. He did not know whether
the psychiatrist had kicked him away; if he had jack-knifed
backwards of his own accord; or whether the whole encounter

had taken place only inside his head. He raised himself to his feet and sidled back towards the desk. She sat exactly as she had done before, with her hands laid flat down before her on top of the desk and her face inscrutable.

"Why do you hide your eyes?"

"Photophobia," she replied. "Please sit down, Mr. Collins."

Lee did so. He shook his head to try and clear it.

"Here . . . did I touch you up just now?"

The woman laughed and laughed. "What can you have been using?"

"What?"

"What drug? What drug have you been using?"

"Ethyl alcohol."

"Besides that."

"He forces a fistful down me in the morning and another fistful at night. They're very colourful."

"What are?"

"The pills."

"He?" enquired the woman.

"My brother."

"Your brother's visits cause some distraction in the ward. A schizophrenic immediately identified him with St. John the Baptist."

"Our mum thought he was the Anti-Christ. She's mad, too."

"Is that so?" said the woman with a glimmer of interest.

"Yes, but she went mad on purpose." Arbitrarily he decided to give her his dazzling smile.

"Do that again!" she said instantly. Lee put up his hands to his face, startled and ashamed.

"How would you describe your relations with your wife? Are they good or bad?"

"Neither good nor bad. They exist. She's been ill before."

"Ill?"

"Mad, then," said Lee. Tears fell down his cheeks.

"Such mercurial changes of mood!" observed the woman. "Why are you crying?"

"Photophobia."

She switched the light off so that shadows of approaching dusk filled the room.

"She had a breakdown before I met her. I don't know much about it. I think she tried to kill herself then, too."

"Do you think you know much about your wife?"

"She's a silly cow."

"Do you think you understand her?"

"No."

"Why do you think she refuses to see you?"

"She's mad."

"Apart from that."

"She believes in keeping herself to herself."

"Try again."

"Didn't she tell you why?"

"She doesn't say much. She only plays with the ring on her finger and sometimes she smiles."

"Her wedding ring, is it?"

"No, not her wedding ring. She ate her wedding ring."

"Ate it?" repeated Lee incredulously.

"When nobody was looking, yes."

"Then how do you know she really ate it, if nobody was looking."

"She told me she ate it with a good deal of conviction. And it was nowhere to be seen. And she smiled; rather a smug smile, I thought."

"She must have seen me at it, then."

"At what?"

"I was on the balcony, knocking off this chick, wasn't I."

"The night of the suicide attempt?"

Lee nodded.

"Apart from that, was it a normal evening?"

"There was a party."

"During which you copulated upon a balcony."

There followed a silence. After a while, she asked him: "Do you love your wife?"

"Is there a kind of litmus paper you could dip into my heart and test such a thing objectively?"

"So you feel no affection for your wife."

"Don't be facile," said Lee, irritated.

"Why were you having intercourse with this young woman on this balcony?"

"I was drunk."

"I would have assumed you were drunk," she said with some asperity. "But did you act on the spur of the moment or was she an old friend?"

The room seemed so dark to Lee he could hardly make out the colour of the woman's hair though he could see perfectly well that, outside the window, the sky was still light.

"I'd been sleeping with Carolyn, her name is Carolyn – I'd been sleeping with Carolyn for some little time owing to thinking it would ease the strain."

"Did your relations with this girl alter your behaviour to your wife?"

"Oh, yes. I was much nicer to her."

"I see," said the woman in a satisfied voice, as though she had expected him to say this. "Do you feel guilty?"

"Rather guilty," said Lee and gave her his dazzling smile, secure she could not see it because it was so dark. Then they were silent again until Lee said, as if to himself:

"Sometimes she hardly seems alive at all, at the best of times. Annabel, she's like a shadow that sits and remembers and probably the things it remembers never happened."

"It . . ." said the woman reflectively. "How odd you should refer to your wife as 'it'."

"I was referring to the shadow of my wife."

"I see," she said and made a note on her pad. "What is the nature of both your relationships with your brother?"

"Complex."

"Your brother does not seem to be entirely normal," she said gently.

"In our milieu, that's something of a compliment, you bourgeois cow."

"Has it come to personal abuse already?" she enquired pleasantly.

"Abuse or violence, take your choice. But if you took your boots off, I'd kiss your insteps with pleasure."

"I'm sure you would," she replied in a comfortable voice. "Your brother seems to take your wife's fantasies for granted, as if they were real."

"Maybe."

"How do you yourself regard your wife's fantasies?"

"I dunno. What a question. I don't know from one minute to the next what it is that exists for her, it's like a flicker book."

"Does your wife want children?"

"Sweet Jesus!" said Lee, aghast.

"Have you ever discussed having children with her?"

"No. No, I've hardly thought about it beyond the odd scare now and then. Why do you ask? Would you think it was normal?"

"In many circles," she said. "Now you've started to cry again, I can hear you."

"I told you, I have bad eyes."

"But the lights are all out. How can your photophobia affect you? You have no excuse for tears except sentimentality."

"Then turn the lights on again, save me my face."

She did so. She was more black and gold than ever, like a holy image in a very white case and her veiled regard, half-hidden by smoked glass, gave her face an oracular ambiguity so that her blunt-lipped mouth, which might have brought forth snakes, issued slow words with a pregnant weight although now she produced a mere banality.

"Perhaps Annabel should get a job and try to make friends of her own outside the environment imposed on her by yourself and your brother."

"What's that again?" gasped Lee, stunned; he had been anticipating something portentous.

She said: "I don't think your brother is a suitable person to live in the same house as such an unbalanced girl as Annabel. Indeed, it is probably very bad for them both."

"Dear God, do I have to choose between them?"

"There is a condition of shared or, rather, mutually stimulated psychotic disorder known as '*folie à deux*'. Your brother and your wife would appear excellent candidates for it. Will you please stop crying. You are beginning to embarrass me."

"I told you, I can't help it. Here, have I really got to cope with her on my own?"

She shrugged enigmatically.

"What's wrong with my brother?" he demanded truculently.

She threw back her golden head and laughed for a long time until Lee reluctantly began to laugh also for he knew very well what she meant.

"Listen," he said through his laughter. "I feel very bad at the moment and I'll tell you why, if you can't guess. I've a brother who tried to kill me and a wife who tried to kill herself and I was searching, you know? For the causal link and so I found myself."

"Pardon?"

"I'm the plus, aren't I?"

"The plus?"

"One plus one equals two but first we must define the nature of 'plus'. They have a world which they have made so they can understand it and it includes me at the centre; somehow I am essential to it, so that it can go on. But I don't know anything about it or what I'm supposed to do except be bland and indefinable, like the Holy Spirit, and see the rent gets paid and the bloody gas bill and so forth."

"It's a hermetic world, the three of you. Will it really admit nobody else?"

"I tried, didn't I. And look what happened then."

"Well," she said. "I'm not concerned with your brother, he isn't a patient of mine. My, but you really are crying."

"I am the Spartan boy but no fox under my jacket, only my heart, eating itself out."

"How self-indulgent you are!"

"It's not so much that. It's more that I've lost my capacity for detachment. I lost it on that memorable night. And I used to be so proud of it, as well, joking about her nightmares and so on."

With that, he gave her the evil, twisted grin he had always

kept only for his own amusement in the past and saw how it
offended her so much she immediately ceased to be his friend.
Whatever sexual or sympathetic undercurrent in this parody
of an interview that had contrived to maintain it for so long
now vanished. She became brisk and officious. She was clearly
about to send him away with an implicit reprimand.

"Think of it this way. There is a sick girl who needs care and
can turn only to you. Dry your eyes and look out of the
window."

He saw a green park where lay a lake surrounded by weeping willows whose leafless branches trailed in the motionless
water. Dusk was falling but slow figures well muffled against
the cold still interminably walked these melancholy grounds
and Lee thought he had never seen so many people all together
who seemed, each one, so entirely alone. Annabel sat on a
bench beside the lake, gazing at its surface which was as black
as if of some impermeable substance and not liquid at all.
Around her, the silent crowd came and went, absorbed in a
multitude of reflections. Since Annabel wore the skull ring on
her finger, she could see but not be seen. No flicker of the
nerves of her face indicated she watched him approach but
suddenly she drew the ring off and threw it away. The waters
closed over it and concentric ripples spread out without a
sound over the place where it sank. Never before had she felt
the extent of her powers until that moment, when she resolved
to be visible all the time and was rewarded by seeing him
drawn towards her whether he willed it or not, as if she were a
magnetic stone.

"I love you," she said.

She spoke in sweet, fallacious music like the song of a mechanical nightingale and now she seemed to him a ghostly
woman, white as a winding-sheet and shrouded in hair. The
darkening light seemed to pass straight through her almost
dissolving edges and when she stretched out her hands towards him they looked like dried flowers, nothing but veins
and transparency, and he could see the bones of her fingers
through them. The sky was serene and no wind nor flight of

any bird moved in the leafless branches of the trees or stirred the still air of winter.

Lee took Annabel in his arms and she buried her face in his breast but he could not forbear to look behind him, towards the hospital buildings. Silhouetted against a bright window, the psychiatrist watched them through her dark glasses. The light behind her illuminated her flamboyant hair so she seemed all of a piece with the brightness itself and as she raised her arm either in a kind of blessing or, more likely, to draw the blinds as if dismissing all her patients for the night, she seemed to Lee like some kind of inexorable angel, directing him to where his duty lay.

"Do right because it is right," said Lee.

Lazzaro Spallanzani observed division in bacteria; his bladder is preserved in the museum at Pavia, in Italy. Pursuing his biological studies, Spallanzani cut off the legs of a male toad in the midst of its copulation but the dying animal did not relax the blind grasp to which nature drove it. Spallanzani therefore concluded: "The persistence of the toad is due less to his obtuseness of feeling than to the vehemence of his passion."

Like Spallanzani's toad, Lee was not insensitive to his situation but the stern puritanical fervour of his childhood condemned him, now, to abandon himself to the proliferating fantasies of the pale girl whose arms clasped as tight around his neck as if she were drowning. He might have guessed her history would be brief and tragic for she had always worn the blind face of those who will die young and so do not need to see much of life; but the moral imperative, to love her, proved stronger than his perceptions and his natural desire for happiness persuaded him, at first, that his intuitive forebodings were unjustified.

Besides, he was full of guilt.

Now Lee knew they would not let Annabel come home until his brother was expelled from the household, he saw Buzz as if he had never known him. He watched the variously obsessed figure intently. It continued to go busily about the absurd tasks it set itself as if they were perfectly natural. It sharpened its knives; it splashed in its acids; it snipped, stitched and dyed its commedia dell'arte rags; it rolled its joints with a pompous ritual worthy of a sacrament; it squatted for hours on the floor in those hollow, interminable silences with which it passed its excess wastes of useless time, and Lee saw all this as the motions of an unfamiliar object. He marvelled that he could have endured its aberrations so long and began to harden against the thing he saw. Until this time, he had scarcely differentiated between his brother and himself; Buzz was a necessary attribute, an inevitable condition of life. But now the circumstances were altered. Annabel freshly defined Lee as having no life beyond that of a necessary attribute of herself alone, and, in this new arrangement, Lee knew his brother for an interloper who might do harm. So now a cancer lodged at the core of his heart, where Buzz had been. Besides, he found the pictures which Buzz had taken of Annabel in the bathroom, before he called the ambulance.

Once the process of dissociation began, it quickly gathered impetus. He felt a sharp distaste at the close physical contact which had been bred of their extreme intimacy. If, at first, he believed he felt a new distaste rather than a positive revulsion, he could no longer drink from a cup Buzz had used unless he rinsed it out and the casual embraces they had always exchanged so thoughtlessly became intolerable for him. Their affection dissipated with extraordinary speed for, had they not been brothers, they would have had little in common and they could not maintain between them an uncommitted state of mutual forbearance without the sustenance of love. Buzz was helpless, incredulous and a little fearful as he perceived the growth of Lee's aversion and strove to protect himself from pain by jeers, by coldness and by the pretence of disdain. He schooled himself in dislike and waited for the blow to fall.

Lee expected a display of panic and violence when he told Buzz he would have to leave the flat but Buzz, well prepared, showed no anger or surprise. He continued to sit before the fire in perfect silence, drumming his fingers on his knee, while Lee wondered nervously what the unguessable response might be. But, when it came, it was scrupulously cool.

"Going straight?" asked Buzz in a normal voice, though with a touch of contempt.

Lee shrugged. They did not look at one another. Time passed. Coals fell in the grate. It was night-time.

"Where shall I live?" said Buzz.

"We'll find somewhere for you easily," said Lee with false cheerfulness.

"When shall I move out?"

"As soon as you can find a place."

"And will you let me come to see you, now and then?"

"Sure," said Lee, touched and embarrassed. "Of course."

"Sure," repeated Buzz equivocally. He recommenced drumming his fingers and Lee's embarrassment and distress grew with every moment that passed for, if he could brave out his brother's wildest passions, this unaccountable quiet nonplussed him and he feared it might be the prelude to some absolutely unexpected act against which he had no defence. Downstairs, another occupant of the house began to run a bath and the sound of running water drifted upstairs.

"Lee . . . who shall I talk to?"

"It's not that you talk to me, much."

"But you're always there. And she, there's always Annabel to talk to."

"I'm not divorcing you, for God's sake. We'll still be here, both of us."

"You'll ask me to dinner once a month, perhaps, will you?"

Lee realized his brother's attack was cunningly directed at his sentimentality and began to lose his temper. The fantastic room became abhorrent and the dark figure who sat on the carpet took on the aspect of a giant, hairy toad squatting upon his life and choking him, since this obscure being was a more

fitting inhabitant of the room than himself. Yet the room be-
longed to Annabel; she had painted her ambivalent garden on
the walls and installed Lee in the midst of it whether he
matched her colours or not. Lee broke out in confused fury.

"She's mine."

"Is she?" said Buzz in sardonic enquiry, turning his hard,
brown gaze upon his brother. At this precise moment in time,
Lee ceased to love him. The few remaining bonds snapped
altogether and at once as they knelt before the fire and bick-
ered about the girl who, like a Victorian heroine, had come
between them. Yet Lee still had not the faintest idea what he
could do with her once he got her to himself or how he might
make some reparation to her, in order to relieve his guilt. He
might, perhaps, clean out her room and throw her things away
for he half believed her some malleable substance on whom
the one who rescued her from her phantoms could impose
whatever form he pleased.

Since he was racked with pity for her, he chose to try to
rescue her for fear of what she might become if she were left to
herself or to the unscrupulous mercies of another, for he did
not know she had plans of her own and would finally choose to
attempt to save herself.

"Mine," repeated Lee and, rising, swept the mantelpiece clear
of all its assorted rubbish with a sweep of his arm. The rubbish fell down around the fireplace; the skull of the horse
shattered in shards of bone and the pottery Prince Albert
snapped in two at the waist. Buzz continued to look at him
with those opaque eyes which were, in no sense, the mirrors of
his soul. He offensively took out and lit a cigarette.

"Turning me out of our home," he said. "What would our
auntie think?"

Lee's heart contracted and he would have lashed out if Buzz
had not been his brother.

"No point in consulting the dead," he said with an attempt
at calm.

Buzz threw his cigarette into the fire and kicked the coals
with his booted foot. As he rose, he towered above Lee. His

coat of long-haired fur took on the appearance of scalps, his hair shook out like that of a brave and his endless, emaciated shadow flickered across the ceiling as if the shadow of his influence dominated the room. His appearance was so fearful that Lee braced himself for the shock of impact or even the cut of a knife but he received only a mouthful of empty threats, as he would have expected in the old days before he lost his detachment.

"Do anything to her like you did last time and I'll get you, I really will."

"You're too bloody inefficient," snarled Lee, freshly infuriated at this dramatic flourish, but Buzz was out through the door before the shaft struck home and when Lee came back from work next day, he found not one of his brother's possessions remained in the flat. Every last rag and scrap of paper was gone and he had not left a note of acrimonious farewell or the gift of his new address which might have hinted at the possibility of a reconciliation. Only a few blotches on the floor showed he had ever lived there. His dark room echoed to Lee's footsteps with a hollow sound.

He took a suitcase for her things to the psychiatric hospital and, now he was in full possession of his faculties, the building struck him by the witty irrelevance of its grandeur to its purpose. One approached it through wrought-iron gates; a double drive swept round on each side of a defunct fountain in the form of a triton who raised up a scallop shell to spill no water any more, only a stain of rust into the marble basin below. On either side of the building stretched pleasant lawns and formal beds of standard rose trees on which a few withered blooms still languished. He saw the lake where he had found Annabel was not a lake at all, only a lily pond in the shape of a tear. All served as a decorative prelude to a harmonious Palladian mansion whose present use was indicated only by a discreet notice board, half hidden in a privet hedge. A young boy in a long dressing gown and several mufflers who lurked on the porch glared mutinously at Lee as he ascended the wide, gleaming, marble steps to the front door.

"This house was built in the Age of Reason but now it has become a Fool's Tower," said the boy. "Are you familiar with the tarot pack?"

Lee with his suitcase was so intimidated by the mansion that he felt like a travelling salesman and could only smile and nod ingratiatingly for he was eloping with the duke's daughter; but when she saw him, she grasped his hand with a strangely passionate pressure and suddenly kissed him. He scanned her face for signs of change but her pale, haunted composure was that of the morning he first woke to see her. He glanced down at her bare hands.

"I'll buy you a new ring," he said.

"One with a moonstone?"

"Maybe," he replied, with a sense of foreboding.

"I'd rather spend the money on something else," she said with the air of a child with a secret plan.

"On what?"

"First of all, on a taxi."

He did not hear her instructions to the driver and found himself unexpectedly in the dockland among mean, steep, cramped streets and low, dark shops. Annabel's features grew unusually animated; she glanced at him from time to time with a repressed, anticipatory glee. From the window, Lee saw a gaunt figure emerge from a doorway folded in the wings of a black cape like Poe's raven named Nevermore but the taxi turned a corner and Buzz, if Buzz it were, was gone. The taxi deposited them on a main thoroughfare by a shop window above which a sign read: ARTIST IN FLESH.

The window was full of coloured photographs demonstrating the full range of the art of the tattooist. Men turned into artificial peacocks displayed chests where ramped ferocious lions, tigers or voluptuous houris in all the coloured inks which issued from the needle. One man had the head of Christ crowned with thorns in the centre of his bosom and another was striped all over like a zebra. Some had flowers, memorial crosses and the words: MOTHER R.I.P. A young girl coyly raised her skirt to show a flock of butterflies tattooed along her thigh. In the centre of the window hung a very large photograph of a man upon whose entire back was described a writhing dragon in reds and blues; and every scale and fang of the beast, each flame it blew from its nostrils, was punctured into the skin for good and all unless he were unpeeled like an orange or pared like an apple. Lee experienced a sympathetic crawling of the flesh; sure, now, of her purpose, he glanced in astonishment at Annabel, who smiled seraphically and pushed at the shop door.

Lee did not know whether this ordeal was a piece of retribution or a rite of passage; nevertheless, he underwent it. The tattooist wore a prim, white, surgical coat and cleansed the ritual of a little barbarism by his care for hygiene, although the clinical asepsis of his shop and the gross attention he paid to the points and sterility of his needles affronted Lee, who could have wished for more atrocious pain, torrents of blood and an ultimate, festering wound to compensate Annabel in full for the skill with which she had devised this baroque humiliation, if she had intended to humiliate him; and, try as he might, he could think of no other reason for the exercise.

Shirtless in an enamel cubicle, he let them write her name indelibly in Gothic script and circle it with a heart so now he wore his heart on the outside, laid bare for all to see. A man in the window had a sacred heart on his left breast and Lee was now equipped with a new heart, also, as if the old one had been cut out, hand-coloured, pressed flat and re-consecrated entirely to Annabel, no longer his own to do with as he pleased. His new, visible heart was drawn in rosy red but, for her name, she chose the colour green. The needle attacked him like an electric bee and he stung and sweated beneath it, biting his lower lip, while she watched the artist plying his tool with intense concentration, her colourless mouth ajar and the tip of her tongue protruding between her teeth. When Lee put his shirt back on, she made him pay and smiled once again, far more radiant than she had been as a bride. Weak and sick, Lee went out with her into the morning and she took his hand in hers, her long, narrow hand which was always nervously moist and unnaturally warm.

"You'll never deceive me again," she said with pale conviction. "What other girl would make love to you now?"

Lee realized he had credited her with more emotional sophistication than she possessed. She believed only that she had signed him; the mark was no more than a certificate of possession which gave him the status of any other object in her collection. She had not intended to humiliate him and was hardly capable of devising a revenge which required a knowledge of human feeling to perfect it. Nevertheless, he had been humiliated, even if it were no concern of hers. In wet weather, the tattoo seemed to throb and burn him; in dry weather, it itched intolerably and he was always nervously conscious of her name under his left nipple, shuddering as it did at every beat of his heart. Annabel was very pleased with the effect. Perhaps, he thought, it was a bad-conduct medal.

So they began their life alone together in the knowledge she had won a major victory over him and Lee could no longer pretend that he had rescued her. She sustained her conviction of supremacy so strongly, if in perfect silence, that soon he began to act as if he had indeed been utterly vanquished and let go all the acquaintances he had managed to keep. He ceased to visit anywhere outside the flat and spent all his free time with her. He became as silent and decorative as the statue with which she had always compared him while their home rotted around them, suffused with purgatorial gloom.

She never mentioned Buzz's name and he never came to see them. Lee sometimes thought he would never see his brother again for as long as he lived. He had no desire to see his brother but a visit from him would have proved that the past had existed. And now he had no other evidence that his life could once have been other than the way he lived now. His family photographs were not objective evidence that the beings in them had ever moved in a real, accessible dimension. His guilt had devised its own punishment. He acknowledged that she was far cleverer than he and began to fear her a little for he could not alter her at all, although she could change him in any way she pleased.

And now Annabel had docketed him securely amongst her things, she began subtly to evacuate herself from the room which had been her whole world, leaving Lee marooned there in miserable isolation.

Now she had two rooms, her unseen world extended its physical boundaries, though it seemed she no longer needed to populate it with as many real objects as before, perhaps because she had impressed her sorrow so deeply on the essential wood and brick of the place she knew for certain nobody could ever be happy there again. She no longer exchanged confidences with the figures on the walls. She did not bother to buy any more furniture or even to fill up the mantelpiece with bunches of leaves and berries from the park stuck into the necks of milk bottles. She lay in bed for hours while Lee was at work, sometimes drawing her pet apocalyptic beasts in her sketchbook but, more and more, merely gazing into space, absorbed in thought. The window remained boarded up and the room was always dark and shady.

Some days she did not get up at all and, if she did, she did not bother to dress or wash but lounged around all day in her nightdress, the very image of mad Ophelia, her disordered hair often caked with watercolour or gobbed with breakfast egg. But now she knew who mad people were and how they behaved, she became a little self-conscious and sometimes she looked like a blurred imitation of her former self. She did not take the drugs which had been prescribed for her and flushed them down the lavatory to conceal this omission from Lee. She kept none of her after-care appointments with the psychiatrist, but took good care to dress herself neatly on certain days of the week, as if she were going to the hospital, and Lee believed her.

Accustomed as he was to dealing with the sick, Lee fed her and cared for her, although, in herself, she seemed much the same as she had always been. Besides, he had few patterns of

normal behaviour with which to compare and contrast her
ways.

One day, she roused herself sufficiently to go downstairs
and put his alarm clock in the dustbin. She said that the tick
irritated her. After that, there was no more means of telling
the time except for Lee's wristwatch, so he was often late for
work, although the days he passed at the school were scarcely
different from the nights he passed at home. Both were barren.
He felt as though all his vitality had drained out through the
perforations of the needle. Each morning on the stairs, he
passed the blonde girl, Joanne, and the swift, fascinated distaste in her glance instantly defined him as a debauched,
shameless and abandoned person. Her look made Lee nervous
and a little wistful. But she never missed crossing his path on
the staircase and he was always aware of her precociously
slumberous gaze fixed on his face when he gave her form their
weekly lessons on current affairs and political institutions.

Seated at the round table in the bleak middle of a Sunday
afternoon, he marked a pile of fifth-form essays on the British
Constitution and found, written in a round, childish hand,
only the following words on one sheet of paper: "They say this
is a free country but I am not free in any way so stuff your free
country." It was difficult to mark Joanne's essay or to guess at
the impulse which prompted it, though he thought she would
not have submitted it to any other member of the staff. He
scrawled "amplify" at the bottom in red but she did not do so; it
seemed the written word was not Joanne's medium. She had a
name for waywardness but Lee paid no attention to staffroom
gossip though he noticed in class she was always biting her
nails and her nails were brown with nicotine.

An unhappy adolescent will clutch at any straw. Joanne,
who was dissatisfied, incorporated her schoolteacher in her
own illusory web where, quite unknown to himself and entirely without his consent, he led a busy, active life of high adventure and almost continuous sexual intercourse. She had never
received much real affection. Her mother was dead and her
father an alcoholic. When she was a small child, she found a

wounded pigeon beside the railway line. Its breast and leg were hurt. She nursed it until it grew better and exercised it by allowing it to fly round and round her room. At first, as it learned once more how to fly, it blundered about from mantelpiece to chest of drawers like a raw beginner, bungling every movement, but soon it gained confidence and swooped around beneath the ceiling with the heavy grace of pigeons. It slept in the bottom of her wardrobe. One night it escaped from her room and fluttered downstairs into the kitchen where it sat on the plate rack of the gas stove, cooing, until the sound irritated her father, who kicked it to death.

She was an enthusiastic competitor in minor beauty contests out of a poignant, though unconscious, desire to be publicly acknowledged a pretty girl, yet she had a certain optimism and thought she might easily satisfy her desires as soon as she was sure what they were.

Lee sank more deeply into a melancholy so alien to his nature it never occurred to him he might be unhappy for he associated unhappiness with a positive state, with scarcely tolerable grief or furious sorrow authenticated by a death or a disaster, not with this unmotivated absence of pleasure that dulled the colours of the approaching spring and took the dimensions from the things around him so everything was reduced to flat, ineffectual shapes. He raised his arm and no shadow fell for Annabel had taken out his heart, his household god, squashed it thin as paper and pinned it back on the exterior, bright, pretty but inanimate.

Yet, always on the point of disintegrating, he contrived somehow always to hold himself together for he sincerely believed that, since the world was so full of a number of things, it was a moral imperative to be happy as a king. This was the final modification of his puritanism; that if he had enough to eat and a roof over his head, he knew he ought to be content even if the king he always thought of in connection with the smiling couplet he repeated to himself every morning was Mad King Ludwig of Bavaria. He lost his self-consciousness for it no longer served him any function and he revealed the aggressive reserve which had always lain beneath his acquired ease of manner. He ceased, almost immediately, to be charming but his beautiful, collected walk changed, or, rather, intensified in character. He strode along with more determination and far greater arrogance now he knew there was nowhere to go.

If his fatal sentimentality demanded that the promises he had made her and the anguish they had shared should, in some way, unite them, he could see with his own eyes that no union had been achieved. Because they spent so much time in silence, it was always possible for Lee to deceive himself they shared an unspoken and profound closeness; only when he occasionally spoke to her did the space between them become apparent and sour. By Easter, he had almost given up talking altogether and smiled only in fits of extreme absence of mind.

Their life passed in a diffused dreariness and Lee could not guess the subject of Annabel's reveries for she took good care not to speak of the absent brother. Besides, she did not suffer from the loss of her playfellow for, since she no longer saw him every day, every day he became more real to her and, though she did not long for him, she waited for his physical return with a certain irritation that it was delayed so long. On the other hand, he might return to her in some other shape. Sometimes she thought of him as a mean, black fox and sometimes as a metamorphic thing that could slip in and out of any form he chose, so surely he could briefly inhabit a bird perching outside on the balcony, for he had no fear of heights. Then, again, he was equally at home in subterranean regions and could have become a mouse she sometimes heard, gnawing the interior of the wall. She remembered the game they had played with his father's ring and thought it very likely he could shift his shape and come to visit her, if only with the other shadows, at night. She grew more friendly with the night-time shapes of things, for now they might possess identities.

Although she hardly budged from her bed, she often, in her turn, visited him in his new room. He had found himself a dark and brooding habitation where light filtered thickly, if at all, through blackened windows on to his piled relics and everywhere among the knives and jars of acid hung photographs of herself. She spent far more time in this imaginary room than she did in her own home, which seemed to her now not a home but a transitory lodging. She threw away Buzz's ring only in order to deceive her husband for she had decided to embark upon a new career of deceit and she knew, if she were clever, she could behave exactly as she wished without censure or reprimand, almost as if she were invisible whether she wore the ring or not. Lee no longer dared be angry with her no matter if she stole, forbore to wash, or pushed him away in bed because he was so frightened of the possible consequences.

When she was two or three years old, her mother took her shopping. Little Annabel slipped out of the grocer's while her mother discussed the price of butter and played in the gutter for a while until she decided to wander into the middle of the road. A car braked, skidded and crashed into a shop front. Annabel watched the slivers of glass flash in the sunshine until a crowd of distraught giants broke upon her head, her mother, the grocer in his white coat, a blonde woman with dark glasses, a man with four arms and legs and two heads, one golden, the other black, and many other passers-by, all as agitated as could be imagined. "You might have been killed!" said her mother. "But I wasn't killed, I was playing," said Annabel, no bigger than a blade of grass, who had caused this huge commotion all by herself just because she could play games with death.

However, this was not the memory of a real event but of a particularly lifelike dream she had under sedation in the hospital although she now believed it to be perfectly true. In the hospital, she could create confusion by a gesture as simple as gulping down her wedding ring; she learned how uncommon she was and so she acquired an aristocratic sense of privilege and, with it, an aristocratic sense of disdain, for all around her she received hints and intimations that her fantasies might mould the real world. She leafed through the *National Geographic* magazine in the lounge and saw pictures of long-

horned steers so she decided to brand Lee like the cattle of the
Old West as a first test of her occult powers.

When she abandoned drawing completely, she paradoxically
appeared to rouse from her physical lethargy. First, with a kind
of abstracted wilfulness, she took to wandering around the
streets all day; then, one afternoon, she found what she was
seeking, a sign advertising the post of an assistant in the window of a draper's. She went in and was hired on the spot. At
first, Lee thought this action was a hopeful sign. Instead, it was
the beginning of a period during which she mimicked Buzz's
pattern of casual labour in her own fashion.

She drifted haphazardly from one undemanding, unskilled
job to another, working sometimes as a waitress, sometimes
packing biscuits in a factory before moving on to a fish-and-
chip shop or a department store. She seemed to want to try her
hand at anything. She earned a little money for herself but she
had given up buying things so there was nothing to spend it
on. She kept the notes in an Oxo tin bound with an elastic
band on the bedroom mantelpiece and, with the small change,
she bought chocolate bars, cream cakes, sugar buns and other
sweet, unnecessary things she consumed immediately, as if it
were pocket money and she were twelve years old. It never
occurred to Lee to touch any of her money. It could have
turned to dead leaves the moment she put it inside her tin.

He lost his first optimism as he saw she grew no closer to
the common world by mingling with it; rather, she enhanced
her own awareness of her difference from it and grew proud. He
learned to treat her desultory employments with a weary in-
dulgence even if he were always apprehensive about her for he
no longer had any notion of how, in a new set of circumstances, she might behave. But Annabel felt a nascent sense of
clarification. She had never felt exhilarated before but now she
felt herself stirring. It seemed to her that the concealed shapes
which had so long menaced her were casting off their ambiguous surfaces and revealing, not the perfect shapes of fear she
had so long suspected beneath them, but soft, indeterminate,
interior cores. The world unshelled itself or she unshelled the

world and she found, beneath the crust of spiked armour, a kernel of plasticine limply begging to be rendered into forms. As she grew more confident this was so, she drew a final picture of Lee as a unicorn whose horn had been amputated. Her imagery was by no means inscrutable. Then her sketchbooks were put away for good.

She longed to share the discoveries she had made with Buzz but she was not impatient to find him again. Her new theory of magic presentiments assured her he would appear again when the time was ripe. She guessed the institution of a new order of things in which she was an active force rather than an object at the mercy of every wind that blew; no longer bewitched, she became herself a witch.

Lee knew nothing of this access of a confidence as strange to him as her former terrors.

As if she was determined, now, to inhabit only incongruous places, her disinterested career in the world took her to work in a local ballroom, one of a chain which operates throughout the provinces. For her duties, she wore a sheath of pink, yellow and white printed cotton slit up to the thigh on the left side and she had to pin a bunch of pink and yellow artificial flowers in her hair. The manager selected a dress he thought might fit her from a folded heap of similar dresses in a musty cupboard and the fabric smelled of disuse and old, stale sweat reawakened by the warmth of her body; it was in no way her own dress and when she looked at herself in the mirror of the changing room she saw, indeed, a stranger. When she was thirteen, she managed to spend a whole year without looking in a mirror for fear of seeing there a different face from her own but, this time, if she felt a passing terror, it was rather at the memory of this old dread than a suspicion it might reassert itself and she shook with excitement for this stranger in vulgar and whimsical clothes who began to smile a little at her, shyly, quite misrepresented herself. This stranger had an appearance not altogether unlike that of ordinary charm.

Annabel pushed her long hair back from her face and practised the smile Lee used to give her in bed, before he gave up smiling. The effect was enchanting and seemed to express utter guilelessness and a marvellous warmth of heart. So she counterfeited the only spontaneous smile he had and took it away from him, leaving him with no benign expressions left for himself. Equipped with this delicious smile, she entered the ballroom and found a cold, bewitching dazzle of lights. Here, since everything around her was artificial, she and her first, carefully contrived, if tentative, reconstruction of herself as a public object passed for a genuine personality.

Everything in this ballroom was absolutely similar to the interiors of all the other ballrooms in the chain, so it was a synthetic reduplication without an original model and there was nothing in it at all peculiar to itself. The bar where Annabel worked was decorated to represent a grove of palm trees spreading green fronds over small, rustic, wooden tables and low stools. The walls were lavishly garnished with fishing nets and, caught in the hanging folds, were brilliantly coloured, luminous, tropic fish, flowers and fruit. Candles placed inside large purple brandy glasses served not to illuminate but to enhance the primary illusion of luxurious darkness. In the swathes of mauve tulle which concealed the ceiling above the dancing floor hung a rotating, many-faceted witchball upon which a spotlight was permanently directed so roving tracks of light scurried about the floor all the time like shining, flesh-less mice and concealed lighting effects all round the room caught the dancers in sudden, cold, blue blizzards or washed them with crimson.

Smiling her borrowed smile, a false Eve in an artificial garden, Annabel served drinks and washed out glasses, to all appearances distinguished from the other girls in pink and yellow dresses only by her height and her distinctive slimness. But she still rarely spoke and customers and staff alike treated her with a certain circumspection for she had no notion of how to behave naturally except in the way which was natural to her. She worked in this place for five nights out of the week, from seven o'clock to eleven o'clock on Monday, Tuesday and Wednesday and from seven o'clock to one the next morning on

Friday and Saturday. Under these circumstances, she was only infrequently at home when Lee was there. All the time she was away from him, he was afraid for her although he was not sure why and, on the nights she worked very late, he went to the ballroom to bring her home. Then they would take the short cut, through the park. Sometimes, when there was a moon, she would grasp convulsively at his hand but usually she walked quietly beside him while he watched their shadows preceding them along the ragged path like shadows of a nonexistent harmony. One Saturday night, Lee became involved in a fight in the ballroom.

As on the other Saturday nights, she carried her smile through the customers like a person carrying a basin full to the brim with water who has to move very carefully so that not a drop is spilled. Lee arrived at the club before she expected him and she was disconcerted; she hid for a while behind a plastic tree to see what he was like when he was by himself for lately she sometimes wondered if he existed at all when she was not beside him to project her idea of him upon him. His by now a little battered beauty was always at odds with the environment in which he happened to find himself for he still looked more than ever like a handsome outlaw even if he was a schoolteacher by profession, so she was not surprised to see him grow in self-possession in the ballroom, out of self-defence.

Later, watching him closely as she washed glasses behind the bar, she was so sure he was her creature she felt only a little angry contempt and pity when he approached the blonde girl for she could see the fluorescent outlines of his heart and her own name glowing beneath his clothes and knew he could not act independently. By a piece of mental sleight of hand, she rendered the ensuing fight inevitable; she was enchanted by her powers and, laying out the separate events and scrutinizing them as if they were fortune-telling cards, she divined the time was ready for Buzz's return. Soon she might be able to tell the wind when it was time to blow.

Since there was no clock in the house and he had forgotten

to wind his watch, Lee relied on intuition as regards the time and so he arrived at the club only a little after midnight for the unmarked hours passed slowly in his silent room. The doorman knew him well by now and allowed him inside to seat himself at a vulgar table and have his wife serve him in surroundings so reminiscent of his working-class origins she looked like an anachronism, anyway. She wore a smile he did not know was a plagiarism since he had never seen himself wearing it; he knew only that it was sweet, unusual and disquieting for it did not seem to belong to her and might hang in the air after she had gone, like that of the Cheshire cat.

Immensely amplified music from an extremely powerful record player and innumerable confusions of coloured lights contended with one another in the air so noisily that, when a man at a nearby table struck a match and held it aloft for a moment before lighting his cigarette, the small, pure, steady flame amidst the clutter of neon was as startling as a chord of silence. The little fire briefly lit up three faces, two of men and one of a girl with a great deal of flaxen hair which sprayed out like flying snow. She was the girl Joanne and at present she was the object of an unpleasant scene of petty sexual bullying. As soon as the match was out, her companion on her right thrust his hand down the opening of her blouse and ostentatiously fondled her right breast. The girl writhed a little in her chair from embarrassment, not from pleasure, and her companion on her left gave a little, mewing giggle and began to fumble with the fastening of her blouse at the back. Both, though still boys, were rather older than she and had a certain elegance of dress and manner; she was clearly a casual pick-up and they could treat her as casually as they pleased.

She was out of her depth and her first signs of fright gratified them. They laughed at one another across the top of her head and the frantic lights momentarily struck a glittering spoor of tears on her round, white cheeks. When Lee leaned heavily on him and said: "Leave her alone," the boy laughed up at him with the serene self-confidence of the middle class mixed with a man-to-man invitation to tolerance and his hand continued to agitate the girl's breast until Lee hit him on the mouth, which transformed the laugh into a gape of dismay.

Disengaging himself from Joanne, the other stuttered: "Here ... I say ... " as if in self-parody. Joanne leaped to her feet and knocked over the table so that everything upon it, glasses, ashtray, brandy glass and candle, rolled and smashed everywhere; in the confusion, she vanished and both boys set on Lee at once while the lighted candle set fire to a swathe of tulle.

Saturday night is the right time for a fight and Lee, a retired veteran of fights in similar times and places, found himself entering into the old spirit. It was like diving back into the past; it was simple, elementary and unpremeditated experience. It had nothing to do with the person he had become.

The first pause in the action occurred when he was thrust back into a drift of flame and lurched forward into the arms of a man in a dinner jacket with a fire extinguisher who pushed him to one side with a curse and attacked the conflagration with squirts of foam. Many of the dancers continued to move to the music as if nothing were happening for both fight and fire were localized in a small part of the ballroom but those nearby the focus of the table had all become involved in it. Lee saw the boy who had caressed Joanne crawling blindly through a labyrinth of legs and overturned chairs, bleeding from the mouth, and some other person was kicking the other boy, who lay on the floor. A few women screamed and smoke billowed out of the smouldering hangings. Another man in a dinner jacket threw a bucket of sand, cigarette ends and dried vomit over the head of the first boy. Perhaps the man had mistaken the contents of the bucket for water. The lights, meanwhile, continued through their various changes so that the chaos was washed by all manner of romantic colours. Lee decided the time had come to leave and slipped out unnoticed. He felt ridiculously light of heart for the insignificant rough-house in the ballroom had reminded him of how simple he had once found it to act without thought and pay attention only to his immediate impulses and gratifications.

So the fight, or tussle, was by no means insignificant for,

while he took part in it, he quite forgot Annabel and, during the time he had forgotten Annabel, he was happy without even trying to be so. When he was twenty, he would have reprimanded himself for such self-indulgence, for then he had believed that happiness was a quality which resided in its possessor and bore no relation to his environment. But now he was a little older and had learned his theory was difficult, if not impossible, to work out in practice. Had there been sufficient time, he might have thought rather more about the implications of his sudden, unexpected and remarkable attack of happiness and concluded, at last, that he might have to stop loving Annabel in order to keep intact what few fragments of himself he could save. But, as it proved, there was no time at all.

The scrabbling at the door announced a visitor, though nobody ever visited them even if, today, Annabel sat on the sofa with the air of someone waiting for something. The scrabbling persisted and, when neither of the occupants of the room spoke, the door handle turned. It was a warm Sunday afternoon in early June and vivacious sunlight broke against the windows only to shatter on a thick rind of dirt so that a dazzle of blurred light suffused the room and bounced back from sparkling particles of mica here and there in the crêpe veil of dust which covered everything. All the shoulders of Annabel's collection of bottles were padded with the dust which ridged the picture frames and rose up in clouds from the rarely disturbed plush of chairs and tablecover if, by chance, they were touched. Images could no longer force their way through the grime on the mirror and the lion's-head handles on the sideboard wore soft, gritty deposits in each wooden eyeball and curl of mane. Dust hooded the glass case so thickly you could not see that the stuffed fox inside was now diseased; its muzzle was grey with mould and its hide sprouted with thriving fungi.

There was nothing in the room which did not smudge the hand which brushed it, for Lee had not the time nor the heart to clean or tidy anything and Annabel never thought to. The pigments of her landscapes round the green walls were already beginning to fade so faces yellowed, flowers withered and leaves turned brown in a parody of autumn although, outside, glimpsed darkly through clouded glass, the trees in the garden of the square shook out fresh leaf in the bright air of summer. It was as if the spirit of the perverse so thoroughly inhabited the room it could make what difference it chose even to the seasons of the year.

Unsure of his welcome, Buzz edged shyly into the flat, concealing his nervousness by a manner at once sinuous and ramshackle. He narrowed his eyes to peer round furtively to see how things had changed; he saw a room like a nursery abandoned just as the children had left it when they went to school, filthy, full of broken things, the furniture scattered about the floor in a disorderly, careless fashion and dirty clothes spilling out of the bedroom everywhere. He was quite satisfied.

"Hi, Alyosha," he said to his brother and sat down on the floor against the wall at his old, Euclidian angle. He exchanged one or two thin remarks with his brother who sat at the table marking third-form essays on aspects of current affairs and then he and Annabel began again their endless conversation of silences and allusions as if there had been no real intermission in it. She was unusually lively and laughed a little from time to time but she did not try her new smile on Buzz for she thought he would see through it immediately. She and Buzz began to smoke and the sweet, heavy odour drifted through the motes dancing on the air, mingling harmoniously with the rich smell of old clothes in the room.

It grew so close and hot that Lee pulled off his shirt. Buzz saw the tattoo at once and turned his eyes to Annabel with open admiration in them; they both broke into peals of derisive laughter and Buzz kept glancing at the mark from time to time in amazed mockery. Once, before Lee acknowledged any difference between what he did and how he responded to it, he

had witch-doctored Buzz to tranquillity from one of his spo-
radic attacks of hysteria by locking him securely in his arms,
according to the usual practice, down on the floorboards
which had then been white and bare, not smothered up with
ragged rugs as they were now. Annabel crouched watching by
the fire and, when Buzz finally slept, she came and lay down
beyond him, stretching out her hands over his shoulders to
caress Lee wistfully and, as she did so, she drowned both
brothers in cascades of her pre-Raphaelite hair. That was the
only time all three spent the night together.

"Oh God," said Lee to himself in horror. "Was that where I
went wrong?"

But he could not bear to think that she might desire them
both because she thought they were incomplete without each
other. He was jealous only of the shared secrets at which they
hinted with every glance but, even so, his jealousy was as
bitter and humiliating as that which had tortured Buzz during
the nights when Lee and Annabel first made love beyond the
thin partition. Buzz knew this and was happy. Lee went on
marking his books in angry disquiet for now he found he
himself had become the sullen interloper; and, at this point,
his brother and his wife might themselves have believed they
could exclude him from their plottings. But the plot was
woven solely to exclude him and so he remained negative but
essential.

The sunlight occupied less and less of the room as evening
drew on. Lee finished his marking, put on his shirt and prepared to go out for Buzz's lean face grew more and more vi-
ciously malign and the heavy air breathed antagonism. But
Buzz and Annabel got to their feet, also, as if mutually con-
senting to carry on the torment a little longer, and they drifted
downstairs together, out into the golden evening. In the street,
Buzz took care to walk between Lee and the girl to emphasize
how emphatically he divided them. But still they would not let
Lee go.

"I need a drink," said Lee sharply.

Fortunately, there was a group of old acquaintances gathered already in the saloon bar so all three could take their places among them as in the old days and pretend for a while that nothing was happening. The girl, Carolyn, sat with her new lover and saw the Collins brothers and their wife come in. She had not seen Lee since the night Buzz broke her nose. She had hoped she would never see any of them again, trailing behind them their slimy snail trails of squalid passion. Lee recognized her and saw how ostentatiously she refused to look at him; he was glad of that for he was in no mood to cope with further complexities.

The bar was crowded with men and women, many of whom he knew and had often talked with in the past. He sat at a table around which were seated people who might think of themselves as friends of his but who seemed devoted solely to the pursuit of contactless sociability, as if this was the best that could be hoped for from human intercourse, gossiping away as if their lives depended on it and, a few feet away, sat a woman who had loved him once and was still so disturbed to find herself unexpectedly in his presence that she refused to acknowledge him. His wife stared into the middle distance in a state, apparently, of luminous vacancy; her lips drooped open a little in half a smile and Lee remembered coming home and finding her in tears because he was not beside her. In the earliest days of their association, her presence had seemed the key to all enigmas; now she was an enigma herself. She was the only one amongst the whole crowd to whom Lee wished to speak but he could find not one word to say to her.

In the course of a spirited conversation which expressed nothing but a common need to pass the time, Buzz reached out his hand and grasped a lock of Annabel's hair. Everybody noticed but everybody went on talking with redoubled vigour. As, entirely without surprise, she turned to Buzz, he drew her towards him by his handful of her hair and kissed her for a long, long time. Then he pushed back his chair and rose; she took his hand and they went out together. As soon as they were outside the bar, they embraced again. Their single, merged silhouette flashed up against the glass door and vanished.

They left a vivid hush behind them. The disruption of decorum took place so abruptly nobody was in the least prepared for it or knew how the gaping hole in the fabric of everyday behaviour could possibly be repaired. Some kinds of collective embarrassment reach such an orgasmic peak the participants cannot recover easily from the crisis and relapse into prolonged discomfort. Those around the table fumbled with their beer mats and avoided the sight of the presumably outraged husband who lost face so entirely he no longer looked in the least as anybody remembered him, for his mouth was twisted in a vile, cynical grin and his reddened eyes were angry as raw wounds. He pulled himself to his feet, knocking over a chair.

"Don't – " said a woman, clutching at his sleeve; the Collinses were famous for their violent passions. He remembered how useful his dazzling smile had been in emergencies and, after an immense effort, produced it again.

"It's all right, ducks, I haven't the slightest desire to do him over," he said with as much poise as he could. The atmosphere began to ease. The brothers' reputation for picturesque and shameless behaviour made the event more acceptable, a public confession of private deviances their friends had always suspected.

Lee wove his way through the crowded tables, nodding and smiling to acquaintances as he went; he managed to put on a fairly adequate show of insouciance but once he found himself in the open air he collapsed against the wall and slid to the ground. After a while, the gentle pressure of a hand on his shoulder announced the presence of the girl, Carolyn. He was not surprised to see her but guessed she intended to comfort him. This made him suspicious of her. She sat down on the ground beside him and did not say anything for a while. It was a beautiful evening; the sky was deep green with a lonely star or two. He looked at Carolyn sideways and was pleased to see her nose had mended perfectly without leaving any kind of scar.

"It was terrible of them to do that to you," she said. She construed the event in the bar according to the motives she ascribed to Annabel whom she still saw as impelled by a need to punish and shame Lee because of Lee's affair with herself, a perfectly natural interpretation even if quite wrong. She hardly bothered to concern herself with Buzz's motives for she did not know him well and concluded only that he was sick, which excused everything and made it unnecessary to look further for causes of his aberrations. Lee had no desire to discuss his brother's abduction of his wife. He tried to change the subject. He cleared his throat.

"I saw you with that bloke, I thought you weren't speaking to me."

"I was afraid you might do something stupid so I came out, just to see you, to see you were all right."

"Something stupid such as what?"

"I don't know," she said, faltering a little for he seemed so calm and reasonable violence was out of the question, and she might have followed him only from a need to reinstate herself with him. Because this might, in fact, be so, she grew a little uneasy but Lee wanted to illuminate the situation for her in depth. He was deceived by her concern and thought it was for Annabel, since Annabel was his principal concern, and we always think that others must have the same compulsive interest in our private perturbations as we do ourselves.

"She's probably bitten off more than she can handle, see. I've known him longer than she has, I know all sorts of things about him she's never bothered herself with and probably wouldn't understand, anyway, like how he feels about our mum, for instance. Our mum, see, she thought he was the Anti-Christ, he was only so high and she thought he leaked out poisons."

He noticed his schoolteacher accent had vanished completely and found himself talking to Carolyn with the frantic desperation of the lonely; he gave her a last, explanatory sentence and stopped short, from pride.

"But I can't stop her trying it with Buzz, if she wants."

"Then why are you crying?" For his eyes were watering, partly due to the smoke in the bar.

"Of course I'm crying," he snapped. She misunderstood him completely for she did not know about his eye infection and took his tears at face value. She spoke in a muffled, distantly disappointed voice for it is always hard to acknowledge one has been a second-string lover, even when the affair is over.

"You really do love her, don't you?"

Whether he did or not seemed entirely beside the point to Lee and he snarled at her: "Shall we discuss it?" Carolyn picked at a thread in her skirt, chilled at his unexpected irritation, and Lee remorsefully put his arm round her and drew her against his shoulders. She rested her cheek thankfully against his throat but did not look up at him and, after a while, spoke his name rather sadly.

"Lee . . ."

"Yeah?"

"I had an abortion."

"Well," said Lee, at a loss. "Well, well."

There was a pause. During this pause, a very pure moon sailed into the sky. It was now as difficult as it was necessary to carry on the conversation.

"Why didn't you tell me?"

"What could you have done?"

"I dunno. Given you money or something. Been supportive in some way."

He tried to normalize the revelation by giving her a brilliant smile but still she kept her eyes fixed on her fingertips and did not see it.

"Is that all you can say?" she said in a low, almost a choking voice. It seemed to her Lee had forcibly subjected her to monstrous excesses of fear, pain and feeling which, now all was over between them, were like memories of a trip to another planet and she needed a little reassurance that the excursion had not been a waste of time, for surely what had happened to her had been significant; only, she did not know in the least what it could have meant.

"What do you want me to say?" asked Lee gently for he was prepared to say anything that would comfort her if it meant she would go away more quickly and leave him by himself.

"Oh, please," she said. "I did love you, really, I did."

Whether she said this because it was true or because the confession or reminder of the connection which, however briefly, had existed between them might be a clue to the meaning she sought, she did not know; nevertheless, it was a kind of coercion which Lee's sentimentality could not withstand. He began to feel sadly protective towards her.

"When did you find out you were pregnant?"

"Just before Easter. It couldn't have been anyone but you," she added wistfully. Lee's sadness turned into misery.

"She was still in the madhouse, then. Was that why you didn't tell me?"

"Yes," she said with a sudden plucky little jerk of the head that implied hitherto unexplored dimensions of feminine grit. Lee experienced an instant revulsion.

"That was terribly, terribly brave and thoughtful of you," he said so sardonically she was shocked. He decided to undervalue her self-sacrifice as much as he was able.

"I'll tell you what I'd have done if you'd told me. I'd have left Annabel for good and gone to live with you, if you wanted me to, that is, and looked after you and the kid and so on to the best of my ability. Yeah, that's what I'd have done."

She did not believe him at all.

"Come now," she said with a certain irony for she knew she herself had acted for the best. "What would you *really* have done?"

"Oh, it's all hypothetical. That was then and this is now and how can I tell what I would have done, really? I might have moved in with you, that might have been my duty. On the other hand, I might have jumped into the river to escape my conflicting obligations."

"You've become terribly bitter," she said.

"At least mad people don't talk such banalities," he complained fretfully, annoyed by the implication she herself had remained unembittered by misfortune.

"You never cared for me at all, not seriously," she said. Lee was quite befogged by a dialogue taking place in a language he did not fully understand for it was that of defensive emotional exploration. He shook his head to clear it and tried to answer her with a satisfactory degree of truth.

"It was like as if you offered me a one-way ticket to normalcy. So of course I cared for you. And I would have lived with you, if you would have had me."

At that moment, it seemed to him very likely he would indeed have done so, had it not been quite impossible. His voice was so steady and serious she was completely convinced by him and felt an immense nostalgia for her unnecessary misery; besides, he was still beautiful enough and, at the moment, sufficiently pitiable to move her. On the other hand, he was no longer a constant presence in her life but only a visitor from a time that was now gone for good; he was a revenant who no longer affected her. She reverted to the theme of his public humiliation for it was all there was left to talk about.

"It was terrible of them to do that to you."

Lee shifted his attention back to his brother and his wife.

"It's ironic, yes."

"I've got someone else to love, you know," she said almost apologetically and that, too, was ironic.

"Go back to your new bloke, then. He'll be wondering what's become of you."

But she could not leave him alone.

"Where shall you go?"

"Back home and wait for her."

Carolyn was astonished.

"Wait for her?"

"Oh, she'll be back," said Lee with a certain melancholy. "She'll be back in a state of anguish in about two hours' time, I reckon, though possibly a little before."

"Oh, darling, do come back with us," she said with well-bred solicitude for she could patronize him now he was helpless. "I don't like to think of you, deserted, in that dreadful flat."

Either because she had kept an excuse to leave Annabel for good to herself or, perhaps, because he would not stand for criticism of his wife in any circumstances, even if she was out of her wits, Lee now felt richly murderous towards Carolyn. He put on a display of ill-tempered bad taste, pulled himself together and went home.

"Shall I come back for coffee then? Can we watch television or shall I chat with your bloke about abortion-law reform?"

Buzz and Annabel shared a twined silence until the key turned in the door of the familiar but unknown room, and, for a moment, they interrupted their embrace in a mutual hesitation when they found they had arrived so quickly at the locale of its conclusion. Their surroundings were just as Annabel had imagined them; she checked with a mental inventory the peeling walls, bare and lopsided staircase, fissured linoleum underfoot, foetid accumulated reek of years of the greasy cookery of the poor and the single bulb which meanly leaked a dim light. She found she had overlooked no desolate detail. She shuddered with anticipation not so much to know she was near to assuaging a longing but that consummation would be accomplished in the place she herself had created for it.

The windows of his room were pasted over with sheets of black paper and the meagre sticks of landladies' furniture were hidden by the detritus of his obsessions. The stained, brownish wallpaper was pinned everywhere with photographs of Lee and herself, of herself alone and of Lee alone. Lee had once possessed the rare knack of looking exactly like himself when photographed; his self-consciousness made it inevitable. She had not expected to see so many photographs of Lee. They represented, now, a fissure of tiny cracks in her scrupulous imaginary edifice. Nevertheless, she braved out his hundred eyes and stretched at once on the narrow, unmade bed where, as she expected, the sheets were yellow with use. Then began the slow decline of her hopes.

At first, she could not help smiling the easy smile which, if all went well on her own terms, might become her natural expression but Buzz did not speak and did not lie down beside her and, eager as she was to touch him, she grew uneasy. She knew no way to break the sudden constraint between them except by speaking herself and she did not know what to say nor what he might reply. Buzz kept as far away from the bed as the constricted space would allow and his heavy lids drooped down over his eyes with foreboding for, now he had indulged his spite against his brother, he was left to face the consequences of it alone.

If jealousy or, rather, resentment of Lee had primarily moved him, his revenge would still be incomplete unless he recreated the maddening acts his inward eye had witnessed so atrociously as he lay beyond the thin wall, sweating at the sound of their voices. He always saw her only in relation to his brother; his interest in her was based on the knowledge he could utilize her both to defend himself against Lee and also to attack him through her after, first of all, she had usurped Buzz in his own home and his brother's affections and then turned him out of both. Now it came to the testing, he would have sworn their shared games and mutual secrets were only so many exercises in manœuvres although, at the time, he had cultivated them for their own sake, to pass the time; and if, incidentally, he estranged her from her husband and his brother from himself, that served to pass the time, also, in a way that suited his taste for dark corners and circuitous routes. But he only decided to hate his brother when Lee refused to live with him any more, and now, after a few months' passionate imaginings, he believed himself moved only by hatred. He had forgotten or never realized that Annabel had credited him with the attributes of a saviour and had she told him so as she lay on his bed things might have turned out better; or else, far worse.

As it was, he faltered between her real self on the bed and her many shadows on the wall, determined to have her but thwarted by his inability to feel as intensely in situations that were actual as he did in the supercharged events of his imagination. Life rarely rose to the demands he made on it. He tried to stimulate himself with memories of past sexual dreams and encounters and found himself as if rummaging in a forbidden cupboard of grotesqueries until he found a memory of Annabel prone on a tiled floor with her blood welling out through the silk pores of her embroidered shawl while, as he still believed, Lee lay in some other woman's bed. This idea alone filled him with desire.

He had often seen her naked but he had never handled her cold breasts nor touched sufficient of her skin to discover how closely its texture, that of chilled rice paper, corresponded to its colour. Nor had he known she would fling out her arms in an attitude of subjugation or death and lie so unnaturally still. The more he caressed her, the stiffer and colder she seemed to grow as if her huge, grey eyes divined in his the true reflection of the perverse origins of his desire and so she made her body act out the role he had devised although she believed that all she wanted for herself would be to surrender to simple, voluptuous actuality. She wanted this desperately. So they began a duel of mismatched expectancies in which Annabel was bound to be the worst hurt for her hopes had been literally infinite while his, true to his nature, existed only in the two dimensions and glaring colours of melodrama.

But he had not bargained for his own horror which increased with every moment of her passivity and the excitement which contained within it such a high degree of dread. He turned over her limp hand and, seeing the faint, white scars on her wrist, found he could manage to kiss her only to discover her lips were made of ice and her tongue burned like freezing metal. His mother who assured her small, dark son with the infernal conviction of the insane that he was the fruit of all the evil in the world had given him many fears about the physicality of women; all the nightmares that had ever visited him rushed back into his head at once and he flinched back from Annabel's mouth, which numbed him.

"Open your legs," he said. "Let me look."

She did as he asked her, faintly wondering, as she had once been with Lee, and already confronted with a great divergence between her desires and her actuality. Buzz crouched between her feet and scrutinized as much as he could see of her perilous interior to find out if all was in order and there were no concealed fangs or guillotines inside her to ruin him. Although he found no visual evidence, he remained too suspicious of her body to wish to meet her eyes so he caught hold of her shoulders and roughly pushed her down on her face. She was astonished; she felt herself handled as unceremoniously as a fish on a slab, reduced only to anonymous flesh, and she could do nothing to help herself for she knew she had connived in her own undoing. He thrust at her from behind and it was all over in a few seconds; he came as soon as he clumsily pushed his way into her and instantly withdrew, in a convulsive movement like a gigantic wince.

She cowered in his rancid bed. He mumbled something she did not understand and pulled the sheet up over her, to hide her, but when his hand accidentally touched her hair, he jumped back. They had imagined too often and too much and so they had exhausted all their possibilities. When they embraced each other's phantoms, each in his separate privacy had savoured the most refined of pleasures but, connoisseurs of unreality as they were, they could not bear the crude weight, the rank smell and the ripe taste of real flesh. It is always a dangerous experiment to act out a fantasy; they had undertaken the experiment rashly and had failed but Annabel suffered the worst for she had been trying to convince herself she was alive.

She cowered in his rancid bed and whispered: "I want to go home," for the only solace she could envisage was to pretend this bitterest of disappointments was itself a dream and that, when it grew light, Buzz's dark, strange body would revert to the familiar shape of her husband for she had often pretended the one was the other, anyway. Buzz covered his face with his hands and allowed her to dress herself and wander off alone through the dark streets, a fragile, flimsy thing whose body had betrayed both their imaginations.

As she came into the kitchen, Lee was burning his three

precious photographs by holding a match to the tip of each; he watched while the blue flame blackened the picture and then he dropped each withered scrap into the sink and turned the tap so that the ashes were washed down the drain. She took a cup from the dresser, went past him to fill it with water, and drank. Torn between jealousy and suppressed murderous rage, Lee was in an evil mood and quite prepared to eschew compassion; he saw only that she was in a state where it might be possible to injure her and at once struck out.

"But what did he do to you? What did he actually do? Did he ask you to lift up his tail and kiss his asshole?"

She shook her head dumbly and Lee doubled up with unpleasant laughter.

"When he was living with my aunt, it was the summer she died, he brought this young chick back and took her up to his room and I was getting the old lady her Benger's food in the kitchen and there was this crash, this terrible crash, like someone falling downstairs, and the kitchen door burst open, didn't it. And this chick fell right through it, she was stark naked and she was clutching her knickers in her hand and she said: "If he thinks I'm going to do that, he's very much mistaken.""

"I would have done anything for him, if he had let me," said Annabel gravely. Lee saw she did not understand he was jeering at her and opened his mouth to make a more direct and brutal attack; then he shrugged and said nothing for clearly she would pay him no attention. He grew less vindictive when he saw how dazed and spiritless she was and would have tried to comfort her if he had known how and had he ever before been able to succeed in comforting her.

She rinsed out her cup and put it upside down on the draining board. She went into the bedroom, walking extremely carefully, for she was about to play her last hand and must concentrate very hard on repressing her panic; she had decided to seduce him.

Avoiding his eyes, she took off her clothes, hurried and quickly hid herself on the far side of the bed so that he would suspect nothing. He thought she was unconsciously instructing him that now her body was out of bounds and, as he undressed more slowly, he said to himself: "It's probably all over between her and me, she'll probably never let me screw her again." And this was a great relief for the notion he might by chance encounter even so much as a stray limb of hers under the covers that night filled him with disgust. He stretched out bitterly in the dark beside her, resigned to emptiness, only to discover she had been cunningly lying in wait for him all the time.

She flung herself upon him in a startling rush. She glued herself to his mouth, breast and belly, moaning and sobbing. He thrashed this way and that to shake her off but she clung too desperately to be shifted and the dark splintered in Lee's head as, apparently beside herself, she twisted against him in a sinister frenzy, speaking his name relentlessly in a hot, dry voice he had never heard from her before. In the folklore of Haiti, there exist female demons named *diablesses* who are so avid for pleasure they seduce the living only to abandon them at the end of the lascivious night among the white graves of a cemetery. So, in the dark, a changeling Annabel attacked Lee with gross, morbid passion and such a barrage of teeth and nails he struck her on the side of the head to stop her inflicting any more damage. She howled with surprise and affront and, continuing to howl, tumbled down on him in a stinging shower of disordered hair.

"I wish you were dead," said Lee. She stopped howling and murmured indistinguishable sounds as she lavished kisses on his throat and shoulders, until soon he caught her fever, turned her on to her back and penetrated her. First, she twitched a little, and muttered; and then she wound her arms around him with bizarre, conciliatory tenderness, pressing her small breasts against the green name she had inscribed upon his bosom and begging him to stop, for now she was afraid he might take her too far, would take her to a place where she might lose herself.

"Please," she said. "Don't go on, I don't think I can bear it, not now. Not tonight, I was mistaken when I wanted it."

"Oh no, my love," said Lee, intent on the unforgivable. "This time you'll get what's coming to you, you will."

Nevertheless, it proved a mutual rape. She expelled her breath in a wavering sigh and seemed to fall limply away from him but, as soon as he began to move inside her, her response was immediate and, it seemed, out of her control. She cried out in a lonely voice and bit and tore at him so savagely he wondered if he would survive the night for he had never known a more tempestuous performance from anyone and, in the dark, she could have been a stranger. He had never been superstitious in his life before but, after it was over, he turned on the light to look at her, for her behaviour had no place in the order of things.

It was his Annabel, still, although she was as bruised and bleeding as himself. She was his Annabel, compounded of memory, so he stroked her hair remorsefully and pressed his burning eyes against her cool skin; yet he had truly wished her dead, for then he would no longer have to care about her.

"I'm afraid I've invested all my emotional capital in you," he said. "And that's all I can say, though God help the small investor when the revolution comes. Though I wouldn't say I was a small investor. So I suppose it would be even worse."

She did not hear one word and when his eyes met hers, he was struck by their curious expression, one of perplexity mingled with assessment. He knew she must be thinking of his brother and guessed she had been deceiving him all the time although he did not know why.

In his late adolescence, at a party, on a pile of coats on somebody else's bed, he held a girl in his arms and kissed her while Buzz copulated with her, glancing up at him from time to time as if for approval. When Buzz wandered off afterwards he and the girl made love with the enthusiasm of transgressors. He had forgotten her face and never knew her name; he remembered only that something like that had taken place and the circumstances and the residual traces of his brother on the nameless girl's body had given him a peculiar satisfaction. It was an adventure similar to many others at that time when nothing he had done was unnatural, and it had never entered his head for years, not until now, when it seemed he would never again sleep with his wife without his brother's invisible company.

"Once," said Annabel, "I came home and found you and Buzz together on the floor, curled up in each other's arms like happy puppies."

"We've always been like cowboys and Indians to each other, we must have been fighting." But Lee was discomfited to find she could reflect and enlarge upon his thoughts. She paid no attention to him. She invented her own connections between the past and the present.

"He didn't even take his clothes off," said Annabel who had no sense of the ridiculous.

"He's got few, if any, refinements. Don't blame me for his incapacities. He's always been funny with girls, I told you."

"Then how did he get gonorrhoea in North Africa, that time?"

"I hate to think," said Lee. "Though there aren't too many ways of getting the clap that I know of. But he couldn't even put his finger inside a sea anemone at one time, for fear of engulfment."

"Whyever should he want to put his finger in a sea anemone?" she marvelled and lay beside him in a miserable silence for a long while, till he thought she might be sleeping and reached out to turn off the light. At that, she threw her arm over him and pinned him down again.

"Lee ... tell me ... "

"What is it now?" he asked uneasily.

"Is that what it's supposed to be like?"

"No," said Lee in order to hurt her if he could. "That's what it's usually like, with normal women."

Her smile faded, her eyes dilated with woe and she drew back.

"Then Buzz could have made it properly with me if you had been there," she said with exquisite dismay and took her pale web of flesh away from him to the farthest edge of the bed. His eyes became so painful he could not see her any more but could make out only an indistinct mass of brown hair which could have been shaved from an unknown head and dumped on the pillow. The hair began to shudder like a nest of incipient snakes.

"It's no good!" exclaimed Lee and fell from the bed. Though the distance to the floor was no more than two or three feet, he seemed to fall into a bottomless pit and was surprised to hit the floorboards so soon. He dragged down the bedside lamp with him by the flex and left everything behind him plunged in darkness.

Stirred by the odorous breezes of the night, the undergrowth in the park rustled a little as if each bush contained a pair of somnolent lovers and the air smelled sweetly of crushed grass. The summer moon distilled almost too honeyed a light for moonlight and Lee, who would have preferred a storm with thunderbolts, stumbled angrily into this sweet quiescence and, on the crest of a hill, lost all impetus for renewed flight although, when he was a child, he got as far as Southampton in the pursuit of liberty. He collapsed on a bench in the white shadow of the Gothic tower and buried his head in his hands. He felt nothing but the absence of feeling which is despair.

After a while, he heard a faint, shifting patter of footsteps on gravel and then, behind him, the sound of moist, noisy, loud and intimate breathing like the shameless breathing of a bad-mannered child. The breathing was interspersed with small giggles. Lee ignored whatever hovered behind him until, smitten with the urge to perform an infant's trick, it clapped its hands over Lee's eyes. Lee grasped the bony wrist and wrenched it until the sinews cracked. The intruder yelped and Lee, turning to look at him, saw a young boy with wild eyes and floating hair, clearly another mad person who might have been the crazed inhabitant of the Gothic pinnacle which, ap-

propriately enough, served as the backdrop for their balked
encounter. Lee let the boy go and he tenderly rubbed his
bruises, casting reproachful glances at Lee from time to time
although his giggling changed to a soft, wordless whine as he
edged coyly round the bench and gingerly sat himself down.
The sight of his thin face reminded Lee how, when he collected Annabel, a boy on the hospital porch questioned him
about the tarot pack.

"I see you fled the Fool's Tower, then," said Lee who guessed
the boy was adding to his troubles by the use of some sort of
hallucinogen. The boy nodded vigorously and tried to reply
but an incoherent babble of sounds came out of his mouth and
he made no sense at all. A sharp spasm of distress shook him
from head to toe and he shielded his working face with an arm
in a ripped shirtsleeve.

"Do you want a cigarette?"

The boy blindly stretched out his hand. Lee gave him the
remainder of the packet and also a box of matches. The boy
pocketed them without looking at them.

"Do you need any money?"

The boy nodded. Lee found he had two pound notes and
about fifteen shillings in change. The boy accepted the money
without thanks or enthusiasm. Lee wondered what he could
give him and remembered his wedding ring. This time, the boy
displayed a brief flicker of curiosity when he saw the gold
band on his palm. Lee spoke in a leaden, didactic, schoolteacher's voice.

"Me and my wife have fallen into the habit of performing
symbolic actions with our wedding rings. She ate hers."

The boy raised his shaggy head and stared at him. By the
light of the moon, he must have seen the huge, scarlet-pricked,
purplish, diabolical bite on Lee's neck for he raised his eyebrows, leaned forward and touched it delicately and enquiring-
ly with his fingertips. He giggled again, this time with a faint
note of interrogation. He smelled horribly of mud and
excrement.

"She carried on the metaphor by trying to eat me alive," said Lee. "I got away just in time."

Dear God, he thought, I'm starting to dramatize myself. The boy shrugged. He made several thwarted attempts to speak but could produce no sensible sounds of any kind and at last wept unrestrainedly until his scratched, scabbed face was blubbered with tears and snot. Lee thought he must somehow have hired the boy to act out his ugly grief for him, like a professional mourner, now he himself had grown so cold and mechanical, lulled by the strange narcotic of a steady, quiet anguish. He had nothing with which to dry the boy's eyes, either, and so he must wait until the mysterious spring of tears dried up. The boy bobbed about on the bench in an uncoordinated fashion until he let out a wind-bell tinkle of pitiful since joyless laughter, sprang up and darted off the way he had come.

In the sequence of events which now drew the two brothers and the girl down, in ever-decreasing spirals, to the empty place at the centre of the labyrinth they had built between them, this nameless boy performed the function of the fool in the Elizabethan drama, a reference point outside events but inside another kind of logic, the remorseless logic of unreason where all vision is deranged, all action uncoordinated and all responses beyond prediction. Such logic now dominated Annabel.

She searched through her rooms with the sightless hands of a somnambulist until she found the tablets Lee gave to Buzz to make him sleep and discovered only four remained in the bottle. Though they would grant her only limited relief, she swallowed them and chose to lie down on the sofa rather than return to the bed where she had so recently been confounded. In spite of the barbiturates, she slept lightly and fitfully, visited by dreams she always took for memories so that, when she woke in the morning, she recalled how she had been married in church and the dress of black crêpe her parents bought her, an ensemble completed by a thick veil of the kind worn by widowed queens. They pressed a bunch of dead roses into her hands while the organ played "Eternal Father, Strong to Save" and Lee grew in size until his golden body filled the vaulted building and was soon transformed into the building itself.

The morning was as beautiful as the night which preceded it and she prepared a small breakfast in the sunny kitchen. She set out two places and decided that, if Lee came home by eight o'clock, she would not kill herself. At five past eight, she heard his footstep on the stairs but she had already hung his cup back on the dresser and put plate and saucer on the shelf.

When Lee saw her unexpected serenity, he wondered if she had forgotten the night entirely or had subjected it to the force of her imagination and turned it to her own benefit so she could go on. All might continue as it had done before or shift so imperceptibly from bad to worse he might barely notice it. He asked her for money for his day's expenses and she could find none in her bag so she sent him to her money box. It was stuffed so full of notes the lid scarcely fitted any more and after Lee went off to work she shook out all the money on the bedroom floor and sat cross-legged to count it all out by the light that came through the cracks in the boards across the window. There was more than forty pounds in the tin.

Because her wedding dress was black, she chose a long, plain, white dress of cotton with a square-cut neck and long, tight sleeves. In the mirror of the changing room in the shop, she glimpsed the possibility of another perfect stranger, one as indifferent to the obscene flowers of the flesh as drowned Ophelia, so she had her hair dyed to dissociate her new body from the old one even more and then she got her face painted in a beauty shop. She was surprised to see how cold, hard and impersonal this new face was. What notes remained from her shopping spree she tore up into little pieces. It was now the mellow time of late afternoon.

She took out her old sketchbooks and fingered wistfully through them for every stroke of crayon or pencil had once been alive to her; her pictures had never referred to the objects they might have seemed to represent but, to her, had been palpable things themselves. But she could not draw anything any more and so was forced to make these imaginative experiments with her own body which were now about to culminate, finally, in erasure, for she had failed in the attempt to make herself the living portrait of a girl who had never existed. From time to time she started when she heard voices in the flat above or the noises of the street outside seeped thinly through the opaque windows. She was troubled by an over-acuteness of the senses and wondered why they shouted so loudly upstairs or the cars outside made, today, such tigerish roarings. She was irritated rather than disturbed to sense occasionally the almost inarticulate breathings and the infinitely subtle movements of the figures on the walls and her sudden excess of sensibility made the paper between her fingers coarser than sandpaper. She saw pits and bristles where the pores and hairs were on the skin of her forearm. Before she had finished looking through her books, Lee came home again.

"What are you doing here?" she demanded angrily.

He would have said the same himself if she had given him time to speak for at first glance he did not recognize her. By some extraordinary chance, she had chosen to colour her hair the same shade of polished brass the woman doctor in the hospital used but her black-rimmed eyes, sweeping lashes, arched brows, carmined lips and dark red fingernails were those of the earliest memories of his mother, before she took up a more flamboyant style of make-up; she wore a white dress cut like the nightdress in which his aunt had been buried; but she sat among a pile of drawings in a manner which recalled only Annabel and so he finally identified this composite figure with his wife, though he was so dazed with sleeplessness he could have been hallucinating her. While he was out in the plain air of school, it seemed hardly possible she could wholly have transformed herself so that nothing remained familiar about her except for certain spiky gestures of her hands.

He was so struck by the newly adamantine brilliance of her eyes he did not see they no longer reflected anything. With her glittering hair and unfathomable face, streaked with synthetic red, white and black, she looked like nothing so much as one of those strange and splendid figures with which the connoisseurs of the baroque period loved to decorate their artificial caves, those *atlantes composés* fabricated from rare marbles and semi-precious stones. She had become a marvellous crystallization retaining nothing of the remembered woman but her form, for all the elements of which this new structure were composed had suffered a change, the eyes put out by zircons or spinels, the hair respun from threads of gold and the mouth enamelled scarlet. No longer vulnerable flesh and blood, she was altered to inflexible material. She could have stepped up into the jungle on the walls and not looked out of place beside the tree with breasts or the carnivorous flowers for now she was her own, omnipotent white queen and could move to any position on the board.

"Go away," she said to Lee. "Leave me alone."

"Dear God," said Lee. *"Le jour de gloire est arrivé."*

Inevitably, he began to laugh at such a reversal for the revolution which he both feared and longed for had arrived at last and he was reduced to bankruptcy for there was nothing left for him to love in this magnificent creature. All would not, now, continue in the old style for she dismissed him without a blessing.

"Go away," she repeated. "Don't come back, don't ever come back. I don't want any more to do with you."

She was extraordinarily beautiful and radiated a gripping air of excitement; Lee soon ceased to laugh for he was seized with the conviction she had dressed herself up so splendidly only for the sake of his brother.

"Has he been back, then? Did you come to terms, you and him?"

"Why are you waiting?" she said. "Get out."

He was furious to find how much he was weeping, as if his eyes were dazzled and he choked on a farewell, shrugged, dropped his briefcase on the floor and left her to herself, though he had only nine shillings and sixpence in the world and nowhere else to go.

She was hardly aware who he was, unless he were a material-
ization of a picture from her books; she had even forgotten she
had branded him. When she bent down over the page again, a
lock of yellow hair fell forward with a soft plop onto a sketch
of the chief of the Mohawks walking on a roof and she bit back
a scream for she saw a yellow snake and heard a thud. Only
when she touched the snake with her finger did she realize it
was only her own hair though this, too, seemed an unnatural
substance now it was so yellow. Then she became aware of a
slow, rhythmic banging which must be her own heartbeat and
soon she heard the brisk drumming of her pulse. She waited
impatiently for it to grow dark because her excited senses
turned the vigil into an ordeal; when it grew dark, she would
go into the bedroom, seal the double doors with adhesive tape,
turn on the rusted gas outlets above the mantelpiece, lie down
on the bed and suffer herself to be blotted out but she thought,
this night of all nights, perhaps the sun might never stop
shining. At that, she moaned with terror and panic. There were
no clocks in the flat so she could not tell whether or not time
was passing.

Now he had been granted his liberty, Lee did not know what
to do with it. He sat on the kerb outside his former home for a
while, shielding his eyes from the sun, anaesthetized by sleeplessness and shock. Because he could think of nowhere else to
go, he went to the park and slept on the grass for three or four
hours. He woke up in the cool, blue dusk which signed Annabel's order of release. He was hungry and went down towards
the dock road, looking for a café, as she scraped a flake of
varnish from her fingernail while she taped the tops of the
doors and tsk'd with annoyance for she wanted to look perfect
on her deathbed. But then she thought perhaps a minor imper-
fection would make the spectacle even more touching and,
besides, the important thing was to get it all over with and not
mind too much about impressions for the quality of death
would make her impressive enough in itself. She put clean
sheets on the bed for last night's were printed all over with
false passions and she did not want to die in the bedclothes

between which she had used her body and her imagination to extricate herself from her fantasies and failed at it so badly. The arrival of night, on schedule, had given her some confidence and she worked quickly and eagerly. In the café, Lee fell into conversation with two bored lorry drivers playing a fruit machine and, before long, found himself in a bar.

It was a glum and barren place though an old man played upon an out-of-tune piano and a group of exhausted whores now and then broke into song. Lee drank the drinks the lorry drivers bought him and let a whore reveal her teeth to him in thin, smiling chatter that fell on his ears like the pattering of raindrops. Unfamiliar as he was with the phenomenon of rejection, he could only diagnose his condition as one of positive grief modified by indignation and he cast around for some retributive act or, at least, an invitation from a stranger to cancel out his dismissal and restore his self-esteem.

As if on cue, as his indignation reached its peak, into the bar came the girl Joanne, always an unexpected apparition, sulky as ever and more voluptuous than he remembered unless he garnished her with a little extra voluptuousness because his antennae indicated she was available. She was immediately aware of Lee, though she said a few words, perhaps imparting a message, to a middle-aged man seated in a corner with a sodden group before she came over to her teacher and took up such an aggressively defensive stance before him he had no idea she shook with nerves to find him accessible and alone. Her semi-circular eyebrows gave her bland, white, motionless face the look of a screen star of the thirties. The piano player thumped out "Roses of Picardy" and Lee knew everything was stale, boring and inevitable; he would seduce this trusting child to once more validate his amorality and again find himself in a swamp of self-disgust so he gave her his dazzling smile and waited for her to sit down beside him, in order that the action should commence.

She wore a tight, short dress of a vulgar, printed material and Lee, indulging a dislike of her which considerably sharpened his intentions, thought how he had short-circuited the time

scale of the old saw, "From clogs to clogs in three generations."
She was one of the back-street bad girls of his teens and, now
Annabel had deserted him, he would revert irretrievably to
type, throw up his job and education, join, perhaps, the Merchant Navy or go to work on a building site. He was ravenous
for the commonplace. Saturday's fight gave her the chance to
accost him at last; she thanked him in a breathy, almost diffi-
dent manner, shifting from foot to foot, before seating herself
on the torn, plastic-covered bench, taking great care she did
not touch him.

"That's my dad," she said suddenly, indicating the drunken
middle-aged man with a jerk of her head. "He's in here every
night, the old soak."

There was no affection in her voice.

"Where does your mother go?"

"She's dead," she said without emotion. They were the family
of whom the street was a little ashamed, the boozing father
who made complicated deals about second-hand cars and his
farouche, sluttish daughter, who lived discontentedly together
and often brawled in a mean house where there was nothing
that could be remembered with affection. Avid for the crass,
Lee put his hand on her thigh with such a coarse and blatant
gesture she started. She had not expected an advance quite so
soon for he had rescued her from a similar embarrassment a
night or so ago and, besides, he was a schoolteacher although
tonight he looked drunk or somehow subtly unlike the presen-
tation of himself he gave in the classroom. Nevertheless, she
expected something like finesse, at least, and she snapped:
"Hands off!"

Lee was delighted to hear the fishwife clang in her voice and
offered her a drink. She accepted half a pint of shandy and,
giggling occasionally, she sipped it, eyeing him over the rim of
the glass in a manner which brought back his early youth so
strongly he was both attracted and filled with distaste. She was
angry with herself because she knew she seemed gauche but
she could not help it for she was very unsure of herself. When
he gave her a cigarette, she coughed at the first draw and,

knowing she had given more evidence of unsophistication, she became withdrawn and sulky. She huddled morosely inside her skimpy dress and looked at him with barely concealed antagonism. But, when her father left the pub, she relaxed visibly; she could behave more freely.

"He's gone off after a deal," she said and stubbed out the cigarette. As she did so, her susurrating mass of hair brushed his cheek and, spontaneously, without any reference to a putative seduction but only because its friable texture was quite unlike most girls' hair, Lee bit at it to see what such strange, white, flossy hair tasted like. She shivered and tensed, stirred by this unusual advance; then she shrugged, sighed, glanced round to see she was unobserved and kissed him full on the mouth with profligate abandon. Then she sank back away from him on to the bench but she no longer giggled. She stretched out her hands and examined her fingernails, waiting the next move.

Her eyes were pale, ingenuous blue and her fat, soft mouth the colour and somehow the shape of old-fashioned cabbage roses. In conversation, her voice had a harsh, subtly discordant timbre that at times grated unmercifully like the sound of a knife scratched on a plate and her laughter always seemed contemptuous because it was so rasping but she did not speak often and she laughed even less. Beneath the pads of puppy fat which formed a protective mask for the vulnerable forms of what she might become, the lines of her face were inquisitive and, perhaps, demanding. Now and then Lee surprised upon her face an expression of hungry curiosity which might be half desperate to satisfy itself and was probably the explanation of her kiss. Whoever she was, she only played at being a trusting child or else became a trusting child intermittently, when she had no other signposts as to how to act. As she grew more self-assured with Lee and stopped nervously chewing her swollen under-lip all the time, she revealed signs of a sharp, unripe cleverness. Once she was fully embarked on the adventure he represented, she unfolded a few more of her astringent petals and, though she spoke of her father and his ways with a sardonic regret, she did not seem to be unhappy. But she was plainly hungry for new company and, at closing time, it was she who suggested they walk for a while in the park together, the old euphemism, before Lee had a chance to do so.

She had a bounding, springy walk and carried her head so high her voluminous hair followed behind her rather than hung down her back, buoyantly rippling as if imbued with its own share of her energetic grace. She walked like a woman entirely at ease within her skin. Though the sky in the west was still streaked with green and rose, a fornicator's moon beamed down already and, as they entered the park from the south side, Lee, sentimental, cheerful, not altogether cynical and accustomed to making the best of any given set of circumstances, let the guiltless night take control of him.

No shafts of moonlight dared enter the absolute night of Annabel's darkened bedroom as, in darkness, she balanced on a chair to reach the gas taps which were rusted, stiff and difficult to turn. However, she was quite determined. It was an exquisite pleasure to hear the first, faint hiss that announced the inrush of gas into the room. She knew it would take a long time but, like Ophelia, gladly lay down on the river and waited for it to carry her away as if she was light and will-less as a paper boat. She left no notes or messages. She felt no fear or pain for now she was content. She did not spare a thought or waste any pity on the people who loved her for she had never regarded them as anything more than facets of the self she was now about to obliterate so, in a sense, she took them with her to the grave and it was only natural they should now behave as if they had never known her.

But the park was an arena for moonlight and bright as a day without colours. The silver-plated trees cast barely visible shadows on the grass and each blade and daisy, each bud and blossom, shone with an individual, clear, distinct brilliance. The south side of the park was far more luxuriantly wooded than the north and the girl and her man stepped off the path and walked through the moist undergrowth between the bleached trunks of trees, in and out of the stippled light, until

they glimpsed before them the serene white pillars of the miniature temple. All was calm, all was bright. The pale light
magically rendered Joanne's gaudy dress as a brief tunic of
vague, leopard-like blotches and a few twigs and leaves caught
in her hair. She looked very young but also very knowing. He
was in a mood to be easily attracted by any young woman but
anyone would have thought she promised all manner of possibilities as she moved through the dappled wood. She could
have been an illusion, a trick of the moon and the perfumed air
of midsummer's night, and, indeed, in this aspect of a flowering siren, she was the artificial creation of his habitually romantic imagination. He knew quite well she was a wayward
schoolgirl but there are times and places when and where it is
a necessary enrichment to trust appearances; and, besides, the
knowledge of the tough flesh under the veneer of moonshine
was consoling for, whatever she was in reality, she was, one
way and another, real.

Annabel was falling asleep, now, slipping into a deep sleep
which was a prelude to a coma which was a prelude to nothing
and she felt her exterior fading as her outlines ceased to define
her. Lee was free to lie down in the grass beside the temple
with an amorous girl on the far side of the Gothic north, and
when it was late enough for her father to be sleeping in his
bed, she took him home with her. They went down into the
city through the amoral gates which neither permitted nor
denied access, as though the gates themselves negated a moral
problem by declaring it improperly phrased. Joanne listened at
her bedroom door for her father's snoring while Lee took off his
clothes. Her walls were covered with pictures of pop singers
and a sash or two from beauty contests hung over the bed; her
orange-box furniture was trimmed with frills of mauve tulle
but the dirty underwear she kicked hastily beneath the bed
proved she was a slut at heart.

But she was a sensitive slut and, now she had got him where
she wanted him, she was overcome with belated reticence. She
tentatively approached the bed with the hazy movements of a
nude walking under water, shaking out the filmy hair that

settled on her shoulders in a prickling mass; she always enjoyed smuggling a boyfriend into the house under her father's nose and there was the added temptation of forbidden fruit about this one – her teacher! a married man! – but all at once she was shy of him, because she had inscribed his name again and again at the back of her exercise book for the sheer pleasure of writing it down, had even tried out "Joanne Collins" on the flyleaf of her civics textbook, then speedily erased it. And she knew enough to know that not by one word or gesture must she reveal she had such a young, foolish crush on him. So she covered her face with her hands and smiled between her fingers in almost an embarrassed way.

Even though all Lee wanted was a little comfort, he felt his heart begin to melt, an experience to which he was no longer accustomed. He held out his arms to her.

She ran her finger over the tattoo on his breast but she did not mention it; three in the bed was one too many for her and she switched off the light so as not to see how he wore his heart on the outside, nor the name on it. In the palpable darkness, all turned out very simple and satisfactory; they were pleased with one another, even though, in the helplessness of sleep, he clung on to her like a drowning man and she had not guessed he would be so desperate for love. That made her uneasy.

She woke him early; he must be out of the house before her father woke and she should finish some neglected homework. "Sweet Jesus," thought Lee. "I've knocked off one of my fifth form." He probed his conscience for the first twinge of guilt, as one investigates with the tongue a tooth one suspects to be on the point of aching but, try as he would, he could feel no regret. This puzzled him; he was so used to the bulky apparatus of sin and guilt and had forgotten these concepts had never entered his mind until he met Annabel. He arranged to see Joanne in the evening.

"What about your screwy wife, though?" she said with a certain reserve.

"I shouldn't bother your head about her, ducks," said Lee

carelessly. "After all, she chucked me out, didn't she."

He had left Annabel in such apparent strength of mind. He had not deserted her for she had rejected him. And, if one should do right because it is right, why should she have been forced to simulate a life-likeness that did not satisfy her? But now she lay in her ultimate, shocking transformation; now she was a painted doll, bluish at the extremities, nobody's responsibility. Lee returned to the house only to retrieve a little money and a few clothes. He found her in the bedroom. Buzz crouched at the end of the bed, at the feet of the bedizened corpse.

"I think you should stand with your foot on her neck," said Buzz. "Then I would take your picture with your arms crossed and, you understand, your foot on her neck. Like, in a victorious pose."

Flies already clustered round her eyes. Buzz had chopped down the boards over the windows but the smell of gas pervaded everything and she was plainly far beyond recovery. Lee struck out at his brother, who crashed from the bed on to the floor. Then they began to squabble drearily as to which of them was most to blame, for nothing but death is irreparable.

# AFTERWORD ⟿

$L$ove was written in 1969 and the people in it, not quite the children of Marx and Coca-Cola, more the children of Nescafé and the Welfare State, are the pure, perfect products of those days of social mobility and sexual licence. Originally I'd intended to write a little about the novel and how I feel about it after nearly twenty years, how I feel about what seems to me now its almost sinister feat of male impersonation, its icy treatment of the mad girl and its penetrating aroma of unhappiness. And the ornate formalism of the style, that has something to do with where I first got the idea for *Love*, from Benjamin Constant's early-nineteenth-century novel of sensibility, *Adolphe*; I was seized with the desire to write a kind of modern-day, demotic version of *Adolphe*, although I doubt anybody could spot the resemblance after I'd macerated the whole thing in triple-distilled essence of English provincial life.

Then I thought that perhaps the best way of discussing the novel would really be to write a bit more of it. I've changed a lot since 1969, and so has the world; I'm more benign, the world is far bleaker, and the people in *Love* would now be edging nervously up to the middle age they thought could never happen, they thought the world would end first.

I can't resurrect Annabel, of course; even the women's movement would have been no help to her and alternative psychiatry would have only made things, if possible, worse. The novel ends so emphatically, on such an irrefutable statement, that there is something a little tasteless about taking her husband

229

and brother-in-law and the lovers and doctors out of the text
that is Annabel's coffin and resurrecting them. But good taste
is not a significant attribute of this novel, anyway.

Bit parts first.

Although *the philosophy lecturer's wife* appears only in a
cameo role, I feel I did not fully do her justice in the days when
I thought that mothers had only themselves to blame. I did not
understand why she was so furious. I do, now.

She became a radical feminist in the early seventies and now
lives on a remote farm in Wales with three other women, two
beautiful AID children (neither of them hers) and a flock of
goats. She knows Lee Collins's second wife, Rosie, and also
Joanne Davis, q.v., from Greenham Common, but she thinks of
her life as a heterosexual as a bad dream from which she is
now awake and, besides, Lee was only one of many unsuccess-
ful solutions to her discontent and she never could remember
his name unless she looked it up first.

Her husband obtained custody of their three children; she
did not contest him. He gained his soul at the price of promo-
tion and publications. He remains in the same job, even in the
same flat, but his children rise up and call him blessed and
though they are now almost grown he still runs a "Single Fa-
thers" workshop at the Community Centre of which the coor-
dinator is Rosie Collins.

Lee, incorrectly, suspects them of conducting a sedate and
reticent affair. It is worse than that. They have discussed it
and decided not to. But it is worse than *that*, even, for the
philosophy lecturer's seventeen-year-old son is sleeping with
the Collinses' fifteen-year-old daughter on the very bed under
the reproduction of the blue-period Picasso harlequin, now
somewhat faded. (There is an admirable consistency to provincial life.) Rosie took her to the family planning clinic, but does
not tell Lee, as she believes he is capable of homicide where
his daughters are concerned.

*The peroxided psychiatrist* left the NHS for private practice
shortly after the events described in this novel, though not
before prescribing Lee, after Annabel's suicide, tranquillizers

of such strength in such quantities that he became a virtual zombie.

She is now on the board of directors of a consortium that runs a chain of extremely expensive detoxification centres for very rich junkies. She is also a director of three pharmaceutical companies, hosts a radio phone-in on neurosis and is author of a nonfiction bestseller, *How to Succeed Even Though You Are a Woman*. She is a passionate advocate of hormone-replacement therapy. She drives a Porsche, rather fast.

*Joanne Davis* had too much brute sense of self-preservation to have anything more to do with Lee after she found out what had happened. While he was absent on compassionate leave, she removed herself from school and ran away from home to London.

A man she met on the train got her a job as a hostess in a near-beer club in Soho. From there she graduated successfully to stripping and made a modest killing as a model in the early days of soft porn magazines in the seventies, putting sufficient by to take out a mortgage on a flat in one of the mansion blocks along the Finchley Road and make the down payment on a sports car. This comfortable life came to an abrupt end when she became pregnant as the result of a cash transaction with a minor Saudi princeling.

After her abortion, she felt that if her life was indeed worth more than that of the child she had been carrying, she could no longer continue to take off her clothes for money but must find some other work. No job that did not involve her sexuality offered enough income to keep up the repayments on her smart flat and car; flat and car went. She was soon radicalized.

After much encouragement from new friends she made when she was living in squats, she talked herself onto a course at a polytechnic and has for some years been a social worker for the London borough of Lambeth, specializing in the care of the elderly.

She is a favourite with her clients, who call her Blondie, but she doesn't have much time for men under sixty-five years old except for her adored baby son, conceived in a fit of absence of mind after a demonstration in support of the miners' strike in the summer of 1984. She and her baby live in a communal house in Tulse Hill. She stood unsuccessfully as a Labour candidate in the last local elections. She lost to the Alliance but has been promised a safe ward next time.

She knows Rosie Collins from Greenham Common but the name Collins isn't unusual enough to jog her memory and she never has any reason to think of Lee; why should she? Nor the time, as a matter of fact.

*Carolyn* . . . is now a TV presenter with one of the commercial channels. After her first marriage, to a television journalist, came unstuck, she married a young barrister who was just beginning to make a name for himself; he has now done so. They have a house in Kentish Town, cottages in Suffolk and the Dordogne, and a full-time nanny for their daughter, Emma. Carolyn's son by her first marriage, Gareth, is at boarding school. She admires David Owen.

At first I thought there could be no positive future for *Buzz* but prison, either for dealing or for committing grievous bodily harm. That is because the essence of naturalist fiction is plausibility; in order to create the willing suspension of disbelief, the writer is forced to allot his or her characters lives that are the most plausible, not the most like life, which, since it is not the product of the human imagination, holds infinite surprises. It would be plausible, and morally satisfying, to dispatch Buzz to prison for some years, though God help the other inmates; but real life goes something like this:

In 1969, Buzz was still waiting for his historic moment, which is why he is the least resolved character in the novel. You might have taken him for a wilting floweroid if you had met him then but, in fact, he was simply waiting for punk to happen, and if he could have contrived to get through the next four or five years without death or addiction, he would become rich and famous.

He added a third z (Buzzz) and managed a few early punk bands with some flair but he had always enjoyed throwing parties almost more than anything and found his metier when he imparted the very quality of "The Masque of the Red Death" that characterized his most successful thrashes to the clubs he managed in London and, from 1977, New York, where he has also dabbled in real estate with some success.

He now lives a life of paranoid seclusion in a midtown penthouse, surrounded by a covey of leather-clad acolytes. His videos are spoken of with bated breath. He was early into graffiti and runs a specialist gallery on the upper East Side, besides the notorious performance-art venue in SoHo and a bondage joint in the East Village. Wim Wenders is rumoured to be considering a treatment based on the search Buzzz undertook for his father in the Apache reservations of the Southwest in early 1985, as a follow-up to *Paris, Texas*.

The brothers are no longer in communication. Their endless, pointless quarrel as to which of them was responsible for finally pushing Annabel over the edge was never resolved, became slurred and desultory on Lee's part and was abandoned when Buzzz moved to London shortly after Lee was taken in hand by the young woman who later married him. Nevertheless, Lee is the only human being his brother ever felt one scrap for and he admits to himself, and occasionally to startled companions, that if there is one thing he would like to do before he dies, it is to fuck him. There is as much menace as desire in this wish.

The portrait by Robert Mapplethorpe reproduced in the Sunday colour supplements two or three years ago shows he has not changed, much, except for the ring in his nipple.

*Lee* was rehabilitated from a slough of guilt, misery, impotence, self-pity and drug and alcohol abuse by a stern and passionate young supply teacher of English, who was at that time a member of the SWP (or IS as it was known then). He still believes it was his first name she found so irresistible; certainly little else about him was attractive at that time.

Rosie fought to reclaim his soul for the revolution and his body for the use of women with missionary zeal and by the time, around 1972, she reluctantly came to the conclusion that the revolution was not imminent in Britain, their first child was on its way. Her father, a South London newsagent, offered them enough money for the deposit on a small house if they legitimized the grandchild. So their fates were sealed. Lee lives in a street that is the twin of the one in which he grew up; his aunt would have approved of his wife. He vaguely marvels when something – Jimi Hendrix on the radio, perhaps; a glimpse of his former philosophy tutor – reminds him of his hot, glorious, cruel youth.

Lee turned out to be rather a good teacher. He works extremely hard in a huge (2,800) comprehensive school, is active in the union and, at home, does most of the cooking as Rosie is not talented in that direction. He is too tired to be unfaithful, even if the opportunity arose.

When he and Rosie first lived together, they spent much time analysing the catastrophe of Lee's relationship with Annabel. Initially, Rosie thought it must have been a simple tragedy of propinquity – three people who should never have had anything to do with one another forced together by circumstances beyond their control, such as birth and love. She did not want to blame Lee, nor Lee to blame himself. But, as she encountered and absorbed the women's movement, she found she had no option but to do so, blaming him for sins of omission and commission, and, especially, for raising his hand to Annabel, that frail, tragic creature.

By the time of the three-day week, the ghost of Annabel was exerting such pressure on them that Rosie could endure it no longer, scooped up her little girl and left home. Lee endured their absence with unexpected stoicism, keeping up the mortgage repayments, staying away from drink and women; each night he stepped inside the empty room where the torn poster of Minnie Mouse in aviatrix's garb still fluttered forlornly on the wall and stared at the empty cot with such intensity he might have been attempting to teleport its rightful occupant home by sheer force of will.

All the same, it takes a lot to make a man admit he has been a bastard, even a man so prone to masochistic self-abnegation as Lee. And, at the period of his very worst behaviour, he had no idea of how big a bastard he was being. Nowadays he can hardly bear to think his daughters might meet young men like him; he does not know that one of them already has.

Rosie finally resolved her argument with him to her own satisfaction by deciding that, yes, he *was* a hypocrite, but if she were to remain a heterosexual, then she could go farther and fare worse. Besides, the little girl adored her father and made her mother feel dreadful about keeping them apart. So they returned home in the period of muted, and, as it turned out, illusory optimism following the Labour victory in the 1974 elections.

By then, Lee had recovered his looks and spirits. Even now, past forty and running somewhat to fat, he is still a physically glamorous man, or he would have no meaning. Rosie would never own up in public to the pleasure his blond, dishevelled presence gives her because, in their austere circles, it would not be considered a sound basis for a lasting relationship. But it has served its turn where Lee and Rosie are concerned. They quarrel a good deal, but he is always grateful to her, in spite of what he says, for bringing him out of his private chamber of horrors, even if sometimes he resents it; Buzzz has made a small fortune out of the very same chamber of horrors, after all.

A second little girl followed in due course after the family was reunited. (The third, a latecomer, is still in arms.) Lee was astonished by the violence of his passion for his children. Rosie got the job at the Community Centre. Lee moved to another school as deputy head of department. The minutiae of everyday life consumed them.

Why should Lee be rewarded with a stable relationship? Might it not be almost as much a punishment as a reward? What sane person would voluntarily choose a life of hard work, ideological integrity and compulsive domesticity in the English provinces over one of terminal chic in New York City? Rosie's lips go thin and white when their lifelong disagreement takes this turn. *She* would, for one. She remembers how Lee drove his first wife mad and then killed her. She reminds him of this; she and Lee share a rare talent for the unforgivable. She suggests that degeneracy runs in Lee's family. They row fiercely. The adolescent daughters in their attic room turn up the volume of the record player to drown the noise. Upstairs, the baby cries. The telephone rings. Rosie springs off to answer. It is the Women's Refuge. She begins an animated conversation about wife-beating, raising two fingers to her husband in an obscene gesture.

The screaming baby is plentifully extruding a foul-smelling substance similar in colour and consistency to spinach purée. Lee inspects it anxiously, as a Roman soothsayer might have peered at entrails. He cleans her up, muttering to himself about Rosie's shortcomings as a mother in order to obscure his worry. If this keeps up, the baby must go to the clinic first thing in the morning. He paces the room for a while, pressing her hot, miserable weight against his breast, on which there is still a tattooed heart; Rosie has grown so used to it she doesn't notice it any more. Suddenly the whimpering baby yawns hugely, quiets and sleeps, looking all at once like a blessed infant.

Her father kisses her moist, meagre hair and lays her down upon her side. The older girls, trained in deference to her tyrannic sleeps, snap off their loud music but, cold-eyed strangers that they have become, continue to discuss in muted whispers their parents' deficiencies as human beings.

Oh, the pain of it, thought Lee, thinking about his children, oh! the exquisite pain of unrequited love. The only authentic wound, the sweet curse they inflict on you, the revenge of heterosexuality.

*Angela Carter*
*London, 1987*